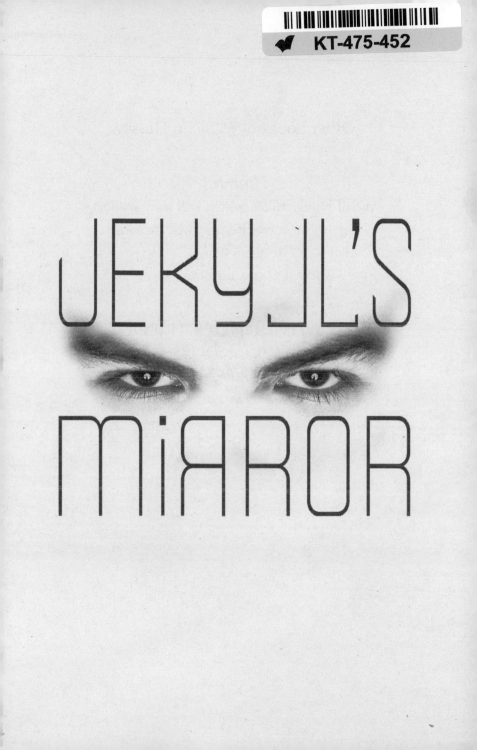

Other books by William Hussey

Haunted
'A nail-biting chiller, which will leave readers
begging for more. Be prepared for some
sleepless nights.'
Micheal Grant, author of *Gone*

THE WITCHFINDER TRILOGY
Witchfinder: Dawn of the Demontide
Witchfinder: Gallows at Twilight
Witchfinder: The Last Nightfall

WILLIAM

'An amazing read.' *Alex Scarrow*, author of the *Time Riders* series

JEKYLL'S

MIRROR

HUSSEY

OXFORD
UNIVERSITY PRESS

Dedicated to the memory of Kate Williams—
kind, generous and eagle-eyed copy editor of my books
and a thousand others

OXFORD
UNIVERSITY PRESS

Great Clarendon Street, Oxford OX2 6DP
Oxford University Press is a department of the University of Oxford.
It furthers the University's objective of excellence in research, scholarship,
and education by publishing worldwide. Oxford is a registered trade mark of
Oxford University Press in the UK and in certain other countries

Data available

ISBN: 978-0-19-273251-4

1 3 5 7 9 10 8 6 4 2

Printed in Great Britain

Paper used in the production of this book is a natural,
recyclable product made from wood grown in sustainable forests.
The manufacturing process conforms to the environmental
regulations of the country of origin.

'... whatever he had done, Edward Hyde would pass away like the stain of breath upon a mirror.'

Robert Louis Stevenson
The Strange Case of Dr Jekyll and Mr Hyde

1
Wrath & the Fire Girl

Daylight glared against the half-turned blinds and laid prison-bar shadows over Samuel Stillhouse. In the silence of the psychiatric nurse's office, Sam fixed a stubborn gaze on his reflection trapped within the window.

'Are you listening? C'mon now, Sam, speak to me.'

A boy of seventeen if you read the date on his birth certificate, much older if you believed the desolation in those denim-blue eyes. Once he'd been called 'Calamity Sam': long-limbed and gangly, apt to bump into the largest of obstacles and trip over his own oversized feet, the nickname had suited him fine. Different now, more careful in all things, he had acquired a kind of grace as he moved like a ghost through the world.

'You won't talk to me, will you?' Nurse Larry sighed.

The first cloud he'd seen in days crawled across the summer sun and, as the room fell to shadows, so Sam's reflection darkened.

'Then there's no point going on. Now I think you should tell your aunt that we've stopped our sessions, but of course that decision has to be yours. If at some point in the future you feel . . . Sam, are you all right?'

1

No. Not all right.

He was in the kitchen again, his nerves singing their old raw tune as he pressed his back against the door. The bad man was lumbering down the stairs. Though the barrier of the door did not protect Sam from the sounds, it at least softened their savagery: the thump of bare feet, the slam of a sweaty fist on the bannister, his name being hollered in the hall . . . then her key scraping the lock. His mum's shift had finished only twenty minutes ago, but his father's beer-drowsy voice was all accusing:

Where've ya bin, ya dirty little . . . ?

Nurse Larry rose from his chair and, for the first time in six months, placed a comforting hand on Sam's shoulder.

'Why don't you talk to me, son? Tell me what exactly you're afraid of.'

Sam reeled into the present. 'I'm not your son! I'm not anyone's . . .'

He lashed out and caught the papers stacked on Larry's desk. In a storm of scrawled patient notes and police printouts, Sam's records scattered across the floor. He had not meant to strike out at Larry nor send the papers flying; for all his sullen silence, he liked and admired the psychiatric nurse. Standing over Larry while he collected the pages back into their folder, Sam wanted desperately to apologize. *It was an accident, mate, and me not talking to you, it's nothing personal. I just can't . . .*

BOY FOUND BESIDE MOTHER'S BODY. HE'D TRIED TO RESUSICTATE BUT INJURIES MEANT SHE DIED INSTANTANEOUSLY

Part of the Vulnerable Witness Interview made by the officer first on the scene poked out from the corner of the file. The drum of his heart quickened and skin prickled over Sam's bones. He could sense it again, blood caking in his hands as he looked deep inside, searching for some response to the horror that lay sprawled before him. All he'd found was a glare too harsh to understand.

Now, looming over the nurse, eyes stinging, fists clenched, he sensed it again: the Wrath coiling within. Frightened, Sam tore himself away and ran. No one in the day care centre attempted to stop him. A mental health care patient fleeing his appointment was not an unusual sight and, as Larry always said, Sam was perfectly free to refuse treatment.

Then why come here at all? a small voice whispered as he wheeled through the double doors. *Because the idea of me 'getting help' makes Aunt Cora feel better,* he answered. *She doesn't need to know that I just sit there while Larry prattles on.*

Sam flew into the string of streets that would lead him back to school. Aware of his background, the headmaster of Pendleton Grammar had authorized him time off to attend these appointments. Mr Matheson was the only teacher to be fully briefed about his new pupil when Sam had arrived a few weeks before the Christmas holidays, and so no one else should have had any idea of the things contained in Nurse Larry's file. But the truth has a way of tracking you down, and with the internet at curious fingertips, the full story could not stay hidden for long.

'We were all sorry about what happened to your mum,' said sixth-form party animal Charlie 'Chugger' Ridley at the beginning of the summer term. 'Anything we can do, buddy, just say the word.'

Trapped in the crowded common room, he had endured the hugs and kisses of most of the sixth-form girls, the shoulder-squeezing and backslapping of every boy, their condolences sharp as a viper's bite. If only they knew his cowardice.

The Wrath was cooling and Sam wandered through drab streets where boarded-up pubs reared blindly over charity shops and dusty newsagents. His heart had just settled when the voice called out to him.

'Penny for them.'

Dazzled by sunlight, he squinted at the figure across the street. The girl who'd addressed him (there was no one else on this baking thoroughfare) wavered like a flame in the heat haze. Yes, his artist's eye insisted, very like a flame, with her short canary-yellow dress, her sleeveless orange jersey and that fountain of sunset hair spilling over her shoulders. Even her scarlet lips, parted now as she called to him again, gave the impression of fire.

'I said "penny for them",' the girl repeated, a smile wrinkling her freckled nose.

'For what?' *American*, Sam thought. *Deep South, by the sound of that*—he swallowed—*that hot, warm drawl.*

'Your thoughts, of course.'

Was she making fun of him? Sam had always been fairly comfortable around girls, and was savvy enough to know when he was being teased. This didn't seem like teasing.

'Who are you?' he called.

'Why don't you come find out?'

With that, the fire girl ducked down a narrow alley that ran between a pharmacy and a small building with a flaking front door and black tinted windows. Even if he hadn't been intrigued, he would have followed, for the heat was almost unbearable and that slim envelope of darkness seemed to offer the only hope of relief. Reaching the mouth of the alley, he paused, his gaze flitting to the little shop on his left. He had noticed it many times, the peculiar sign over the door never failing to draw his eye:

PHANTASMAGORIUM

By the words stencilled onto the windows:

SPECIALIST TRADERS IN RARE ARTEFACTS

VIEWING BY APPOINTMENT ONLY

Sam guessed that it was some kind of antique shop, full of the kind of quirky bric-a-brac his mother had loved to collect (and his father had loved to break). But then what to make of that strange, almost theatrical name? Although he couldn't explain it, *Phantasmagorium* struck Sam as an unbalanced word—a thing of mists and substance, surface and depth, truth and lies.

'Hurry up, Samuel Stillhouse, I'm waiting.'

He dragged his gaze back to the alley. It hadn't rained in over a fortnight yet there were pools of water on the flagstone path, and the moss-furred wall of the Phantasmagorium was damp to the touch. His vision still adjusting to the gloom, Sam groped his way along the path and was about to call out again when his reaching hand closed around the girl's wrist.

'Sorry, I—I didn't see you there.'

She took his hand and held it firm. 'Come with me.'

5

All the playfulness had gone out of her voice, as if the alley had somehow sunk its darkness into her words. The drawl was gone too and, although still richly suggestive of the Deep South, her accent was now clipped and deadly serious.

'How'd you know my name?' he asked, and received no answer.

She drew him on until they dipped back into the pitiless sunlight. Only now did Sam see the girl fully. *Beautiful*, he thought, *and just a bit freaky*. A tower of jade, amber, silver, crystal, onyx, amethyst, and rose bangles reached up to the elbow of her left arm while from her right shoulder a green serpent tattoo snaked its way down to the hand still grasping his, its forked tongue splitting between her forefinger and thumb. The girl's brilliant red hair was decorated with multi-coloured beads which flashed in the light, though none were brighter than her startling green eyes.

'What are we doing here?'

'*Shhhh.*' The tongue of the snake lashed out as she placed her finger against his lips. 'What do you feel?'

She had brought him to an area of open waste ground that stretched out for almost an acre behind the shops. A grit-salted breeze blew here, tearing their eyes and crackling against the rear of the Phantasmagorium; a simple blank wall which, unlike the back of every other building, was untouched by graffiti. Sam wondered what it was about that particular shop that kept the taggers at bay.

'Feel?' he echoed. 'I don't . . . '

She pulled him to the edge of the wasteland directly behind the antique shop. The ground was concrete, bits and pieces of litter tumbling listlessly over its grass-cracked surface. *This is crazy, what do you expect me to . . . ?* Although the words had formed in his head, Sam never had chance to speak them because, at that moment, he felt it:

Darkness singing in the air.

2

The Gorgon's Invitation

Sam had never enjoyed horror films, his life at home had been frightening enough without seeking out fictional terrors, but still he understood the atmosphere of scary movies: it was best born at night, in crumbling cemeteries and forlorn forests. It certainly wasn't supposed to creep out of nowhere on a hot summer day behind a row of boring backstreet shops. Nevertheless, he felt an icy prickle at the nape of his neck and a rasp of dread sank like black oil down his throat.

'What does it mean?' he swallowed. 'What is this place?'

She looked at him curiously. 'A dull little shop tucked away in a dull little pocket of a dull little city . . . ' Then she nodded, as if satisfied. 'Be seeing you, Sammy.'

He barely had chance to blink before the alley shadows doused the fire girl's flame and she was lost to him again. Sam took off after her. His footfalls echoed both ahead and behind, an unsettling acoustic trick that made it seem as if he was following the girl while himself being pursued.

'Wait!' he called to the glimmer ahead. 'Who are you?'

Bursting into the light, he found the street empty; from end to end, nothing to be seen except the sun burning in the blank gaze of every building. Every building, that was, except the one directly behind him. He saw it from the tail of his eye, the tinted glass shunning the glare as the Phantasmagorium held him like a mirror, his face stark amid the blackness.

Get out of here, he told himself. *Go now, don't look back, this place is very wrong.*

Sam ran. Ran through the city's silvered streets, down to the platinum thread of the canal where half-submerged shopping trolleys glittered like pirate treasure sinking into the sea. Ran in a daze until he passed through the rusted gates of Pendleton Grammar, sun-gilded now so that they looked brand new.

'Sam? Are you all right?'

Miss Crail stood in the reception hall, exercise books cradled in her thin arms. The English teacher cast a concerned glance over her favourite pupil while Sam strived to summon a smile.

Less than half an hour ago he had waved goodbye to sessions with Larry; now he wondered if a psychiatric nurse wasn't exactly the person he should be talking to. He knew the origin of his anger and, much as he tried to ignore it, he could at least rationalize its existence. Who knew, Larry might even think it a natural response to what had happened to him . . . Sam mentally shook himself. He must *never* allow anyone to catch a glimpse of the Wrath. To do so would be to invite people like Larry to entertain it, to sympathize with it, and that would lead to disaster. Still, at least the Wrath made sense, what had happened just now did not. Was he losing his mind? Running away from a perfectly ordinary antique shop just because he sensed something wrong in the atmosphere? But if that inexplicable eeriness had been a delusion then the girl must also be a figment of his imagination, and she had seemed so . . . *real*.

'Miss Crail,' Sam said at last. 'Let me help you with those books.'

They passed through the corridors of Pendleton, the bare walls of the old school radiating cold as if the stonework still held shards of winter deep within. When Sam first arrived here during the heavy snows of December, he had stood open-mouthed, his gaze playing over mullioned windows and white-capped chimneys. Pendleton had seemed a fairy-tale place, as unlike his old sink estate school back in London as it was possible to imagine.

At the door to her office, he handed Miss Crail her books and turned his steps towards the library. He had not gone far when she called him back. During his first weeks, Sam had found the head of English more than a little scary. Standing just under five feet in her sensible black shoes, Amelia Crail had a reputation as the school gorgon, her stare enough to turn the most unruly pupil to stone. Beneath this fearsome mask, however, Sam had gradually uncovered a kind and committed teacher, always willing to go that extra mile for her students.

'Sam, I have something to . . . That's to say, an opportunity has arisen that might . . . '

If he hadn't just encountered the mysterious fire girl, this would certainly have been the strangest thing Sam had experienced that day: Crail tripping over her words and avoiding his gaze.

'You all right, Miss C?' he frowned.

She looked up at him and gave a rare smile. 'You're a good kid. Had a hell of a time of things, so I've heard. I can sympathize. I have a daughter, you see, and she . . . ' No one would ever believe him, but in that moment Sam saw a flash of tears moisten those pebble-hard eyes. 'Look, something's come my way from which I think you could really benefit. You'd be getting in on the ground level of a new academic scheme that could help shape how future generations are taught about one of our major writers. It's the sort of thing universities would love to see on an application, plus you'd be helping me out.'

Living carefully day to day, Sam hadn't given much thought to life after school. He knew he would have to start making plans soon if he wanted to get in, and as Aunt Cora probably expected it of him, he guessed uni was the next logical step. Perhaps going away and studying somewhere would be good for him. *Another new start?* whispered that sly inner voice. *That's right, you keep running, little Sammy. Run as fast and as hard as you can . . .*

'What would I have to do?' he murmured.

A muddle of emotions confused Miss Crail's features until at last her natural authority returned.

'Last week I asked you to do some preparatory reading for one of next year's set texts.'

'Yeah,' he nodded. 'It's a short book; I've almost finished.'

'Good.' Her thin lips appeared to tremble. 'The book is, of course, a literary classic as well as being a brilliant dissection of man's nature—both light and dark.'

The deep cold held within the stone of the school seemed to reach out and chill the sweat at the nape of Sam's neck. He gave involuntary shiver.

11

'*The Strange Case of Dr Jekyll and Mr Hyde.*' Miss Crail turned her back on Sam and moved into her office. 'That is the text which will form the basis for our experiment. You will meet me here tomorrow after school and we will begin . . . '

She faced him again, the tears so completely absent from her eyes that Sam wondered if they had ever been there at all.

'Project Hyde.'

3
Blazing in the Wasteland

LOVE   **HATE**

The words hovered before little Sam's tear-blind eyes. He
was kneeling, as he always was in this moment, his hands
clasped together in silent prayer. He prayed to God, to
Father Christmas, to the Tooth Fairy, to the Prime Minister,
to Mr and Mrs Bradbury who lived next door, and who
must surely hear the kind of things that went on under this
roof. Most of all Sam prayed to the man who loomed over
him, tattooed knuckles standing up like sharp cliffs on the
back of those big, bulging fists.

Keeping very still, Sam waited to see if the Wrath would
win. It always seemed to when his mother was its target
but sometimes, when it had Sam in its sights, his father
would shake himself free of its power. Then one of those huge
hands would reach out and a beer-flavoured voice would
whisper, I'm sorry, Sammy, I'm sorry, and Sam would hug
his father fierce, as if his tiny arms had the strength to keep
this good man with him always.

But this had not been one of those times. Sam's mother was
at work and in his dad's red-rimmed gaze he had seen the
Wrath dancing its scary jig. The bad man advanced and . . .

The dream jarred. Changed. Erasing **H A T E**, *a new word began to crowd those huge knuckles:* **PHANTAS**—*And then Sam saw a figure behind his father, where no figure had ever been before . . .*

He woke as usual, lathered with sweat and biting down on his fist to silence the scream. Piece by piece, his room came into focus: the drowsy bubbles in his glass of water, the dog-eared corners of his library copy of *Jekyll and Hyde*, the Spider-Man poster above his bed assembling its bold colours out of the night. Slowly, Sam turned his thoughts inwards and examined the dream with all the caution of a man probing the edges of a terrible wound. It was a nightmare of early memory, one among the hundreds that tormented him, only this time it had been different.

He pulled back the sheets and went to his drawing board. Clicking the halogen light clamped to the corner, he found the furious eyes of his superhero creation, Carrion Wrath, staring back at him. Beneath that hawkish cowl and billowing cape lurked the relentless Benjamin Bradley. Mild-mannered caretaker by day, ruthless vigilante by night, Bradley's alter-ego prowled the city's rooftops in search of what he called, *'Those men whose hearts are dead to love and kindness: the carrion of humanity!'* In another time, in another city, Sam's father had worked as a caretaker.

He tore the latest incarnation of Carrion from his sketch pad and grabbed a fine point pencil from the jar on his desk. The end of the dream was collapsing inside his mind, the already shadowy figure losing its shape and cohesion. In the seconds that remained, he sketched the rough outline of a man—tall, thin, arms dangling in an almost apelike manner, his hair . . . Too late, the vision was gone.

The pencil fell from his fingers and Sam squeezed his temples. He needed air. In an echo of the old Calamity Sam, he skipped perilously around the room, pulling on a pair of jogging bottoms and a faded Iron Man T-shirt. The flat was quiet, Uncle Lionel asleep in the bedroom next to Sam's, Aunt Cora snoring softly on the sofa. Smaller, darker, heavier set, Cora did not look much like his mother, though occasionally a furrowed brow or twist of the lips would catch him unawares and remind Sam that Cora Kremper and Maria Stillhouse had been sisters.

At this hour, it took only a few minutes to summon the urine-stained lift and travel the thirty-one floors to the ground. When the doors trundled open, Sam stepped into the empty courtyard and under the Bluffs' bleak shadow. It seemed that the night was too muggy even for the tower block's hollow-eyed drug dealers to ply their trade, and so Sam walked alone, his thoughts returning again to the fire girl. Earlier in the evening, he had decided to dismiss her as a random crackpot (*You're a fine one to talk*, his mind had echoed back). A crazy person fixated for some reason on the Phantasmagorium, who had decided to share her paranoid delusions with a stranger, but that explanation seemed too easy and she continued to haunt him.

Sam wandered into Old Town and one of the many Victorian alleyways that carved a winding path through this modern city. Cobbles scraped beneath his Nikes and the electric lights housed in antique lampposts threw yellow blocks against the high walls. All this place needed was the clatter of a horse-drawn carriage, the distant shriek of a policeman's whistle, and it could be a scene from *Jekyll and Hyde*. Yes, Sam could just imagine the good doctor swallowing down his miracle potion, transforming into the sinister monster and skipping gleefully down this dark passage . . .

'Don't mess me about. You gotta have a phone, a purse, summat. Give it now or I'll start choking.'

The voice bounced from wall to wall, shivery and excitable. Keeping to the shadows, Sam turned a corner and found himself at the abrupt opening of the alley. Either by accident or unconscious desire, his wandering had brought him to that forgotten scrap of ground behind the Phantasmagorium. In the wasteland stood two figures, one in hostile pose over the other. The mugger was a big, barrel-chested man dressed in a black T-shirt and jeans and with a dirty check scarf masking his lower face. His hand was around the throat of his victim and he was pushing her hard against the Phantasmagorium's back wall. A security light from one of the neighbouring properties flashed into life and the beads in the fire girl's hair shone like a constellation of trembling stars.

'I mean it,' the mugger growled. 'Pretty little things shouldn't be hanging round this part of the city at night if they don't want trouble. So you pay me to go away or maybe, when I leave you bleeding in the gutter, you won't look pretty no more.'

With that, he threw the girl onto the hard concrete. Even from his position on the far side of the wasteland, Sam heard the dull smack of her skull.

'You gotta choice now, girly: option A, you hand over some cash or cards. Option 2—'

The girl hawked up a mouthful of blood. 'I think you mean "option *B*".'

The mugger dipped his hand into his jacket and pulled out a flick blade. 'Option 2: you keep what's yours for a few more seconds, then I stick you between the ribs and take it anyway. S'up to you.'

Flat on her back with the mugger standing over her, the girl shrugged.

'Can I make a counter offer? Option 3, or C, depending what suits your moronic system best: I get the boy standing behind you to drop you like a sack of potatoes and I live to fight another day. How's that grab you?'

'Huh—?'

Sam had moved in a daze across the moonlit wasteland, his anger motoring him on fast and silent feet. As he walked, the scene before him seemed to alter, resettle, and alter again in a kind of nightmarish kaleidoscope. While he was here, approaching the mugger, he was also in the hallway of his old house, the kitchen door clicking softly shut behind him. His mother's screams had stopped and she now lay in an unflinching huddle on the floor. Towering over her, fingers dripping red, his face a blank and bewildered mask: the bad man. Sam had then felt the presence of the Wrath for the first time—felt it as he guessed his dad must feel it, blinding and insatiable. In that moment, he might have killed his father, but terror of this newborn anger had held him back.

It did not hold him back now. Sweeping low, he caught hold of a piece of broken pallet roughly the length of his forearm. It felt good in his hand. As the thug turned towards him, Sam could barely see the widening eyes nor hear the piggish grunt. Most of what he saw and heard was the victorious rush of his rage. Blazing, burning, blistering, it banished all the grief and hatred, all the pain and injustice, all the monumental misery and petty frustrations he had endured since his mother's death. *This is the time*, the Wrath urged him. *Do it! Do it! DO IT!*

A roar, half-bellow, half-sob, accompanied his swing. The wooden weapon caught the mugger a heavy blow to the temple, the scarf was ripped from his face and, just as the fire girl had foretold, he collapsed in a groaning heap. Sam quickly helped the girl to her feet before turning back to her attacker. He raised the cudgel above his head and brought it spearing down into the man's stomach. A follow-up blow to the shoulder resulted in a muffled gasp, a further smack to his ribs and the monster who would have murdered the girl was now begging her to make this madman stop.

'That's enough,' she ordered. 'Listen to me, Sam, just put it down.'

It was not easy to let go of such delicious rage. With a supreme effort, Sam threw the cudgel across the wasteland.

Bruised and battered, the mugger had just enough energy to chuckle. 'You two are dead. I catch up with you again, you'll be begging for the mercy of my blade.'

'Boring now,' the girl sighed, and executed a swift kick to his injured temple, knocking the thug unconscious.

'Are you OK?' she asked, turning to Sam.

His anger was retreating. He could feel its fire seeping out of his veins and cooling in the secret chambers of his heart. When the girl reached for him, he swatted her small hand aside.

'I'm fine.'

She shrugged, a loose smile on those ruby-red lips. 'Thanks anyway, for the rescue.'

She skipped across the wasteland, a fairy figure dancing through the weeds.

'Wait.' Sam stumbled after her. 'Who are you? Why are you here again? What is this place?'

She reached the mouth of the alley from which Sam had emerged.

'You have a lot of questions.' *Trick-trick-trick* went her bangles and beads as she plunged into the shadows. 'That's good, but are you sure you want the answers? If you do you'll have to follow this red rabbit a long way down its hole.'

'Just tell me,' he called, pursuing the glimmer.

'I will soon, Sammy, I promise.'

'I'm Sam,' he shouted, his voice a strident echo. 'Just Sam . . . Only he called me Sammy.'

'Your father.'

He turned a corner and came to a sudden stop. Ahead of him, a long stretch of cobbled walkway illuminated by those old-fashioned electric lampposts. Four such posts separated him from the girl. Her face was cloaked in darkness and yet he thought he could see sympathy in those startling green eyes.

'How'd you know about my dad?'

'I know a lot about you, Sammy.'

'I said don't—'

'Like it wasn't just *him* who used that name. She called you Sammy, too.'

'But how do you know? Please, just tell me.'

She removed one of the amber bracelets from her

wrist and tossed it to him. The smooth resin felt warm and soft between his fingers.

'A keepsake, until the next time we meet.'

'That's not good enough.' He held up the bangle. '*This* isn't good enough.'

'I'm sorry. I'll be seeing you again real soon, I promise.'

'Stop!' he cried. 'Who are you?'

'My name's Cassandra.'

And then she was moving again.

Sam did his best to keep up, dodging lampposts, groping at the empty air. His cry of *Cassandra!* echoed back to him as the drum and throb of the city began to sharpen. Up ahead, a block of light showed the end of the alley. He took a huge breath and tore out into the street.

A flash of blue lights. A siren wail and a screech of tyres. Sam's feet were swept from under him as, tumbling forward, he hit the bonnet of the car and saw the startled face of a policeman staring back at him. His shoulder bounced off the glass, the windscreen cracked like warming ice, and the face behind it fractured. Then he was careering backwards and bounding smartly off the tarmac. Coming to rest with his head pillowed on the pavement, he glanced groggily down the street. A shadow moved in one of the doorways, a red-headed girl with stars in her hair.

'C—Ca . . . '

The policeman stood over him. 'Try not to move. Ambulance is on its way.'

'Cass—'

'What's that?' the copper frowned.

Sam pointed a shaking finger.

But the fire girl was gone.

4
The Devil Behind His Eyes

Like an old man shrugging off the aches and pains of his bed, the lift lurched its way through the Bluffs, depositing its passengers almost directly outside Flat 3113. The policeman pressed the buzzer and Lionel Kremper opened the door.

Sam's uncle, sallow and rat-faced, stood blinking in the dawn-dark shadows. A piece of toast hung from his mouth and he was already dressed in the peppermint green uniform of the local supermarket. From his self-important air anyone might think that the title 'Manager' adorned his nametag instead of the jam-smeared word 'Cashier'. Lionel's gaze switched from PC Markham to his nephew and focused, without sympathy, on the cuts and bruises discolouring Sam's face.

'Don't look so worried, Sir,' Constable Markham smiled, misinterpreting those downturned lips. 'Sam here took a bit of a tumble this morning, but we've had him checked out and the right number of brain cells still seem to be rattling around inside that thick skull of his. I just wanted to make sure he got home OK.'

'What on earth has he been doing?' Lionel said, throwing his toast crumbs to the pigeons that had gathered in the walkway. 'Anything *criminal?*'

'Not at all,' Markham soothed, again misreading the note of hope in Lionel's reedy voice. 'What with the heat last night, Sam just couldn't sleep. He went out for a breath of air and, before he knew it, he'd wandered into Old Town and got himself lost. Kid tells me he only moved to the city recently.'

'Six months ago,' Lionel snapped, 'he should know his way around by now.'

'Well, he realized you'd be worried if you woke and found his bed empty, so decided he better get home sharpish. Next thing he's head-butting the bonnet of my car.' Markham gave Sam a friendly pat on the shoulder. 'He's a good kid, Mr Kremper, and a hell of a sprinter judging by the way he rocketed out of that alley.'

Sam thanked the officer and sidestepped around his uncle and into the flat. He tried to ignore the triumphant smile flickering at the edges of Lionel's butter-greased lips. *Maybe he'll let me go back to bed for a couple of hours and it'll all be forgotten . . .* Some hope. He had reached his bedroom door, head thumping, bones aching, when he was called back to the lounge. He found Lionel hunched over Aunt Cora, who was still fast asleep on the sofa. As his wife stirred, Lionel made a supreme effort to erase the smirk and replace it with an expression of grave concern.

'Wharisit?' Cora stretched her eyelids. Then, catching sight of Sam, tore back the blanket and rushed across the room. Her quick nurse's fingers assessed his injuries and a little of the tension went out of her. 'Nothing serious. Oh Sam.'

'I'm fine, Aunt Cor, really.'

'He was brought home by the police,' said Lionel, relishing each word. He recited the story Sam had fed PC Markham in a tone that suggested he didn't believe a word of it. 'Who in their right mind would walk around that part of the city after dark? Unless, of course . . .'

'What?' Sam grunted.

'Oh, I don't know. Got yourself into a gang, maybe? A bit of late night vandalism? Or have they started you off dealing a few ounces of weed?'

Anger began to twitch at Sam's fingertips and he almost wished he still had that piece of broken pallet in his fist. He made to step forward and Cora caught him by the arm.

'Go to your room.'

'No. I won't let him say those things about me. I would never—'

'I know that, Sam. Go to your room and get some sleep, I'll check on you later.'

The smirk slipped as Lionel stood isolated in the lounge, his fingers fumbling at that ridiculous nametag. Behind him, the sun glared through the curtains like a scarlet eye, Lionel Kremper cast as its thin, elliptical pupil.

'You don't honestly buy that absurd story, do you?'

Inside his room, Sam listened to the muffled voices and their strained argument.

'Not so loud! And yes, I do believe it. Why must you always think the worst of people? That poor boy has been through the most hellish experience I can imagine and you still won't give him a chance.'

'He's dangerous, Cora, surely you can see that?'

'Don't be absurd!'

'It's *in* him.'

23

'Not this again! Please, Lionel, spare us your attempts at amateur psychology. He agreed to go into therapy, he's doing well at school, he helps out with the housework. God above, it's a miracle he's as well-adjusted as he is.'

'It's not psychology. I've told you before, it's—'

'Don't say it, I'm warning you.'

'Evil. You honestly can't see it, Cora? The devil behind that boy's eyes?'

Sam fell onto the bed and pushed the heels of his hands against his ears.

'Surely you do. After all, he's the spitting image of his father . . . '

In the early morning dimness of his room, Sam did not need a mirror to see the truth of his uncle's words. The cyan flecks in his eyes, the wiry wave of his hair, the strong cut of his jaw, the slight prominence of his canines: all of it inherited from his old man. Even his knuckles, broad white cliffs when his fists were clenched, were the same, for although they were unmarked with LOVE and HATE, Sam still sensed anger scratching beneath them.

Looking back, Lionel's suspicion had been obvious ever since he and Cora had been called to the hospital on the night of Maria Stillhouse's murder. After a masked forensic officer had taken scrapings from under his fingernails, Sam had been allowed to wash the dried blood from his hands. He'd let the tap run until the water scalded, then spent almost fifteen minutes soaping and scrubbing, soaping and scrubbing. Later, when Cora sat beside him and touched the tender flesh, folding her unsteady hand into his, Sam had refused to meet her gaze. Instead he let his eyes wander, taking in everything and nothing, until finally they rested on his uncle.

He had only met Cora's husband twice before. Once at their wedding, where Lionel had told the four-year-old Sam to stop sucking his thumb and stand up straight for the photographs, and then at his grandmother's funeral ten years later, an occasion on which Sam Stillhouse senior got drunk in public (something he rarely did), and had punched Lionel full in the face. And so, on that night in the hospital, only hours after his mother's murder, when the police had explained to Cora and Lionel that Sam would need somewhere to stay, Sam had seen the fear and mistrust stamped upon his uncle's features.

It's *in* him . . .

He woke with the girl's name on his lips. Aunt Cora removed her hand from his shoulder and placed a cup of steaming tea on his bedside table. He groaned as she pulled back the curtains and a flood of merciless daylight washed into the room.

'That's a pretty name. Cassandra. Wasn't she some kind of mythical princess who went bonkers because no one believed she could see the future?'

'Huh?' Sam clacked his sleep-dry tongue. 'Oh. Right. Dunno.'

'And there's me thinking you were smart.' Cora sat on the edge of the bed and brushed her nephew's long fringe back from his brow. 'Were you out meeting this Cassandra last night? I don't mind if you've got a girlfriend, but don't sneak off in the wee small hours without telling me.'

'She's just a friend.' *Is she? You don't know anything about her. She flickers into your life, makes a few cryptic comments, then disappears again. How can you believe anything she says?* He still had no idea why Cassandra had been hanging around that old antique shop nor if the unsettling atmosphere of the place had been real or some kind of infectious paranoia passed on by the fire girl. Was she crazy? Maybe, but that didn't explain how she knew so much about him.

'A friend,' Cora nodded, 'that's good. I'm glad you're making friends.'

'What are you talking about?' He took a gulp of tea. 'I've got loads of mates. I went to the cinema last week with Charlie Ridley and I had a kick about with—'

'Don't kid a kidder, kiddo.' Cora smiled sadly and went to the door. 'You're keeping up with your therapy sessions, aren't you?'

'Course,' Sam said, hating the lie.

'That's good.'

'Cor?' He looked down at his hands, suddenly recalling the tackiness of his mother's blood between his fingers. 'I . . . I just wanted to say thanks, for taking me in and looking after me. You didn't have to, and I know it's caused problems between you and Uncle Lionel. I'm really grateful, that's all.'

Cora closed her tired eyes. 'You don't ever have to thank me, sweetheart. And your uncle? He just never anticipated having a kid around, that's all.' The call of Cora's hospital pager hooked her attention. 'Crap biscuits! I'm late for my shift. You better get moving too, mister, midnight wanderings through Old Town do not excuse you from school.'

Sam was in the shower when he heard the front door snap shut behind his aunt. Aside from the drum of water, silence reigned in the Kremper flat. He thumbed moisture from his eyes and picked up the amber bracelet from the soap dish. He'd taken it out of his pocket before heading to the shower, feeling that, in some way, it was important to keep it near.

En route to school, Sam made a decision. Whatever was happening to him was real. He had the evidence of the amber bracelet, confirming the girl's existence, as well as a splinter he'd found embedded in his palm, suggesting that last night's adventure wasn't some crazy dream and that he really had wielded the broken pallet. Now all he had to decide was what to do about it. Carrion might have known. Faced with such a mystery, Sam's superhero detective would set about assembling the facts and making a plan of action.

An idea. He stepped quickly off the main street and ducked into the entrance of the city library. Under that cool Victorian archway the glare of the sun vanished and he could focus on his phone. He soon found the little shop's website, a simple page with only that odd name and a telephone number highlighted in red. So far, so ordinary. Frustrated, Sam turned and looked through the glass doors into the library's murmuring oasis. He had always loved these places. Whenever the bad man appeared, summoned by those dark potions his father bought from the off licence, Sam and his mother would seek shelter in the local library. They would curl up together in the children's section and find a haven in the warm world of books. Libraries made Sam feel safe, but they were also places of knowledge and power. Here he could discover all kinds of information about the Phantasmagorium: news reports, planning permissions, the history of the building, maybe even . . .

But he was already late for school. The mystery would have to wait.

5
Gathering of the four

'You have a Jekyll and Hyde personality, Sam.'

In the heat of Miss Crail's cramped office, where four students had gathered around a book-strewn table, Sam felt a sudden wave of claustrophobia. The blinds were drawn, the raging sun shut out, the shadows of bookshelves thick at his back. He could almost feel their weight pressing down on his shoulders like hot black hands as they leaned in and whispered, *She knows, she sees. The Wrath, it's in you . . .*

'Come on,' *tssk'd* Miss Crail, 'we've all heard the expression, what does it mean?'

The shadow-hands lifted and Sam looked down at the book in front of him. Sitting on the bone-dry grass of the playing fields, he had finished *The Strange Case of Dr Jekyll and Mr Hyde* during morning break. The words of author Robert Louis Stevenson had acted like a spell on his senses, drawing him away from this simmering city and into the chill of a Victorian nightmare; a place where it seemed entirely possible for a man to brew a potion and change his face.

'All right, Charlie Ridley, what do you think the phrase means?'

Bleary-eyed after another night of partying, Charlie shrugged. 'I guess it means that one minute you're all sweetness and light and the next you've got a serious case of the evils. Had a girlfriend like that once. She'd be kissing me, nibbling my ear, basically all over me, and then,' he snapped his fingers, 'she was like a cat trying to scratch out my eyes. Proper mental.'

'Thank you for that vivid story,' Miss Crail sighed. 'And I can see by the pristine state of your book that your insight into *Jekyll and Hyde* goes no further.'

'Do we need to actually read it?' Martin Gilbert grunted. 'We all know the story: this smart-arse doctor thinks he can separate good and evil. He takes a mixture and transforms into a monster called Hyde who goes on the rampage. What else do you need to know?'

Doreen Lackland cleared her throat. 'Actually it isn't that simple.' She glanced through the reams of notes in front of her. '*Jekyll and Hyde* was a phenomenal success when it was published. People were fighting to get their hands on copies, sermons were preached about it, even Queen Victoria was said to have read it. The story seemed to touch something very deep in the human psyche.'

'The monster inside.'

Doreen cast Sam a curious glance. 'Go on.'

'I just mean that it's a horror story where the monster isn't something outside ourselves.' Sam licked his lips. '*Frankenstein*, right? *Dracula*? They might have themes that tell us about human evil, but this book is about the potential in all of us to become the monster. I think that's what people found so frightening.'

'Good,' Miss Crail approved. 'And, of course, the Victorians were obsessed with the new theory of evolution. Charles Darwin had shown them that, for all their science, art, and progress, the human species was really a descendant of apes rather than angels. Now Stevenson was saying that, with a little prompting, society could easily degenerate into a kind of animal chaos.'

'Exactly,' Doreen said, pushing her spectacles onto the bridge of her nose. 'The story has all these layers but we only think about it as a tale of good versus evil because that's how it's entered popular culture through films and plays.'

'Then what is its true message?' asked Miss Crail.

'Hypocrisy.'

All eyes turned to Sam.

'I think the mistake is to believe that Dr Jekyll was a good man. In the story, he admits he isn't. That's why, in the end, Mr Hyde becomes the stronger personality, destroying Jekyll in the process, because Jekyll is, like all of us, a mixture of light and dark while Hyde alone is entirely evil. It's Jekyll's hypocrisy, his failure to express all sides of his personality, that dooms him. D'you see? If Jekyll had been able to show his true self to the world, warts and all, then Hyde would never have existed. Forget the potion, it was his failure to admit who he really was that created the monster.'

'We must live with the balance of what we are.' Miss Crail stared into the middle distance. 'Yes indeed . . . Well, I suppose I ought to tell you why you're all here.'

Exactly the question Sam had been asking himself: *Why has Miss Crail put the four of us together?* They seemed a mismatched bunch, drawn from different classes and, if Sam was brutally honest, from very different skill levels. At the very top end there was Doreen Lackland, president of the debate team, editor of the Year Book, Chairman of the Young Historians and, if there was any justice in the world, future Prime Minister. The butt of a thousand jokes, Doreen seemed to sail above the tide of her schoolmates' cruelty as she set a course for a glittering horizon.

After Sam, Charlie was the next step down on this short but plunging ladder. Standing six foot three in his bare feet, the captain of the hockey team was a boisterous but gentle giant, popular with students and teachers alike. Academically, Chugger coasted comfortably along highway 'C' and, although his teachers would occasionally hassle him, saying he had the brains to switch lanes into 'B' or even 'A' territory, trying harder would mean partying less, and Charlie loved to party.

The last rung was occupied by Martin Gilbert, and here was the real mystery. Sam could understand Miss Crail including Charlie in her special project, maybe thinking that the responsibility might spur him to take his education more seriously, but Mouldy Martin? It wasn't that the kid was dumb exactly, he just couldn't be bothered, and that seemed to apply to all areas in his life. Sam doubted that a comb had ever scraped a path through that knotted bramble of hair or if his school shirt, stained with the splodges of a hundred lunches, had been changed since September.

Echoing Sam's curiosity, Doreen said, 'I think we'd all like to know why you've selected such an . . . ' she cast an uneasy glance around the table, 'eclectic group.'

'That's easy,' Chugger smiled and tapped his chest, 'you gotta have some beauty to go with the brains. Not sure why you're here though, Mould.'

Martin scowled.

'It's not for you to question the merits of anyone here, Mr Ridley,' said Crail in her sternest tone. 'I've drawn you together because I feel that you each bring unique qualities to this experiment.'

Sam frowned. 'Experiment?'

'Ah,' the teacher flustered, 'perhaps I've been thinking too much of Dr Jekyll and his potions! I am developing Project Hyde as an academic tool to help students studying the book. Its aim is to show the continuing relevance of *Jekyll and Hyde* to the modern world. One of the themes of the text is how the anonymity given to Dr Jekyll by his potion allowed him the freedom to indulge his dark side.'

'The potion transforms,' Doreen nodded. 'Gives him a new appearance so that he can do things that he would never be able to in his own skin.'

'Exactly. Hyde is the face of evil but he is also the face of freedom. There is something in our modern world which allows us all the freedom of Dr Jekyll's potion; the ability to shrug off our identities and form entirely new ones.'

Miss Crail looked around the table. Everyone was surprised when Martin answered.

'The internet.'

'Exactly. I'm sure that all of you have created online versions of yourselves on various social networking sites, but here's a question: are these "personalities" an accurate reflection of your true selves or have you crafted them to reflect the person you would like to be? A perfection, an ideal? And are they all consistent or do you present different faces to different audiences? It's not true anonymity, people know your name, see your pictures, but it is *still* a transformed you. Now imagine a darker possibility: there are people on the internet called "trolls". They create new personalities online then use the mask the net provides in order to engage in the most cruel behaviour, bullying other online users, sometimes with tragic consequences.'

Doreen nodded. 'There was a girl in the papers recently. She'd been targeted by a cyber bully who tormented her until she . . . Well, she killed herself.'

'All because of a few mean words?' Martin snorted.

'It's psychological torment,' Doreen snapped. 'An assault on everything the victim holds dear.'

'And, when investigated, it often emerges that the cyber bully is the kind of person who would never say or do these things normally. They behave well at school, do their homework, respect their parents. Sometimes they're even adults with good jobs and happy families. But logging on is today's equivalent of taking Dr Jekyll's potion, allowing pent-up and repressed darkness to escape.'

'They're hypocrites,' Charlie said quietly. 'Like Sam was saying with Dr Jekyll, they're probably people who don't show their true faces to the world, and so they take out their frustrations on other people.'

'And this is how Project Hyde hopes to show the relevance of the book to students today.' Miss Crail handed each of them a slip of paper with a web address and password. 'In the initial stages you're to work in pairs—Charlie and Martin . . . ' Chugger groaned. 'Sam and Doreen.' The President of the debate society gave Sam an appraising glance before nodding stiffly. Miss Crail continued, 'As I've told you, this will be a significant achievement to put on your university applications. I anticipate the project to take two or three weeks and I want you to begin immediately.'

'But begin what, Miss Crail?' Doreen held up the slip of paper. 'Is this all we have to go on?'

'There's a virtual moderator that will take you through the project. I don't want to say any more about it as too much information will spoil the experi— . . . experience. The only thing I ask is that you commit yourselves *fully* to Project Hyde.'

Summoned by the afternoon bell, Miss Crail rose from her chair and headed out of the door. Martin Gilbert grabbed his slip of paper and disappeared after her. Sam, Charlie and Doreen lingered as a thunder of feet passed by.

'Bit weird,' Chugger said at last. 'But if it improves my chances of getting into a good uni with minimal effort, I guess I'm OK with it, even if it means spending time with Mould.' He gave a mock shudder. 'OK Jekyll geeks, catch you later.'

Before Sam could make any study suggestion, Doreen piped up. 'Could you make it out to my house by 7.30 this evening?' She jotted down her address and the details of the most convenient bus route. 'You live somewhere by the Bluffs, don't you? I'm afraid my father wouldn't let me visit that part of the city. No offence, of course.'

'None taken,' Sam smiled. Doreen's directness struck many of her schoolmates as snobbery but Sam saw only a smart efficiency with no malice behind it.

'Excellent.'

Sam picked up his bag and followed her to the door.

His thoughts had already moved away from Project Hyde and back to the fire girl.

6
The Experiment Begins

With each stop taking it further away from the Bluffs, the bus emptied. Sam sat towards the back on lighter-scorched seats, the tired engine rumbling through his feet. His laptop bag rested against his chest and his phone was in his hand, the number for the Phantasmagorium illuminated onscreen. His thumb hovered over the call tab.

Homework had eaten away the early evening hours and he hadn't had time to visit the library as he'd planned. Maybe this more direct kind of research would do just as well? He could call the shop, pretend to be an interested customer, ask a few questions. That way he might figure out what Cassandra found so fascinating about the place. His thumb flinched and he drew it back. The memory of that ominous atmosphere prickled his skin and he found the idea of speaking to whoever owned the dreary old shop somehow dreadful . . .

No, he would go to the library tomorrow.

The bus left behind the choking city, moved through tree-lined suburbs and soon found itself trouncing along country roads. His thoughts full of Cassandra, Sam saw little beyond the mud-splashed window. What did she want from him? And who was she, anyway? All he really knew was that, after two brief meetings, he could think of nothing but the fire girl. To reassure his aunt, he'd pretended to make connections—at school, with Nurse Larry—while in truth he'd kept everyone at a distance. Now, intrigued by a perfect stranger, he'd lowered his guard and, as he'd always feared, the Wrath had come roaring out of him. He remembered the pallet in his hand, how good and right it had felt, and he shuddered. He couldn't allow himself this kind of connection. Not ever.

Sam checked the address Doreen had given him— *Merridown House, Herring Pond Lane. Get off at Catchpole Corner.* It sounded like something out of some corny fantasy movie. He moved down the bus and checked with the driver, a grizzled old geezer who looked a bit like his mental picture of Captain Ahab from *Moby Dick.*

'Catchpole? Next stop.'

Disembarking, Sam stood for a moment as the blue-grey fumes of the bus settled around him. It was just after seven and the sun still sizzled over the dusty cornfields. Cutting away from the road, a tree-tunnelled lane ran beside the belly of a dried-up river. Sam decided that this must be Herring Pond Lane and stepped into its lush green mouth.

As sun-drunk birds began to flutter to their nests and unseen creatures crackled homeward through the bracken, Sam started to wonder if Doreen had been playing some kind of prank—surely no one lived in this wilderness—and then he stepped out of the tree tunnel and into the courtyard of Merridown House. A grand pile of sandstone bricks, Doreen's ivy-clad home was probably small by manor house standards, but it was still a mansion to Sam. He crossed the courtyard and approached the imposing porch with its huge oak door. Before he could try the bell-pull, the door swung open.

Doreen hovered on the threshold, plucking at her cardigan with bitten-down nails. The self-confident president of the debate team had vanished and in her place stood a strangely timid creature. She didn't acknowledge Sam's presence, just glanced over his shoulder at the sleek Bentley parked in the drive.

'He was supposed to be at his Rotary Club meeting,' she said, more to herself than to Sam. 'He wasn't supposed to—'

'Doreen, who are you talking to?'

The voice came out of the medieval darkness behind her, and Doreen started as if someone had prodded her with a sharp stick.

'Who is *this*?'

The hiss of that last letter had a snakelike quality entirely fitting the man who slithered into the light. About forty years of age, Mr Lackland possessed the thin, almost invisible lips of a serpent. While only a few black wisps covered his shining scalp the large hands folded across his chest were very hairy indeed. He flicked one manicured finger towards Sam and the Rolex on his wrist jangled.

'Don't just stand there gawping, Doreen, I asked you a question.'

Sam felt anger billow in his heart. While Doreen quailed under her father's glare, he sought out the tell-tale signs: the sleeves of her jumper pulled down well past her wrists (to hide bruises?); the way her hand always seemed to cradle her left side (to ease the pain of pummelled ribs?); the tears welling in the corners of her eyes (tears she didn't dare let fall). Sam thrust out his hand.

'My name's Sam Stillhouse, I've come over to work on a school project.'

Unbalanced by Sam's directness, Mr Lackland took his hand.

'Quite a grip you have there, my boy,' he grimaced. 'So what is this project?'

'W-well, it's like Sam said, Miss Crail has devised a new . . . ' Doreen stopped to swallow. 'A new teaching aid, and we've been selected to trial the project. It's only a two week thing, it won't interfere with my other commitments.'

'I don't think this is a good idea at all,' Lackland said, looking at Sam with all the distaste of a peacock sizing up a common house sparrow. 'Must I drill it into you again, Doreen? If you're to get into my old Cambridge college then you must focus on your studies. I've already allowed you one afternoon off this month to visit your mother—'

'But Daddy . . .'

Despite the anger sizzling in his veins, even Sam shivered at the look Mr Lackland threw his daughter.

'What have I told you about interrupting your elders?'

'I'm sorry.'

Sam interjected, 'I think what Doreen meant was that Miss Crail's project is going to be a recognized credit on our uni applications.'

'That so?'

'Yes,' Doreen said eagerly. 'And I promise to keep up with all my other work.'

'Very well then.'

The snake fell back from the door and ushered Sam into his lair. And what a lair it was. A great dark-panelled entrance hall decorated with immense oil paintings and finely-woven tapestries stretched away into the shadows. For the most part the historical artwork had a military theme, with cavalry officers on horseback, their rearing, grimacing mounts almost life-size. Also hanging from the walls was an array of antique weaponry—sabres and cutlasses, crossbows and battle axes, maces, broadswords, and war hammers.

'Are you interested in history, Sam?' Mr Lackland said, beaming up at his instruments of death. 'I can trace my family all the way back to Agincourt. These are some of the weapons they wielded. One must be ruthless, you understand, if one is to maintain one's position in society.'

'Yeah,' Sam said drily, 'I think I get it.'

'Come on.' Head down, Doreen led him to the wide staircase where mahogany posts had been carved into leering, scroll-tongued lions. 'This way.'

Her room was a high-ceilinged chamber just off the landing. Expensively decorated, it housed a four-poster bed that would have taken up every inch of Sam's bedroom back at the Bluffs. Apart from the pretty furnishings, which had probably been here forever, there was no character to the place. A few textbooks sat on the desk next to a pricey Apple laptop but there were no posters on the walls, no keepsakes cluttering the dresser tops, nothing to tell Sam who Doreen Lackland really was. *She's keeping herself hidden*, he thought, *because if she has nothing on display, if she keeps everything that's important deep inside, then he can't touch it.*

A window not much wider than an arrow slit looked out over the sun-dappled fields. In the distance, Sam could see the city's dirty gleam, like a mote in the eye of the landscape.

'Doesn't your mum live with you?'

Doreen sat at the gilt-edged table that served as her desk.

'My mother has . . . emotional difficulties. She spends most of her time at a clinic where they can monitor her behaviour. I see her, when I can.'

Sam thought of the proud, haughty snake downstairs; how his venom had clearly poisoned his wife and was now working its way through the veins of his daughter. He wondered if, a few years from now, Doreen would be receiving treatment at the same clinic as her mother. For six months, Sam had worked at toughening the sinews of his heart, keeping himself safe and everybody else shut out. Now he allowed a little of the pain to show.

'You know what happened to me, Doreen. I used to live like you, always scared of putting a foot wrong. I should've told someone but I left it too late.' He knelt beside her and tried to catch her eye. 'Too late for me and for my mum.'

'He's not like that,' she said in a small voice. 'He . . . he just wants me to do well.'

'And he has to bully you to achieve that?'

'It's all about results.' She sat up primly in her chair, the mask of the president of the debate society back in place. 'Now, shall we make a start?'

Sam's own mask was soon reapplied, those hard sinews strengthened again. If she didn't want his help, then fine, she'd just have to find out the hard way. The bitterness of this thought stung him and he wondered again about those words of Uncle Lionel: *It's* in *him* . . .

Doreen opened her laptop while Sam took a seat next to her and fired up his battered old Dell. Following her lead, he typed the Project Hyde website into the address bar. An almost featureless welcome page requested their passwords. When they clicked 'enter' the page disintegrated like pixelated snow and unveiled an entirely black second page. Then a single spark of illumination flickered in the centre of their screens and an old-fashioned lamppost, much like the ones in the alley behind the Phantasmagorium, came into view.

Doreen frowned. 'What is that?'

Standing beneath the lamppost, his features emerging gradually from the shadows thrown by his top hat, an animated man blinked back at them. Although clearly a computer-generated character, the details of his face—pocked skin, cold blue eyes, grey whiskers reaching almost to his jutting chin—were sharp enough to give the impression of reality. His mouth began to move and a posh, haltering voice came through Doreen's speakers. As Sam's laptop lagged a fraction of a second behind, he muted the volume on his Dell.

'My name is Gabriel Utterson, lawyer and friend of Dr Henry Jekyll . . . '

'*Jekyll and Hyde* is told from Utterson's point of view,' Sam said.

'I know,' Doreen replied waspishly, 'I've read the book. Twice.'

'I'm here to act as guide and moderator on your journey through the world of Project Hyde, the purpose of which is to demonstrate the continuing relevance of

Robert Louis Stevenson's story. In essence, how each of us holds within a Mr Edward Hyde and how, with the promise of anonymity, this dark self will come out to play.'

Light flickered at Doreen's window: the sun vanishing behind a fist of clouds.

'In order to satisfactorily complete the project you must undertake a series of simple online tasks. For each you'll be rewarded a golden key, which will be stored in your 'Hydeaway Purse'. Only those with a sufficient number of keys will receive a testimonial certificate. Now, if you're ready to begin, we will create your Hyde avatars.'

The screen turned like the page of a book, and Sam and Doreen were presented with a series of options and questions, similar to the way you might build a social networking page. They were then asked to provide an identity for the program, not their real name but a 'Hyde' alias. Doreen chose 'Mary Merridown' (she shrugged, 'I'm not very creative'). After a long pause Sam couldn't resist the itch at his fingers and typed 'Carrion Wrath'. Before Doreen could ask him about his curious selection, Sam stirred.

'Miss Crail barely understands how to work her email,' he frowned. 'This site must have been designed and built for her. How did she even begin to pay for all this?'

'Maybe she got a grant from somewhere,' Doreen shrugged.

After filling in some mundane details about their views on this and that, their favourite bands, movies, books, and so on they were asked to upload a photograph. This would be their 'Hyde image', which only they would see. A second image would be generated by the program to act as their public appearance. Utterson then explained how the role-play game worked: Project Hyde would generate an entire host of other 'game players', each as artificial as Utterson himself. Doreen, Sam, Charlie, and Martin's Hydes would then be prompted to interact with these characters but, unlike with normal networking sites, they'd be encouraged to be absolutely honest in their interactions. If a certain character posted a status that irritated or infuriated them then they had to tell the character *exactly* what they thought of them. In the safe, anonymous environment of Project Hyde they must let all aspects of their personalities, light and dark, breathe.

'I don't get it,' said Sam. 'So we put up posts slagging off a few fictional people, what's that going to prove?'

'I think I understand,' Doreen said, her nail-bitten fingers hovering over the keys. 'In the book Jekyll hides his true self from his friends, right? It's that hypocrisy that makes his Hyde so strong and violent when he transforms. Maybe . . . ' she hesitated, 'maybe we're all hypocrites, showing one face to our family and friends while at the same time pushing down our darker selves. Project Hyde will show us what we'd be like if we took Jekyll's potion and were allowed to say and do whatever we wanted.'

'But it isn't real.'

'Right. It's a game. But haven't you ever played Monopoly with a bad loser?' Her gaze wandered to the door. 'It all starts off friendly enough, everyone joking and groaning as they take a hit, but then someone's laughter becomes a little strained, and . . . ' She turned back to the computer. 'Games can tell you a lot about a person, Sam.'

Outside the red sun dimmed and the first traces of evening stole into the room. When they had both finished setting up their Hyde avatars, the screen folded over again and they were introduced to a kind of forum. 'People'—the fake characters made up by the program—were already sending and responding to posts.

'It's amazingly detailed,' Doreen marvelled. 'All the usual stuff you find on social networking sites: "I love my cat!", "Can't wait to watch *EastEnders* tonight", one girl distraught because her boyfriend's cheating on her . . . Just remarkable.'

Suddenly Mr Utterson popped up in the corner of the screen.

'Time to get started. Doreen, tell me what you think of this—'

A post was plucked from the body of the forum. It read:

> Some nerd at school 2day actualy CRYED when the teacha red out sum POWTRY. She said it was 'reely moving'. Lol! Wot a loozer! Ha ha ha!

Doreen considered for a moment before typing her response to Utterson:

> I don't think much of it at all. Just a pathetic individual with no common decency.

The Utterson animation nodded. 'Then tell her so.'

Doreen hesitated.

'Come on,' Utterson laughed, 'she's not a real person. It's all part of the game.'

Doreen considered for a moment, then retyped what she had written in a comment box under the 'girl's' status. Before she posted, Utterson popped up again.

45

'Is that *all* you would like to say? Surely a rather feeble response. Haven't *you* been hearing similar insults all your life?'

'How does it know?' Sam wondered.

As if in response, Utterson went on. 'The Project Hyde program has analysed the personal information you have inputted and developed an understanding of you as a subject. Doreen Lackland, alias Mary Merridown, would, if she were able to comment freely and anonymously, post a more *rigorous* response. To earn your first golden key you must do so.'

Sam could see the battle written across Doreen's features. She was not naturally a mean person, but she had promised her father that this project would benefit her educationally. She typed –

> You are a cruel, absurd little airhead. Well done to the girl in your class who *cried*, it shows she has a soul. Something you are clearly lacking.

'Better,' Mr Utterson approved, 'much better.'

Sam noticed the change as soon as the message was posted. Doreen's rigid posture relaxed and something like victory lit up her features. A response from the 'girl' flashed onscreen—a baffled and defensive message asking who 'Mary' was. Doreen typed like a demon, piling on a stream of clever and cutting insults until her target was pummelled into silent bewilderment. Sam couldn't help laughing at Doreen's brilliantly witty gibes and he had to admire the ingenuity with which the program manufactured the girl's responses.

A golden key flashed on screen and deposited itself in the 'purse' at the top of the page.

'Excellent work,' Utterson approved. 'And now, Samuel, it's your turn . . .'

'Oh damn!' Sam muttered, glancing at his watch. 'I gotta run or I'll miss the last bus.'

'But you haven't got your first key,' Doreen said, 'and Miss Crail told us to work together.'

'Right. Except maybe we should get on with it separately, now we've run through the set-up.' He shoved his laptop into his bag. 'It's a real hassle getting out here, and if you can't come to the Bluffs—'

'Of course.' A hint of disappointment shadowed her features. Doreen jotted down her number and handed it to Sam. 'Call me. Perhaps we can collaborate over the phone. I must say,' she laughed, 'it really is a most *interesting* project . . . '

7
This Hungry Path

He soon forgot all about researching the Phantasmagorium.

Even the fire girl blazed only rarely in his mind.

Sam had a new obsession.

It began almost as soon as he returned from
Doreen Lackland's. Cora and Lionel were both pulling
evening shifts and so Sam sat alone in his room,
flipped open his laptop and started work on Project
Hyde. At first he found the make-believe forum only
mildly distracting, checking the stream of fake status
updates from the computer-generated personalities as
he chomped through a bag of crisps and doodled in
his sketch pad. A smog-red moon boiled outside his
window while far below the muffled soundtrack of
the estate—shouts, sirens, a screech of tyres, the blare
of music—continued on its never-ending loop. Though
he was still amazed by the program's ingenious ability
to create such a variety of fictional people, all with
their own photographs, profiles, and individual online
voices, Sam felt his eyes begin to droop. It had been a
long, long day.

Then Mr Utterson popped up on screen and highlighted one of the scrolling updates. Sam fished his headphones wearily from the drawer and plugged them into the laptop's port.

'So good to see you again, Samuel. Now please tell me, what do you think of this . . . ?'

The status read:

> Just saw this white chick holding hands with a black guy. They was kissing! It was gross! I say 'there aint no black in the union jack'! Blacks and whites shouldn't never mix.

'How does reading something like this make you feel?' Utterson coaxed. 'Rather vile, is it not? Why not tell this grubby little racist what you think of him?'

Sam's fingers twitched over the keyboard. He hesitated only for a moment, allowing a white spark of rage to cool and harden around the fine and cutting words that sprang from his mind and raced to his fingertips. Then he typed. The message was short, brutal, devastating in its wit and outrage. He dragged his chair closer to the desk and hunched over the screen, the glowing surface of which mirrored the smoky moon that hovered above his shoulder like a watchful face.

> Who the hell are you anyway?

flashed the racist's response.

> I don't like blacks, that's my business. Butt out unless you want me to find you and do you some damage. England 4 da English!

Sam's smile turned wolfish. His fingers danced over the keys as he laid down a string of comments, countering the bigot's increasingly dumbfounded responses with facts and figures that proved the stupidity of his small-minded views. After half an hour, Sam's foe had exhausted all his hateful rhetoric and, complaining that he was being picked on, had withdrawn from the field of battle. Still smiling, Sam sat back in his chair and surveyed his posts with pride. It hadn't been all that difficult, dealing with a nasty little racist like that, and now he found that his anger had burned itself out and that a kind of calm had settled over his mind.

'Well done, Samuel,' came Mr Utterson's voice through the headphones. 'You have earned your first golden key . . .'

Sam slept well that night. No cold sweats, no bad dreams, no black memory to stalk the emptiness behind his eyes. He woke early, the sun's first rays lapping hungrily at the window. His gaze fell on the laptop and he pulled back the sheets and went to sit at his desk. While the old Dell creaked into life, he thought about the experience of last night and wondered at the soothing effect it appeared to have had on him. It was mental really, getting such pleasure from whopping the virtual ass of some racist character that didn't exist, but the thrill of the moment and the peace afterwards couldn't be denied. Now he wanted to experience it again. Licking his lips, he logged into Project Hyde.

That day he turned up an hour late for school. The next, he missed it altogether.

By the end of the week, Sam was catnapping at his desk. Project Hyde consumed him, though in his short bursts of clarity he could not explain why, other than it made him feel good. He no longer needed the guiding hand of the moderator Utterson, now he could seek out his own targets. At first they were of the same type as the racist, and he dealt them all the same quick wit and righteous anger. The sexist, the homophobe, the snob, those that posted discrimination against the poor and disabled, abused the elderly and the disadvantaged, those who laughed at suffering children and neglected animals: all were subjected to the itch of his fingertips.

Meanwhile, homework piled up and meals went uneaten. A few days into the project, Cora poked her head around the door and asked if he needed anything. Sam barely glanced up from the screen.

'I'm fine. Thanks.'

'Will you be joining us for dinner tonight?' she asked. 'It's just you haven't had a proper meal since—'

'I told you,' he muttered, 'Miss Crail's given us this project to finish. It could get me into a good uni. I don't have time for anything else.'

A plate scraped against his desk, the smell of a bacon sandwich, and Cora was gone. Sam took an unenthusiastic bite and went back to berating an idiot who thought 'women doctors shouldn't be allowed.'

Time wore on. So far Sam had been able to keep up the pretence that he was going to school. He'd get up, shower, pull on his uniform and then hang around in the stairwell until his aunt and uncle left the flat. Phone messages from the school secretary were deleted from the answering machine and the first letter home was collected and disposed of. Each day Sam would promise himself that this was his last full session on Project Hyde: just a few more posts, just another hour of putting these losers in their place . . .

Soon he started to run out of obvious suspects and his targets began to change. He hunted for them now, stalked the fictitious forum, and when he couldn't find posts that made him angry he'd settle for those that merely irritated him. The harmlessly idiotic, the selfish and attention-seeking, the just plain dumb: anything to soothe the Wrath.

> I keep hearing about this thing called 'The Aborigines'. Are they a new boy band?!

> OMG! Some1 just told me the Earth goes round the Sun! I thought it was the other way round. Im rite and there wrong. Rite?

He dealt with these and a hundred others. Someone complaining that their 'crap-for-brains' daddy hadn't bought them a sufficiently expensive mobile phone was given a short, sharp lesson on world poverty. Another posting details about her relationship was told just how interesting her latest date with 'cuddly-wuddly Brian' really was to the wider world. Before he knew it, Sam was leaving snide comments under pictures of cats dressed as Christmas elves and plates of home-cooked food

> No one's interested in your dinner, mate. For God's sake, just eat it!

Then there were the updates where he would delight in picking apart the poster's spelling or ridiculing their inability to express themselves clearly. Whatever their faults and foibles, Sam plied them all with the same smart abuse.

Only occasionally would his furious fingers stop in their tracks. In those brief flashes, he'd sense a change within him, a small shift that his obsession with Project Hyde seemed to have masked. It was a strange sensation, and he wasn't entirely sure what it meant or how he felt about it, but then he'd remember how quiet the Wrath had been in these last days and his fingers would dance again. After all, it was just a game and, even if he was moving into increasingly darker territory, that landscape was only a virtual one, so what did it matter?

The game called to him more and more. Free of nightmares he slept soundly, but only in snatches. After an hour of rest he could almost hear the lure of the forum whispering in his ear, drawing him back. Or was it his fear of the Wrath that stirred him from his dreamless sleep? At its slightest twitch his eyes would snap open and he'd be at the laptop again, anxious for the program to spark into life. At intervals Utterson would appear and reward him with more of those animated golden keys, a reward in which he took little interest. In fact he had almost forgotten the purpose of Miss Crail's experiment and now no longer wondered about the obvious lesson it was trying to teach.

'You're looking very pale,' said Aunt Cora one morning . . . or was it afternoon? He couldn't be bothered to drag his gaze from the screen to check his wristwatch. 'I know this project's important but I'm worried you're not eating properly. Maybe if I called the school—?'

'No! I've only got a day or so to go and I'll be finished. Stop fussing, I'm fine.'

'All right,' she sighed, 'but just let me take a look at that hand.'

He barely reacted as she brought in a bowl of warm water and cleaned the old cut he had sustained when handling the broken pallet.

'Looks raw,' she said in a puzzled voice, 'but it doesn't seem to be infected. You'll tell me if it gets any worse? Sam, are you listening to me?'

'Huh? Oh. Yeah. Right. Sure.'

The blazing sun rose and fell, the summer night smouldered, and Sam remained at his desk. He heard nothing from the other participants and thought little of it. Under the cloak of his obsession even Cassandra, bright and brilliant fire girl, had dimmed, as had any interest he might once have taken in the Phantasmagorium. The strange atmosphere he had felt outside its walls was like a memory from another life, dull and far away. And so he progressed, step by lunging step, until he reached a point on this hungry path where he could barely understand what his victims had done to provoke his spiteful brilliance. They were no longer hateful bigots or even mildly foolish. In fact many were like him: the lost, the lonely, the vulnerable . . .

And then, late one night, he read the final message.

Utterson had appeared onscreen and Sam slipped the headphones over his ears.

'You have done well, young man. Remarkably well. Your clever and insightful barbs have made your targets look like fools. I congratulate you.'

Sam smiled a natural smile.

'You have earned yourself ten golden keys. Only two remain and you will be able to claim your reward. So tell me, what do you think of this . . . ?'

A status was highlighted and dragged forward until it filled the screen. As Sam read it, he felt the sting of the Wrath like a hot blade sizzling inside his flesh. For days it had been soothed, now the dragon was awake once more.

Tony and me are back together again! Woohoo! He really is a great guy, so all you haters can just shut up! Tony's never, ever hit me, so stop stirring, OK?! We've had our rough patches, but from now on it's going to be just great for us :)

Utterson's voice whispered to Sam, echoing his thoughts, 'Of course she's going to defend him. You've heard it all before, haven't you? The angry denials, the hollow explanations of cuts and bruises and broken bones, the ready acceptance that *this* time it will be different. She has a child, you know. A little daughter. Look . . . '

Another status from the same user was highlighted and drawn forward:

> Down the hospital again with Tansy. Such a clumsy girl!! Ran straight into the corner of the dining table. Huuugest black eye, bless her!

'Why not tell this weak-willed woman exactly what you think of her,' Utterson coaxed. 'Give her a taste of the punishment she truly deserves. Open your heart, Sam, and let your bile engulf her. *Tell her . . .* '

He could. He *should* . . . grasp this damaged woman in his furious fist and, with mere words, pull her delusions to pieces. Strip away the lies she told herself, tear apart the comforts she whispered to the darkness, trample whatever small crumb of dignity Tony had left as hers. Not to protect her, not to startle her into realizing that her daughter's safety was at risk, not for any good or noble reason at all, but because it would please Sam to do it. The urge rattled inside the empty cauldron of his mind: *Do it, Sam, make her pay for her pitiful love and her cruel cowardice. Write it down, let it go, and destroy her utterly . . .*

Sam jolted back from the desk. A shiver ran through him—the ice-cold chill of reality. It felt as if he had been shocked out of a dream, wicked and yet horribly tantalizing. For the first time in days, his full senses slipped into focus and he tasted the unclean tang at the back of his mouth and smelled the sour odour of his own body. Fingers trembling, he was about to slam down the screen when his eye caught the private photograph attached to his Hyde profile. The picture he had uploaded of himself. It had changed.

He ran to the bathroom. Saw his reflection in the mirror as he had not properly seen it since Project Hyde began. It confirmed the photo: his skin was grey and pinched, his eyes feverishly bright in their bruised hollows. He looked as if he hadn't slept or eaten properly in a week, which he guessed was true.

'Who are you?' he asked the glass, and received no answer.

His grubby fingers tapped against the sink and he looked down, remembering all the spite and bile they had poured into the forum. It didn't seem to matter now that the targets he'd persecuted weren't real, that they didn't have feelings to hurt or ideas that they cherished. He could only think of the dark delight he had taken in tearing into them.

He tried to breathe. Couldn't. Had to get out of here. Now.

He blundered down the hall, thankful that Cora and Lionel were at work and so didn't have to witness his claustrophobic stumble to the front door. The handle slipped through his sweat-slick palm and he fumbled again and wrenched it open. The muggy air choked him, sank into his airways like a moist, smothering blanket. He reeled onto the open air walkway and, just as he felt as if he was going to fall, strong fingers locked around his wrists and he was steadied on his feet.

'You're all right,' the fire girl whispered, drawing him to her flame. 'You're going to be all right.'

8
Reach of the Puppet Master

She drove them to a lay-by café on the outskirts of town. At a quarter-to-midnight the only people occupying the converted shipping container were a couple of lorry drivers exchanging dirty jokes over their fry-ups and a baggy-eyed waitress yawning at the till. Even so, Sam couldn't help noticing Cassandra's constant watchfulness. Every few seconds her eyes would flit to the wide window cut out of the metallic wall and rake the lay-by, the road, and the empty car park of the giant supermarket opposite.

Their drinks arrived with a dramatic thump. Wiping stained hands on her apron, the waitress treated them to a challenging stare before heading back to her copy of *Soap Star Weekly*.

'And I thought you English were famed for your politeness.' Cassandra emptied a sachet of sugar into her cup and took a sip. 'How you doing, Sam?'

'Better. I think.' As he spoke, Sam realized that he was fingering the bracelet she had given him that night behind the Phantasmagorium. Throughout his Project Hyde experience, he hadn't thought of it once; now he took an odd comfort from that soft, warm loop of resin. In a hoarse voice, he asked, 'What the hell is happening? Am I going mad?'

Her gaze flipped back from the empty night and she looked at him with the kind of understanding that, since the death of his mother, only Aunt Cora had come close to.

'You mustn't doubt yourself. Everything that's happening right now is as real and raw as that wounded hand of yours. Trust your instincts, Sammy.'

Without any true conviction he said, 'I asked you not to call me that.'

'Your mother thought it a good name. So do I. Ownership of a name is important, it gives the possessor power.'

He sighed. 'Cassandra, you have to tell me what's going on.'

'OK,' she breathed. 'You want a story? Then you better open that mind of yours so wide your skull creaks. Here goes: my name's Cassandra Kane, I'm eighteen years old and I was born in New York City, though I spent most of my childhood in Louisiana. There's not much more you need to know about me, other than the fact that I'm here to put things right.'

Sam raised an eyebrow. 'For who?'

'My family,' she said, and a dark edge seemed to slip into her tone. 'But we'll get to that. Now, I know you've recently been involved with something called "Project Hyde"—'

Sam sat forward in his chair. 'You know about that? Are you saying it's connected to your obsession with the Phantasmagorium? How?'

'Obsession?' she smiled. 'I guess you could call it that. And yes, that's exactly what I'm saying. But for me 'Project Hyde' is just a name—I've no idea what it means, although I've reason to think it's nothing good. But let's start at the beginning. For reasons I'll explain, I was convinced even before our first meeting that you'd play a key role in whatever Edgar Dritch is planning.'

'Dritch? Who's he?'

She held up her hand. 'We'll get to that. Now, my certainty about your involvement wasn't based on any knowledge of your character or how your allegiances would fall; you might well have ended up being an ally of the Phantasmagorium. All I knew was that you'd definitely have a role to play.'

Cassandra's lips closed like a trap as the truckers folded their newspapers, grunted a goodnight to the scowling waitress and headed out to their rigs. Moments later there came a gasp of airbrakes and the lorries trundled into the night.

'After hearing the name Samuel Stillhouse, I booked a flight to England,' Cassandra continued. 'That was about a month ago—'

'A month!'

She nodded. 'Once I arrived, I set myself up close to the Bluffs and began surveillance. I'd already researched what I could from online reports about your mother's manslaughter and your father's imprisonment. I'm sorry, by the way, for your loss . . .'

Sam looked away, his hand tightening around the bracelet in his pocket.

'After weeks of watching, I found no evidence that you had any connection with the Phantasmagorium. Your day-to-day routine was perhaps a little too predictable for a seventeen-year-old, but I guessed that was some kind of coping mechanism. Maybe something suggested by Nurse Larry.'

'You've been thorough,' said Sam flatly.

'I'm sorry. I understand this must be uncomfortable, but the stakes I'm playing for are huge, and I'm afraid that your private life just isn't a consideration.'

'All right,' he muttered. 'Go on.'

'I decided on a little experiment. I enticed you towards the Phantasmagorium and then carefully watched your reaction. Your shock was genuine and convinced me that you weren't a willing ally of Edgar Dritch.' She paused for a moment. 'You felt it, didn't you?'

He nodded slowly. 'The wrongness.'

'As good a way to describe it as any,' she agreed. 'That place is wrong in all senses of the word, and its wrongness comes from the man behind its walls: Edgar Lemuel Dritch.'

'Who is he?'

'Well, that's the real mind-blower,' she shrugged. 'As far as anyone is able to establish, Mr Dritch is over five thousand years old.'

Sam laughed. He couldn't help it. And yet there was an edge to his laughter, a hint of possible acceptance behind the mirth.

'There isn't any written evidence of Dritch before the eleventh century,' Cassandra continued, 'but the stories go way back. He's a dark magician and, most importantly, a collector of cursed objects.'

'A collector of what?'

'There are certain artefacts in this world in which, via many different methods, strange powers have been contained. The Holy Lance, for example, the spear that pierced Christ's side as he died upon the cross, is supposed to have the power to heal. And then there's the quill of Nostradamus, which is still said to be able to predict the future. These and other objects can be used by a man like Dritch for his own dark purposes.'

'But what's all this got to do with Miss Crail and Project Hyde?'

Cassandra took her mobile phone and held it out between them. 'I've been investigating Dritch for a while now. A few months back I managed to intercept a phone call.'

'You what?' Sam boggled.

She smiled. 'I've always been a tech-head, it was no big deal. Anyway, listen to this.'

She thumbed the screen and a crackly recording started to play. The first voice was familiar, though Sam had never heard Miss Crail sound fearful or nervous before. The second was high, somehow youthful, and with a mocking edge to its tone.

'You promise they won't be hurt?'

'I am not in the business of giving guarantees, my dear. Let us just say I will not harm them personally. But let me be clear, if you refuse to play your part then one thing I can certainly promise . . .'

A choking sob from Miss Crail.

'Now,' Edgar Dritch continued, *'of the four potential participants in Project Hyde, the one I am most interested in is Master Samuel Stillhouse. What can you . . .'*

The recording cut off.

'That's it?' Sam asked.

'That's it,' Cassandra confirmed. 'Your Miss Crail was somehow blackmailed into involving you in Dritch's scheme. And it was the mention of that word—Hyde—that brought me here. It had to be connected, you see? The murder of my father and sister and the theft of the Stevenson mirror.'

'Your family were killed?' Sam asked softly.

Now it was Cassandra's turn to look away. 'My father, yes. And Cassidy, my sister. We were twins, but I was always the big sister. Always bossing her around and . . .'

She fished a silver locket from around her neck and handed it to Sam. Undoing the delicate clasp he found two miniature pictures inside: on the left, a red-haired child sitting demurely, hands folded, a timid smile on her lips; on the right, an identical girl with wild, unkempt locks and a face smeared with strawberry jam.

'Guess which one's me,' Cassandra smiled. 'Not long after those pictures were taken our parents divorced. I was hauled down to Louisiana to live with my mother while Cassidy stayed with Dad in New York. We tried to stay close, but that kind of distance only highlighted the differences between us and we drifted slowly apart. Mom died when I was sixteen, and I guess I went off the rails. I took off for almost two years.' She caught Sam's eye. 'Don't ask about that time, I don't feel much like sharing . . . Last December I was sitting in a diner in Washington State reading the *New York Times* when this article at the bottom of the page jumps out at me: "Antique Store Owner & Daughter Murdered Over Mirror". Then a name: "Cassidy Kane". I was on the next flight home. Dad owned this little place on West 57th, the kind of store where brainless biddies from the Hamptons pay top dollar prices for reclaimed junk. I went to the police and found out that my family had been killed a week before. Far as the cops could make out, the only thing missing from the store was some old mirror. They reckoned it was a burglary gone wrong.

'I hung around for a few months, trying to put my family's affairs in order. The police kept checking in but they had no leads and I got the feeling the case was being quietly dropped. It was hard . . . ' Cassandra took a breath, 'going through Cassidy's stuff, finding the letters I'd written her and the photos of us as kids . . .

'I was packing up the last odds and ends one morning when I came across my dad's appointment book stuffed in a bureau drawer. The cops must've overlooked it. On the night of my family's murder, it seemed that dad had a meeting set up with a man called Dritch. I took the information to the police but they drew a blank, and so I began investigating myself. My father had left me a great deal of money, enough to buy my way into a world I had no idea existed. That's how I know what you're feeling right now, Sammy. Like the crust of the planet's split apart and you've found something dark writhing under the surface. Am I right?'

Sam nodded.

'It took me a long time piece together the story Through certain dealers in occult objects, I learned that Dritch had been to my father's store asking about a certain mirror. Dad told him he was sorry, but that it had recently been bought by another client. When he refused to accept more money for the mirror, saying it was no longer his property, Dritch showed his true colours. He murdered my family and took the mirror anyway.'

'But what is this mirror?' Sam asked. 'And how's it connected to Project Hyde?'

'I've no idea. All I know is that it was transported back to Dritch's headquarters in the UK.'

'The Stevenson mirror,' Sam murmured. 'You mean Robert Louis Stevenson, don't you? The author of *Jekyll and Hyde*.'

'That's the guy. But now I think it's time you told me about this project of yours. What is it exactly?'

Sam felt a rush of shame. How could he explain the hold Project Hyde had had over him? Even though it was a harmless game peopled by fictitious characters, still he looked back on some of the things he had written and cringed. How could he expect her to understand when even he wasn't sure how the obsession had begun?

The shadow of the waitress suddenly hovered over them. 'Top up your coffee?'

'No thanks, we're good,' Sam said without looking up. 'Cassandra, I have to—'

'Top up your coffee?'

'I said no thanks.'

The black shape remained.

'Top up yuh-yer curgh-feeeeee?'

Sam's head snapped sideways and his grip tightened around the amber bracelet in his pocket.

From the edge of her slack lips, ribbons of thick drool threaded down and dribbled onto the waitress' apron. She looked like a puppet supported on limp strings, all the muscles in her body depressed as if they had been placed under a huge gravitational force. The corners of her eyes hung down, exposing the inside of raw and red-etched lids. As Sam watched, a fly landed on her unflinching eyeball and cleaned its legs against that jellied smoothness. She didn't so much as blink.

64

And then the coffee pot fell from her nerveless hand and spilled its scalding contents against her leg.

'Jesus!' Sam cried in sympathy.

The waitress just stood there while red and yellow blisters foamed against her flesh.

'Slorry,' she garbled, working disobedient lips as best she could. 'Clugh-offee's off.'

Mixed with strands of bright red blood, runners of snot cascaded from the waitress's nose and splodged against the tablecloth. Sam felt his stomach roil.

'What's happening to her?'

'My contacts in the occult world told me about something like this,' said Cassandra, scraping back her chair and scanning the windows. 'Dritch has psychic abilities; the power to possess people at a distance. He knows I've been snooping around and must have locked onto my whereabouts.'

'You mean he's here?'

'No. He's tracked me down psychically and taken control of this woman.'

'But what can he do with her?' Sam stared at the teetering figure. 'She's so . . . weak.'

Cassandra was now at the window, double-checking the empty lay-by and car park beyond.

'Doesn't have to be a big thing,' she said. 'Could be something as simple as . . . Oh God . . . '

The headlights of a passing truck sparked through her hair, and suddenly it appeared as if her face was framed with fire.

'Do you smell gas?'

The moment he caught a whiff, Sam wondered how he hadn't noticed it before. He looked to the cooking area behind the counter where the air danced and shimmered, then back to the waitress. Hands shuffling in the pocket of her apron, she took out a tiny plastic lighter.

'Yuh-yes, Muh-ister Dritch,' she slurped, 'I uh-nderstand.'

Her thumb scratched against the wheel.

'NO!'

Before she could strike it properly, Sam knocked the lighter out of her hand. It skittered over the grimy vinyl floor and towards the window where Cassandra crushed it under the sole of her boot. The possessed waitress shrieked, her features contorted, and a fresh wash of blood gushed from her nose. Sam jumped away from the table, avoiding the splashback by inches. And now the torrent wasn't just coming from her nose—blood squeezed through the clenched gate of her teeth and crimson clots began to snail their way out of her ears. Sam imagined the inside of her skull like a pressurized container ready to blow, the psychic force exerted by Edgar Dritch scrambling the poor woman's brain until . . .

'Cassandra, what the hell's happening to her?'

Until blood ran from the roots of her hair and her entire head dripped like a toffee apple drawn fresh from a pan of boiling syrup. The apple bobbed violently on the stick of her neck as she turned and jerked spasmodically down the aisle of tables. Back at the counter, a spell of concentration seemed to overcome her and those once limp arms stiffened with purpose. She was reaching into a drawer, her head glistening under the sickly glare of the café's fluorescent tubes.

'Sam, we need to get out of here.'

He felt Cassandra's hand plucking at his sleeve.

'But we have to help her.'

'It's too late. I'm sorry, Sammy, but we—'

'Muh-ister Dr-Dritch. He says tuh-to tell you. G—gguhhrrr...'

They looked to the far end of the container café where the bright-faced woman stood at her station.

'Gurghd. *G'urghd ni* . . .'

Sam saw the match clamped between thumb and forefinger. The waitress lifted the little stick, ready to strike.

'Goodnight Miss *Kuh-ane*.'

9
A Family of Liars

A final glance at the shimmering waitress was enough to convince Sam that there was nothing to be done except flee. The vinyl floor squeaked underfoot, the metal door retched on its rusted hinges, and they tumbled down the steps and into the lay-by. Thrown up by the tyres of a passing lorry, a shower of grit peppered Sam's face. He did not feel the sting. He ran, Cassandra's hand locked in his, her hair flaming in the lorry's wake.

They reached Cassandra's bottle-green Beetle, tucked away in the shadows on the far side of the lay-by. There they exchanged a puzzled glance and looked back the way they had come. Swinging in the restless warmth of the night, the door revealed the short stretch of the container café, swung back and blocked it from view, then unveiled it again. In that widening and narrowing gap, Sam saw the waitress throw a broken matchstick onto the floor . . . search her pocket . . . scrape a fresh match against her thumbnail . . . and . . .

The voice of the explosion was muted by the metal box that contained it. Even so its fury rumbled through the soles of Sam's feet and flashed tears into his eyes.

Shielded by the car, he did not see the fiery tongues lash out from the doorway but he felt their white-hot spittle rain down upon him. Luckily, the most lethal fragments of shrapnel were absorbed by the Volkswagen and those small pieces that did strike Sam and Cassandra were swiftly brushed away.

'You OK?' she asked breathlessly.

'Think so,' he groaned, helping her to her feet. 'You?'

'Peachy.'

Over the dented roof of the Beetle, they looked back at the café. Just a few moments ago they had been sitting inside those buckled and blackened walls, drinking undrinkable coffee and discussing impossible things. Now the container had been transformed into a flabby, fractured version of its old self, the metal torn into jagged strips and blasted into unlikely curves. A long smoke stack rose up from the holes in the roof, and Sam imagined the atomized remnants of the waitress rising with it.

'Let's get out of here.'

He moved to the passenger side and sank into the seat. With the ring of the explosion still ghosting in his ears, he heard Cassandra's prayer for the Beetle to start. The god of engines was merciful and they were soon speeding away from the lay-by.

'Can't see anything behind us,' Cass said, her toe pressed hard to the accelerator, 'but everyone within a ten mile radius would've heard the blast. Means we've got three or four minutes to get off this road and into the city. I'll have to dump ol' green, of course.' She reached forward and stroked the dash. 'Sorry, girl.'

They left the B-road and Sam watched familiar landmarks flash by, the features of the city suddenly strange and unknown to him. For six months, he'd walked these streets, gazed upon these buildings, grazed his fingertips against the stone skin of the city. Now the fire girl had erupted into his life and shown him the horrors that lurked beneath reality's fragile crust. He stood now before a world twisted and transformed; a place in which every shadow might contain dark wonders that he had once dismissed as superstition.

Such thoughts sifted like sand through his head as the Beetle wended its way into the city's grimmest corners. Before he knew it, they had arrived at the Bluffs.

'You need to get out of the car now, Sammy.'

'What?'

'He's locked onto me.' She teased at one of the onyx bangles around her arm, a nervous tic. 'I have to get myself somewhere safe, lay a false trail to keep him guessing.'

'What about my friends?' he said, trying to push down the panic in his voice. 'The ones involved in Project Hyde. Where will they be safe? And what about me, Cassandra? *He* knows about me now.'

She shook her head. 'He was only able to manipulate the waitress to a certain extent—he wouldn't have been able to use her senses and so wouldn't have seen you. As far as Dritch is aware you're a part of *his* plan, whatever that might be.'

'You don't know that for sure.'

'I don't know anything for sure, but if I take you with me now then he *will* become suspicious. So go home and do what you're best at—*stick to your routine*.'

He looked at her sharply; there was no cruelty in those gentle green eyes.

'When will I see you again?'

'Soon,' she promised. 'Until then, keep your eyes open.'

Sam got out of the passenger door and turned back to the shattered window.

'I can come with you, help keep you safe.'

She looked at him, a sad smile curving those perfectly bowed lips.

'You don't have to save me, I'm already lost.'

The sound of the Beetle trundling away to its final resting place stayed with Sam as he crossed the empty courtyard and summoned the lift. Body jolting with the carriage, he was borne roughly upwards. He could feel himself hanging there, fragments of his old life falling away as the lift ascended. It seemed incredible: a dark magician living in this modern city; a man who had murdered for the sake of a writer's mirror; a mirror that must have some connection with the addictive Project Hyde. A fearful Miss Crail had involved her students in Dritch's strange game, but what was the magician's ultimate goal and why had he decided that Sam must be part of it? It was too much to take in.

Stepping into Flat 3113, Sam sensed the sting of his hand. A red blot had bled into the bandages and the pain was back, nibbling at his nerves. A deep shudder ran through him.

'Where've you been, boy?'

He was almost at his room when Uncle Lionel called him into the lounge. As it was a Friday night or, more accurately, Saturday morning, Aunt Cora would be pulling a late shift at the hospital. The flat was always different without her there: the rooms seemed darker,

71

the air thick and sour. Lionel uncoiled himself from the couch and went to stand in front of the flickering TV, feet planted wide, a can of beer in his fist.

'Is this how it begins?'

He eyed his nephew's hand with all the delight of a scavenger assessing the wounds of its weakened prey.

'What're you talking about?'

'I knew your dad before he married your mother, Samuel.'

It was always 'Samuel', never Sam: his father's name used like a red-hot brand.

'We grew up in the same street, me and that jolly Jack-the-lad. I even remember how he started in those long-ago days.'

'Started what?'

'Showing the rot beneath his handsome smile.' And now Lionel's self-satisfied smirk turned into a leer. 'Everyone loved Samuel Stillhouse, even the teachers who he'd backchat at every opportunity, but *I* knew there was a black heart beating inside him. I tried to get Cora to warn her sister about him, but even she couldn't see past those baby blue eyes. Not until it was too late.' He shook his head in mock sympathy. 'How were they all so blind?'

Lionel set his beer on the coffee table and came staggering towards Sam. Those alcohol-hazed eyes did not possess the hard glint he had seen so often in his father's, yet still Sam shrank back as the thin finger prodded his chest.

'Now it's starting all over again, the sins of the father coming out in the son.'

'Shut up,' Sam whispered.

'I gave you a roof over your head.' Lionel teetered onto his toes, finger jabbing. 'After that monster smashed your mother's brains all over the hall, I took you in, fed you, cared for you.'

'Cared for me?' Sam echoed. 'You never wanted me here. It was Cora—'

'I never wanted children, that's true, especially not one of *his*. But it's my money that puts clothes on your back and food in your belly.'

Sam knew that was a lie. Cora paid for his clothing and for every morsel of food that passed his lips. He'd turned to go back to his room when Lionel caught him by the sleeve.

'And now you repay me by bringing trouble to my door?'

'I'm not in any trouble.'

'Your old man was a liar too. Worst of all, he turned your poor mother into one. She used to bring you round here when you were little; bet you don't remember that. Used to sit in that chair and lie her pretty backside off. "I walked into a door", " . . . tripped down the stairs". She'd even lie about you—"He's so clumsy, Cor, just like me". What kind of mother does that?'

I don't know, Sam thought, *I don't know*.

'But I s'pose she was scared of that charmer back home, and we mustn't speak ill of the dead. But *you*.' Again, the prodding finger. 'You I do *not* forgive. You've been fighting.'

'I haven't.'

'Then how'd you explain turning up at two in the morning, your hand bleeding?'

'I missed the bus after studying at a friend's.'

· 73

'And then you fell and cut your poor hand. *Ahhhh.*'
Lionel pouted. 'So what about that stink on your clothes?
I know what you've been doing, Samuel. I see those little
scumbags outside my shop every night just waiting to
set fire to the bins. You're in their gang, aren't you?' He
swallowed hard, tears welling in his beady eyes. 'They
follow me home, throw fireworks at me and laugh.'

For the first time since coming to the Bluffs, Sam
felt a twinge of sympathy for his uncle. He would never
understand why Cora had married this man, but that
didn't mean Lionel had no right to his share of dignity.
Sam had had no idea about this cruel bullying.

'I'm sorry.' He placed his wounded hand on the small
man's shoulder. 'I didn't know.'

'Know what?' Lionel spat back. 'That you're as bad as
him? I knew it from the moment you were born. You've
got that same handsome face, that same lying smile. Your
soul is rotten, Samuel. Rotten, rotten, *rotten.*'

The movement was an unconscious one; that's what he
told himself as the rat-faced man went flying backwards
into the coffee table. *I didn't mean to push him.* Those
were the words echoing through his head as the can of
beer somersaulted into the air and Lionel flipped head
over heels onto the couch. Showered with amber foam,
Lionel Kremper blinked the room back into focus. At
first a look of fear gripped his features, and then his face
relaxed into that old self-satisfied grin.

'And now you've proved me right,' he panted. 'Enjoy
your last night under my roof, son. Tomorrow you're
history.'

10

Through the forgotten Ways

'Is this Cassandra? She's beautiful.'

Sam woke with his face scrunched against a diagonal plane of sketching paper, his arm slung over the top of his drawing board. Somehow he'd managed to fall asleep while perched on his stool. Cora stood at his side, her weary eyes moving over the paper which, until a moment ago, had been his pillow.

'You've got real talent, you know that? Your mum was no artist, and I can barely draw a convincing stickman. Must come from the Stillhouse side, your dad was quite creative before . . . ' Her features tightened. 'Before the drink changed him.'

Sam looked down at his hand, the bandage crusted with dried blood, his fingers so discoloured with charcoal that they appeared bruised right up to the second knuckle.

'I'm sorry I pushed him,' he said. 'If he wants me to leave—'

'You're not going anywhere.' She draped an arm around his shoulder and drew him close. 'Didn't even try to give your side of the story, did you? You don't have to spare my feelings, sweetheart, I know what he's like. And now you're looking at me and wondering why I stay with him. He wasn't always like this, you know. Disappointment has a way of stirring up bile in a person's heart, and Lionel's had more than his fair share of disappointment. He's been passed over for promotion more times than I can count, and then there's the fact that I can't ever have children.'

'He told me he never wanted kids,' Sam said quietly.

'He *would* say that. Now.'

Sam returned his aunt's hug.

'Just stay out of his way for a few days and everything'll be fine,' Cora said, disentangling herself and wiping a tear from her cheek. 'But Sam, I need to ask you—'

'I'm not in a gang. Not drinking or taking drugs. I've just had a couple of weird days, that's all,' he said. Then, less truthfully, 'There's nothing for you to worry about.'

'Good enough for me,' she nodded. 'So you're finished with Miss Crail's project?'

He gave a wry smile. 'Totally.'

'All right. But listen, if you're going to be out all hours with your girlfriend could you please call and let me know?' Cora gestured at the drawing board. 'Is she your muse?'

Sam stepped off the stool and took in his work of the night before. After his encounter with Lionel, he'd popped a couple of paracetamol to ease his aching hand and then collapsed onto his bed. The only certainty in all this seemed to be Edgar Dritch's ruthlessness. He had already murdered Cassandra's father and sister, and now the blood of the waitress from the container café was on his hands. There might be more of the story to come once Cass had shaken Dritch off, but this was enough to be going on with.

At 3 a.m., Sam had given up on sleep and gone to sit at his desk. The laptop hummed quietly on standby and, crazy as it seemed, he'd felt a sudden urge to flip open the screen and log onto Project Hyde. Mixed up among all the fear and wonder, he could sense a blade of anger striking out from his heart. He felt it then as he had felt it before, furious at the evil of men like Edgar Dritch. Unlike his father, this magician wore a mantle woven of supernatural terrors, but to Sam the two men were brothers cut from the same cruel cloth. Entering Project Hyde and venting a little of the Wrath would give him peace.

It had taken all his willpower to resist that lure. Instead, he went to his drawing board. Still pinned there was the rough sketch of the figure that had invaded his dream the week before: a long-limbed man with a blank oval for a face and a strange, monkey-like stance. Troubled by the sketch, he tore it away and had then stared long and hard at the fresh sheet beneath. His fingers twitched and he began to draw...

'She's the fire girl,' he said now.

Sam took in the wild hair, shaded to suggest a Medusa mane of flickering flames, those wide arresting eyes and the serpent tail coiling around her right shoulder, its undulating body coasting down her arm and splitting between her fingers.

'It's the best thing you've ever done,' Cora nodded. 'Now let me see to that hand.'

After his aunt re-dressed the wound, Sam showered, grabbed a slice of toast from Cora's plate, and headed out of the flat. Far from the Bluffs, the crush of Saturday shoppers propelled him down the high street and to the door of the city library. Under the stone entrance, he took out his phone and dialled.

'Hello stranger. How are you getting on with Project Hyde?'

For a crazy moment, Sam thought about telling Doreen of his night-time adventures. Then sanity reasserted itself. He was faced with the impossibility of putting the others on their guard without any concrete evidence. After all, what could he tell them? That Miss Crail was being blackmailed by an ancient magician? That there was something sinister about the project (but he didn't know exactly what), and that it was in some way connected with an old mirror once owned by Robert Louis Stevenson? Quick as you could say 'padded cell', Nurse Larry would be measuring him for his very own straitjacket.

'To be honest,' he said, 'I've kinda given up on—'

'Hopeless!' Doreen exclaimed. 'Come on now, Sam, it really is a very entertaining program . . . ' Though her tone became guarded, she wasn't able to completely disguise a flutter of excitement. 'Its lesson is simple enough: anonymity breaks the bonds of acceptable behaviour. Still, I've found it to be quite . . . ' The star English student struggled for the right word. 'Addictive.'

Sam's stomach turned at her choice of adjective.

'Yeah, well don't forget the rest of your schoolwork,' he said breezily. 'Miss Crail's project isn't *that* important.'

'I hardly think you need to remind me of *my* obligations. Now.' He heard a rustle of paper. 'I have a window in my diary Wednesday afternoon, shall we meet up then to compare notes?'

It wasn't a question. Doreen Lackland hung up.

Sam passed through the huge glass doors and into the cathedral-like chasm of the city library. Reaching the area reserved for computers, he dropped into a cubicle and entered his library number into one of the whirring PCs. He didn't want to revisit Project Hyde (at least, that's what he told himself), but his need to provide the others with a sane reason to abandon the program urged him on. He typed the web address, entered his password, and the homepage of his alter-ego, Carrion Wrath, appeared on screen. He noticed at once that his personal photograph looked less gaunt than it had the night before and, glancing at his reflection in one of glass display cases, he saw that his eyes had lost their feverish glow and that his face was much less drawn.

Suddenly Utterson appeared on screen. Sam took the headphones from his iPod and plugged them into a port.

'Welcome back. So far you have earned ten golden keys.' The cartoon purse at the top of the homepage sparkled. 'Now, shall we make a fresh start?'

A stream of status updates began to scroll, top to bottom. Utterson selected one and enlarged the text:

> I'm back with Tony! Yay! It's a new start for us and our little girl, so all you troublemakers just leave us alone. HE HAS CHANGED, OK?!!!

'She's kidding herself, of course,' Utterson whispered. 'Her partner has been physically violent, both to her and their child. So why don't you tell this weak woman exactly what you think of her?'

Why didn't mum stand up to him? Why didn't she protect me? Why didn't I protect her . . . ? The old questions roiled in Sam's mind as he wondered how this animated man knew just which of his buttons to press. Utterson claimed that the program had analysed the personal information they'd inputted, and so understood the characters of the Project Hyde participants, but the truth was much stranger: the psychic Edgar Dritch knew all the secrets of their broken hearts.

'She's not a *real* person,' Utterson assured him. 'Come now, tell this so-called mother just how frail and pathetic she is.'

The Wrath tingled at Sam's fingertips.

'Tell her how she's failed her child. Tell her that she's just as responsible as the monster she loves. Tell her. *Tell her.*'

Why not? Wasn't it just a silly game after all? There are no consequences, the Wrath whispered. Let it out, Sam. Let it out in a scream of words.

'He has angry eyes,' Utterson coaxed, 'and slobbery lips that lie. He has big fists with sharp white knuckles, and on those knuckles are written the words . . . '

LOVE   HATE

Sam stabbed at the mouse and screen switched to the library homepage.

He took a few deep breaths, the safe scent of books dusted into each inhalation. While his heart settled he wondered what this act of temptation meant and how it could be connected to Dritch's plans for the mirror. Come to that, what was this supernatural object exactly? He opened a search engine and typed 'Robert Louis Stevenson, mirror'. All he found was a poem about a looking glass given to Stevenson by his writer friend Henry James.

Stumped, Sam turned his attention to Cassandra. After a little research he discovered a newspaper article dated 5 January:

MIRROR MURDER —POLICE BAFFLED

Officers investigating the double murder of father and daughter Edward and Cassidy Kane have today admitted that they are still no closer to identifying the killer. Some time in the early hours of Christmas morning, the Kanes were brutally slain and their antique shop, *Lost Times*, ransacked. It appears that, despite housing a number of valuable treasures, the only item taken was a Victorian mirror. Miss Cassandra Kane, daughter of Edward and twin sister to Cassidy, has refused to comment on the police investigation.

The words became a blur as Sam focused on the picture at the top of the article. He had seen her cocky and defiant, brave and resourceful, but until now he'd only caught glimpses of Cassandra's vulnerability. Here he saw it plain and true, the grief etched into those compelling eyes.

But there was something wrong with the picture. It seemed to be paparazzi shot taken through the window of *Lost Times*. A central aisle of marble-topped tables, grandfather clocks, hat stands and roll-top bureaus led all the way to a counter at the back, behind which a mirrored wall extended the small store to twice its normal size. In front of the counter stood a startled girl. Cassandra had been snapped mid-turn, her cardigan spilling over her bare shoulder, her left hand raised as if to ward off the photographer. Tidy for once, her hair was pulled back in a tight bun and her red lips were drained of colour. It looked to Sam as if the fire girl's flames had been doused.

He puzzled over the picture for a while before turning his attention to the Phantasmagorium itself. Three hours later and he was ready to admit defeat. He had checked every online database he could think of, had scrolled through reams of old newspaper reports on microfiche, had even checked city records dating back to the early nineteenth century: apart from the shop's official website, he could find nothing significant on Edgar Dritch. The man seemed to move through the world like a phantom that left no trace.

And then a display in the local history section caught his eye. Getting up from his desk, he went to stand in front of a large yellowed map that had been carefully pinned to a big freestanding board. It showed the old Victorian sewer system that ran under the city—a network of interconnecting tunnels that roughly followed the streets above. Using his finger, he traced a path from the library directly to the Phantasmagorium.

Sam scanned the whispering landscape of the library. A dozen toddlers were nestled like attentive sparrows on the colourful carpet of the children's section, their mouths agape as a librarian fed them a tale of sea serpents. By the back wall, a gang of college kids twanged rubber bands at each other and ignored their coursework. And there, over in a quiet corner, was the spiral staircase that led to the basement level.

Sam picked up his bag and moved silently to the stairs. This part of the library was out of bounds to the general public, and he felt a curious sense of betrayal as he slipped unseen down the spiral, as if he had broken a sacred trust. In the basement, red-eyed sensors on the walls tripped the lights and a hard white glare flooded the long room. He was in the stacks, a space in which shelves of rarely used books and research materials were pressed tightly together. Passing through a doorway at the end of the room, Sam entered a low corridor blocked off by a hinged slab of iron, like the door of a great safe. To his surprise, this seemingly impenetrable barrier yawned wide at his touch, and he moved beyond it onto a metal platform that jutted into utter darkness.

Sam stopped in his tracks, his hand on the platform's rusty rail. After weeks of relentless heat the incredible chill of this place struck him like an open-handed slap. There was nothing to be seen except the grille under his feet and the lick of light that projected through the doorway behind him. It was like floating in space. Robbed of sight, he could nevertheless sense the vastness of the void he had entered. The drip of faraway water reached up to him and the very air seemed to vibrate with a humming emptiness. Taking out his phone, he used the screen to illuminate the staircase that dropped off the edge of the platform.

Down Sam plunged. Down the rickety stair and into raven-black shadows that clawed beneath the city's concrete mask. As he went, his meagre light chanced upon foundation stones carved with dates that reached back to brutal, long-ago days. Did those above know that they walked upon the primitive bones of their city, Sam wondered? That far below them a darkness from less civilized times stirred?

The phone shook in his hand. He imagined himself reaching the last step only to find Edgar Dritch standing upon a mountain of corpses, like the twisted ruler of some medieval plague pit. And then his trainer slammed against stone and he was at the bottom of the hollow. Looking back, the halo of his phone picked out only a few silver-grey slivers of stair before the darkness pushed it back. Sam pulled the neck of his T-shirt over his nose and turned his light on the passage that stretched out before him.

He stood in the dank, dripping archway of an old sewage tunnel. A channel of putrid water filmed with a toxic-green glaze took up most of the tunnel while a narrow walkway ran along the side. Billows of bluebottles droned over the surface and monstrous rats the size of puppies slipped in and out of the slime. From this stew of pollution, rotting in the bowels of the city, a black and infernal stench rose up.

Sam brought to mind the twists and turns of the map, sucked down a breath of tainted air, and set off again. The flagstones were sewage-slick and at one point he reeled on the lip of the channel. A meaty bubble broke the surface, and Sam imagined some mutant creature waiting beneath, its greedy eye fixed on his flailing body. If such a horror really existed in this forgotten place then it was to be disappointed. His arms windmilling, he managed to regain his balance and collapsed against the weeping wall. Slower now, more cautious, he picked his way down the path, toeing rats into the water as he went.

The corner of the tunnel turned into a wider waterway. The sewage flowed faster here, its course caressed by a thin yellow mist which coiled jealously around Sam's ankles. He moved through this murk until his mental map told him he must be close to his destination. Now he stood for a moment, his phone light pushing at the gloom while the poisonous air scorched his throat. What on earth did he think he was going to find here? A secret entrance to the magician's lair with which he could impress Cassandra? It was ludicrous. He should just—

' . . . indeed, I fully expect my little experiment will cause quite a stir.'

Sam's heart leapt into his mouth. It was the same high, piping voice from Cassandra's recording. It seemed to echo from somewhere above but his light was too frail to reach the source, and in any case he didn't much fancy being discovered. He slipped his phone into his pocket and waited, breathless.

'Yes, any day now,' Edgar Dritch continued, 'though the exact time cannot be accurately predicted . . . No, alas I will be away that Tuesday evening . . . Yes, my flight to Munich leaves at nine o'clock on the fifteenth, but I shall return the following afternoon . . . Ah yes, the poor, dear children. But aren't they always the ones to suffer?'

Laughter, cruel and hysterical, shivered down from above.

'The mirror? Yes, it will be safe enough while I'm away. I keep it under lock and key, of course, and who would be fool enough to try to steal it from my Phantasmagorium . . . ? What's that? Oh wheels within wheels, my old friend. The project, the mirror, the children—one day, when it's all over, I'll explain it all and you will marvel at my cleverness.'

11
Hideously Human

If Sam expected the jack-knifing events to continue apace he was to be disappointed. Returning to the Bluffs, he washed the stench of the sewer from his body, and waited . . .

And waited.

And waited.

As the tortoise hours of Sunday crept into the beginning of the week, and Monday's monotonous minutes ground into Tuesday, then Wednesday, so Sam's anxiety mounted. During sleepless nights, his imagination conjured scene after dreadful scene, one in particular inspired by his favourite artist: he saw Cass being dragged down a shadow-rich alley by a fantastic William Blake dragon, the name 'Dritch' etched onto its scaly back.

It wasn't just the idea of losing Cassandra that made him anxious. Lionel hadn't spoken to him since their fight. He had been overruled by Cora on the issue of Sam remaining at the flat, and so he now watched his nephew with all the intensity of a muzzled dog waiting for its chance to bite. Maybe Sam was becoming paranoid, but it seemed that his uncle's sidelong glances became even more suspicious during Saturday's evening news, which carried the report of an explosion that had killed café waitress Theresa Trimble. Although the cause seemed to be an accidental gas leak, the police were keen to speak to a young couple who might be able to assist with their inquiries. When sketches based on a trucker's description flashed on screen, Sam felt his skin prickle. To his artistic eye, the likeness was vague at best. Still Lionel treated him to a curious stare. Was he connecting the time of Sam's arrival back at the Bluffs with that strong scent of burning that had clung to his clothes?

As Wednesday dawned, an exhausted Sam realized that it was now only a week until the fifteenth, the date when Dritch planned to be away from the Phantasmagorium. While he unravelled the bandages from his injured hand and re-dressed the still-throbbing wound, he asked himself the question: If there was still no sign of Cass would he dare to enter Dritch's lair alone? It seemed that whatever the magician was planning, the Stevenson mirror was a vital part of his scheme, but then would Sam even recognize the looking glass if he saw it?

The city continued to suffer under the cruel sun. Now into the third week of the heat wave, Sam noticed how the people around him were starting to transform. In the beginning they had welcomed its rays like the sun-worshippers of old, now they prayed for rain. On the news there had been reports of road rage attacks caused, so the experts said, by the sweltering heat. Dipping into the cool corridors of Pendleton, Sam reflected that Robert Louis Stevenson had made a mistake with his story—Dr Jekyll didn't need a potion to change into Mr Hyde, he just needed three weeks in the sun.

On his way to English, he ran into Charlie Ridley. It was the first time he'd seen Chugger since their meeting with Crail and, to his horror, he saw the same dark stamp of Project Hyde that he'd noticed on his own features. Bruised rings circled Charlie's eyes and the healthy glow that usually suffused his cheeks had been replaced with a chalky greyness.

'Hey Charlie,' Sam's greeting sounded timorous in his ears, 'how's it going?'

'I'm good,' Chugger assured him, a guarded smile trembling at the corners of his mouth. 'What's happening with you?'

'Not much.'

'How . . . ' Chugger wiped a finger across his lips, removing a blot of spittle. 'How you getting on with Crail's project? I started it with Mould but we decided to work separately. He couldn't stand my hockey stories and I couldn't stand his . . . Well, I just couldn't stand *him*.' The laugh was on the knife-edge of hysteria. 'I've got eight gold keys in the bank so far, only four more to go and I get . . . Well, I'm not sure if there's a prize, but it's fun, right?' He hesitated, an expression somewhere between shame and defiance muddying his usually open features. 'I mean, it's pretty lame, posting comments to people who don't exist, but it's kinda . . . liberating, don't you think?'

Liberating. Yes, that's the word. Despite all he now knew, Sam once again felt the whisper of Project Hyde; that itch at his fingertips that had so soothed his anger.

'People think I'm this lunkhead who's only good with a stick and a ball,' Charlie went on. 'Good old Chugger sinking the brewskies and snogging every girl in sight.

But we all have a private face, right? The face we don't show to friends and family . . . ' He tried to suppress a shiver. 'That face can have sharp teeth, Sam. It can gnaw at you because it wants—it *needs* to be seen. This thing of Crail's, it kinda relieves the frustration. I don't know if that's part of the lesson it's supposed to teach us, but it helps, taking your frustration out on something while keeping the face secret. You know what I mean, don't you?'

Oh yes, I do. God, I do.

'Charlie, the thing is . . . ' Again, Sam was struck by the impossibility of putting Charlie and the others on their guard. Despite what he had heard in the sewer below the Phantasmagorium, he still had no hard evidence that there was anything sinister going on. 'Look, I've stopped working on Project Hyde and—'

'Then why'd you let me stand here talking like an idiot!' Even with his recent weight loss, Charlie was an intimidating presence and, for a moment, Sam thought that good old Chugger would knock him to the ground. But then the tension seemed to flood out of him and he slapped Sam on the shoulder. 'You really ought to get started again, mate.'

'My thoughts exactly,' snapped Miss Crail. 'Sam. My office. Now.'

His anger forgotten, Charlie gave his friend a goodbye grimace as Sam followed Miss Crail through the winding hallways and into her cluttered domain. Crail slammed the door and turned on him like an enraged scorpion.

'So you've given up, have you? May I ask why?'

'I've been busy.'

'Is that so? Tell me, am I a figure of fun to you?'

'What?'

'Do you find it amusing to mock my work in this department?' She marched up to him and thrust her beaky nose into his face. 'How many hours did I spend helping you when you came to this school, answering your moronic questions and marking your pathetic essays? Now when I ask for a little help in return, you throw it back in my face.'

Miss Crail's reputation for strictness was legendary but this was something else. Her carefully pinned hair had come loose and a veil of grey locks swept untidily over her flushed face.

'You *will* engage again in this project, Mr Stillhouse, are we clear?'

'Crystal,' he answered through gritted teeth.

'Good. Now there's no point in you coming to class,' said Miss Crail, tidying her errant hair back into its neat bob. 'I want you to go straight to the library and start work.'

She held open the door. As Sam passed, the English teacher took an uncertain breath.

'Wait . . . Perhaps I was a little harsh just now. You are a *very* gifted student and it wasn't fair to suggest otherwise. It's just this thing is important to me. Much might hang on the outcome.'

She looked back into the office where the framed portrait of a young woman hung on the wall above her desk. The room was such a clutter of books and posters, art prints and mugshots of famous authors that Sam had never noticed the picture before. Now he saw the resemblance between this young woman and Miss Crail: they had the same birdlike nose and sharp, unsmiling eyes, yet there was also a suggestion of kindness in that granite face. Were they mother and daughter, he wondered, and, if so, was the younger Miss Crail a factor in the mystery? The teacher was being blackmailed by Edgar Dritch to engage her pupils in Project Hyde—what if her daughter was being used as leverage?

Afternoon lessons had begun and the corridors of Pendleton breathed stillness. Sam was debating how he could possibly take part in the project, thereby diverting Crail's suspicion, when he heard the sound of crying coming from down the hall. He followed it past vacant classrooms and the empty gymnasium, eventually tracing its source to the drama studio and a trembling curtain.

The girl hiding there was about thirteen years old, her freckled face splotchy with tears. She looked at Sam with all the fear of a field mouse staring up at a swooping owl. He took a step back from the curtain and raised his hands, as if to say, *Hey, I won't eat you, promise.*

'My name's Sam, are you OK?'

A fresh sob rattled the girl from head to toe.

'You're gonna be all right. Here, look.' He took a packet of tissues from his bag (for some reason Cora slipped a fresh pack in every week) and handed them to her. While she wiped her eyes, he asked, 'Do you want me to get a teacher? Mr Matheson, maybe?'

The girl shook her head determinedly.

'Good call. I'm not sure I could stand a dose of Matheson's BO either.' That won him a smile. 'So what's your name?'

'Gail. Gail Matthews.'

'Cool. You know if teachers aren't your style I'm a pretty good listener.' She looked down at the tissue scrunched in her hands. Sam knew the signs, had seen them often in the bathroom mirror and his own tear-streaked face. 'Has someone been hurting you?'

'Not h-hurting,' she stammered.

'Not physically, but they've been saying stuff, right? Calling you names? Someone in your class?' Again, she shook her head. 'A kid in another year? A teacher? OK, someone else ... Is it someone at home, Gail? Your mum, your dad?'

'No.'

'Then who?'

'It's not anyone I know. It's someone out there.' She made an airy gesture towards the windows. 'I keep blocking them but somehow they keep breaking through. They say things about me. Terrible things. Things I'd never—'

The door of the drama lab squeaked open. 'There you are! You're late for our meeting. Carrion Wrath and Mary Merridown are needed in the library pronto ... Oh, who's this?'

In the blink of an eye, Gail Matthews had become the frightened field mouse again, this time recoiling from a puzzled Doreen Lackland. With fresh tears in her eyes, she threw Sam a reproachful glance and darted for the door.

'Gail, what's wrong?' he called after her, but she had already vanished into the school's labyrinthine corridors.

'What was all that about?' Doreen asked as she marched Sam to the library. 'Upsetting Year Nines doesn't seem your style.'

'Someone's been upsetting her,' Sam growled, 'but it isn't me.'

They took a seat at one of the study desks in empty library, and Doreen nodded, her voice low and thoughtful. 'Bullying is an awful thing. It takes away the victim's sense of self-worth. My father . . . '

She shook her head and pulled the laptop from her bag. It seemed to Sam that she was operating on a kind of autopilot, flipping back the screen and entering her password to gain access to the school's Wi-Fi. Like Charlie, there had been a dramatic transformation since he'd seen her last. The same dark circles bruised her eyes and her cheeks stood out in sharp ridges. Trembling fingers clicked the keys as she summoned the Project Hyde website and 'Mary Merridown's' homepage. Sam sat back from the desk, suddenly wary of the lure of the program.

It was only as the page loaded that Doreen seemed to come to her senses. She twitched her head towards Sam, then focused on that area of the page which he had suddenly homed in on. Too late, she slammed down the screen.

In that brief glimpse he had seen the private photograph Doreen had uploaded onto her Hyde profile. No longer resembling the plain Jane president of the debate society, this was a vision of something warped and oddly repellent, its metamorphosis much more advanced than Sam's had been. There was an impression of ugliness, he thought, but nothing definitely hideous. And suddenly he remembered Robert Louis Stevenson's story and the devilish Mr Hyde, who everyone agreed was disfigured but whose exact deformity no character could describe.

'Has your picture changed?' Doreen asked with a hollow laugh. 'I confess, I don't really understand the point of it.'

'Doreen, I . . . I've stopped working on the project.'

The same guarded, almost aggressive expression that had overcome Charlie now tightened Doreen's features. It was as if they had thought of Sam as a member of some trusted, mystic circle only to discover that he had never understood their silly rituals and had been laughing behind their backs.

'Then you don't know.'

She grabbed her bag from the table and shoved the laptop under her arm.

'We were supposed to be working as a team. I will not fail this assignment, Sam. I will *not*.'

Sam sat alone in the silence of library, head in his hands. When he shut his eyes the face of Doreen Lackland imprinted itself behind his closed lids. Not the enraged, emaciated face he had just seen but the face of her Hyde avatar. A face made all the more hellish because it appeared so hideously . . . He spoke the word in a whisper—

'Human.'

12
Drawn by the Bad Man

'In our main news this morning, an inexplicable tragedy has rocked the Scottish town of Balfour. We go now to crime correspondent Naval Bhasin.'

The TV picture switched to a man in a yellow mackintosh standing on a promontory of jagged rocks. To his right, a churning stretch of slate-grey sea, to his left, a short pier jutting out into the shallows. A snapping police cordon guarded by a uniformed officer made a rough circle around the tumbledown structure.

'It was here that, at five o'clock this morning, a man walking his dog made a gruesome discovery.' Naval Bhasin gestured to the rusted ironwork suspended four metres above the shore. 'The body of local schoolboy Lance Newton was found washed up beneath this half-demolished pier. Lance's hands had been tied behind his back and the word "Loser" had been written in marker pen on his forehead.'

'Oh my God,' Cora murmured.

Sitting beside her, Sam dropped his spoon into his bowl of cereal, his appetite suddenly gone.

'Police want to speak to twelve students from Balfour Academy,' the reporter continued, 'all of whom disappeared in the early hours of this morning. Most simply vanished, but a few were confronted by their parents as they tried to leave home. One of those was Thomas McAdam. His mother had this to say—'

When the picture changed again, Cora gasped. 'What on earth's happened to that poor woman?'

Mrs McAdam sat up in her hospital bed, a blood-stained bandage covering the right side of her face. Her left eye, the only one visible, was round with horror and full of tears. Flashbulbs went off, shocking moisture onto her cheeks.

'All I want to say is this: it wasn't Tommy who killed that boy. He's a shy child, frightened of his own shadow. The other kids would tease him about being so small for his age and . . . Well, he's a good boy.'

'Where do you think Tommy is now, Mrs McAdam?' asked a reporter. 'Is he with the other children who disappeared?'

'I don't know.' She shook her injured head. 'Tommy didn't have many friends.'

'But it was your son that attacked you last night?'

'I thought it was him . . . at first. He was small, you see, and he was wearing my son's pyjamas. I was only half awake and I asked him what he thought he was doing, wandering around the house at three in the morning. He—*It*—it told me to mind my own bloody business. That voice was *not* my son's. I screamed, and that's when it attacked me.'

'Did you see its face? Are you sure it wasn't—?'

'It looked *nothing* like Tommy. That thing must

have abducted my son and the other children. Then it drowned that poor boy under the pier . . . '

'The police say you've been unable to provide a clear description of your attacker.'

Mrs McAdam's shaking fingers went to the side of her head, where blood had spread like a Rorschach test.

'I can't describe its face,' she whispered. 'It was awful, ugly, but not in any understandable way. It was just . . . wrong.'

The picture returned to Naval Bhasin. The tide had come in and the reflection of the murder pier wavered in the dark waters.

'One final puzzle in this already perplexing tragedy is the fact that, although these children went to the same school, they don't appear to have been friends. And so this morning the town of Balfour is asking the question: how can twelve seemingly innocent and unconnected children be involved in such a brutal crime?'

A senseless mystery, a face indefinably deformed: it had to be a coincidence, didn't it? The Phantasmagorium was based in this city while the town of Balfour was over three hundred miles to the north. Sam shook his head. What was happening here and now was puzzling enough, he didn't need to go looking for mysteries.

He picked up his bag from the hall and set out for school. Pearing down every side street and alleyway, Sam only vaguely noticed the sun's relentless lick on the back of his neck. He searched for Cassandra and for that stranger's face that might turn out to be the black magician himself. All he saw were the wilting masses plodding the pavement and throwing murderous glances at the sky.

At Pendleton, he snagged the blazer of a Year Nine student and pulled him out of a line filing into the assembly hall.

'Do you know someone in your year called Gail Matthews?' Ever since their encounter in the drama studio, Sam had been keeping an eye out for the girl.

'She's home, sick,' the boy said, smoothing his ruffled blazer. 'Why'd you care anyway? Gail's a freak.'

Squatting down, Sam levelled his gaze with kid's. 'You know who else is a freak, little man? *Me.* And the thing with us freaks is, we stick together. So if you've got a problem with Gail you've got a problem with me, understand?'

'Yeah,' the boy mumbled. 'Sure.'

Sam watched him scuttle into the hall. Somewhere inside he could feel the Wrath licking its lips, savouring this tiny appetizer while still hungry for a more substantial meal. It had been so quiet during those days and nights of Project Hyde, and now Sam wondered: had it really been sleeping or instead gorging itself on all those smart, snide comments he'd posted? The thought made him sick to the stomach.

Apart from running into Martin Gilbert in the lunch hall, the rest of the day passed without incident. Picking listlessly at his salad, Mouldy Martin looked to be in even worse shape than Charlie and Doreen. He appeared skeletally thin and the stench radiating from his unwashed body was almost enough to put Sam off sitting next to him.

'If you don't eat it soon I reckon that tomato will evolve legs and make a run for it,' Sam said, opening a bag of crisps in the vain hope that the aroma of salt and vinegar might mask Martin's eye-watering odour. 'You OK, Mould?'

'Think you're funny, calling me that?' Martin turned angry eyes on him. 'Just because my family's poor you think you can take the piss?'

'No.' Sam blinked. 'I'm sorry, I didn't think you minded.'

'Why? Because I've never stood up for myself before?' Martin thrust his food across the table and onto the floor. Salad scattered and a host of heads turned in their direction.

'I'm not taking it any more.' Jumping onto his seat, he swept the lunch hall with a seething glare, his lips drawn back over painfully red gums. 'You've all pushed me and pushed me and pushed me, and now I'm pushing back. *You hear me?!'*

Giggles erupted around the hall. Sam tried to reach up to him but Martin batted the calming hand away and leapt down from his seat. At the door to the outer corridor, a concerned Mr Wardell attempted to block his path. Martin Gilbert, the sullen butt of a thousand jokes, punched the geography teacher full in the face. The giggles stopped dead and a few screams broke out as Wardell staggered back, his nose spuming blood. Meanwhile, Martin made good his escape.

As he left for home later that afternoon, Sam heard that 'Madman Mould' had been arrested but that Wardell didn't want to press charges. Obviously the poor kid had suffered some kind of breakdown. In the car park, he saw Miss Crail getting into her rusted-to-hell Nissan Micra. Their eyes locked and Sam prepared for that booming voice to ring out. Instead she bowed her head like a weary penitent, got into her car, and sped off through the gates.

It was Friday afternoon and the sun-crazed city seemed almost delirious. Car horns honked as office workers fled from its boiling built-up heart into the cooler suburbs. Those forced to live around the Bluffs prowled the pavements like caged animals, bubbling with a directionless kind of anger. Sam stepped cautiously around a ring of teenagers that had congregated in the courtyard and headed for the lifts. Backs turned, shoulders hunched, they watched him pass through narrowed eyes.

He was thinking about everything he had heard and seen that day, certain now that the time had come to tell the others all he knew, when he noticed the man at his side. Lionel stared dead ahead and poked his finger at the already illuminated lift button. Once inside the flat, he disappeared into the bathroom while Sam went to the kitchen and gulped down a pint of water. School shirt clinging to his sweat-slick body, he found himself longing for the chill of that subterranean stairway beneath the city library, sewer stench and all. Memories of that darkness led to thoughts of Edgar Dritch and the date of his absence from the Phantasmagorium. Only four days to go . . .

The corner of a letter lying on the worktop caught his eye, and suddenly the magician was forgotten. As if moving through treacle-thick air, Sam approached the table, reached out to the pile of unopened mail, and plucked the third letter from the top. The scarlet stamp and familiar handwriting had the power to force him to his knees, and all at once Sam found himself sitting cross-legged on the floor, the envelope in his lap. His thumb brushed the stamp—**STEMIST MOOR PRISON**—and the firm letters making up his name.

The flap came away in a jagged tear. Inside, six sheets of unlined paper, folded twice and slipped with care into the envelope. The care of a man who had many, many hours in which to perfect his letters.

Dear Sammy

I don't know if you got my other letters. The screws say I can write all I want but you wont ever receive one cos you're said you never want to hear from me again. I don't blame you, son, but I'm going to keep writing anyway. Because I love you. <u>I do</u>. With all my heart and soul

'NO!'

He crushed the pages in his fist and threw them across the kitchen. The terror in his mind had vanished, burned away by the heat of the Wrath. It raged within in him now, its fury as bright as the sun that beat through the flyspecked window. He covered his mouth with his hand, as if to stop those razor-sharp rays from escaping his lips. He must never let that happen. Must never allow the Wrath to be seen.

One of the balled pages had landed by his feet and now began unfurl like a flower. A dark, hateful flower with lies printed on its petals. Except this page, the last, had no writing on it. Instead a pencil sketch was slowly unveiled. In all his childhood years, Sam had never seen his father draw so much as a stickman, but now he remembered Cora saying that Samuel Stillhouse had been quite creative. Before.

'No,' Sam whimpered. 'Please, no . . .'

It was a moment drawn from memory: three figures hand in hand on the riverbank, shaded by the wispy arms of a willow tree. They were smiling. It had been a good day. They had laughed and played and the bad man had stayed away. The hand marked **L O V E** had brushed little Sam's cheek and wiped grateful tears from his mother's face. *This is a new start*, the good man had promised. *If you and Sammy stay with me, I know I can stop drinking and we can be a proper family again.* A kiss for his mum. *I love you.*

'No, no, no.' Sam shook his head, but the words rang inside his mind, clear and strong: *And I love you, little man. Know why?*

Why? Bright eyes, desperate to know.

Because we're peas in a pod, you and me. Two sides of the same coin. And you know what? Little Sam shook his head. *We'll always be together.*

Always.

'Sam? What are you doing down there?'

He kept his eyes fixed on the crumpled sketch as Cora bent down and picked the envelope from the floor.

'Stemist Moor . . . Oh Jesus! I'm getting on the phone to that bloody place right now!' He heard her storm into the living room and snatch the phone from its cradle. While waiting for the call to connect, she whispered, 'He's got a letter from his father. Go see if he's all right . . . What? For God's sake, Lionel, just do it!'

The pencil figures stared back at him, their hopeful smiles somehow mocking.

'Want a cup of tea?' Lionel spoke from the doorway.

'Yes, this is Cora Kremper . . . Well, I'll tell you what I'm phoning about, shall I? After that animal you've got caged up down there bashed my sister's brains in, we made it clear that Sam didn't want to have any contact with his father. Right . . . Well, he's just received a letter and now the kid's in pieces . . . A clerical error? Are you kidding me!'

Lionel took the sketch from the floor and threw it into the bin.

'Why did you do that?' Sam blinked up at him.

'That's where the rubbish goes,' Lionel shrugged. 'Now, do you want a cup of tea?'

'Tea?' he sneered. 'No, I don't want tea.'

'Then what *do* you want? Someone to sit down there with you and dry your tears? Come on, Samuel,' Lionel said, his voice not unkind, 'you know better than most that's not the way of the world. You get kicked, you fall down, you get up, you get kicked again. Same old cycle until one day you just don't get up any more. That day comes for us all, but I don't think it's come for you just yet. Whatever else you are, you're a fighter.'

Sam leapt to his feet and thrust Lionel against the fridge, rattling the bottles inside.

'You don't know anything about me.'

'No,' Lionel agreed. 'But I knew a lot about him.'

Sam loosened his fingers and backed up into the hall. Cora was still pouring expletives into the ear of the governor of Stemist Moor Prison when he slammed the front door behind him and plunged down the stairwell. The temptation was suddenly very strong, his anger screamed to be released, and he reached into his pocket and took out his phone. Even with everything he now knew, it took all of Sam's determination not to connect to the net and log onto Project Hyde.

By the time he pounded the last step, he was breathing hard and drenched in sweat. Outside, he ran straight into the circle of teenagers he'd seen earlier in the courtyard. Clearly the leader of the gang, the largest of them peeled away and placed his gigantic hands on Sam's shoulders.

'Where you running to, blood?'

Sam looked up at that grinning, tattooed face and waited for the inevitable punch or the bite of a blade between his ribs. Instead, the gang leader guided him to the centre of their circle. A crowd of faces smiled back at him, mischievous but not unfriendly. He'd seen most of them in and around the Bluffs, harmless pranksters for the most part, hissing their tags onto bins and spinning skateboards over benches.

'What do you want?' Sam asked.

'S'not what we want. *She's* the one calling the shots.'

The gang parted.

There, at the heart of this motley crew, the fire girl burned.

13
The Boy and His Troll

'Thanks Weevil.' Cassandra bumped fists with the gigantic gang leader. 'I'll take it from here.'

''K. Later, Red.'

With a snap of his fingers, Weevil's followers dispersed like a cloud of smoke, skateboards clacking on concrete as one hooded tendril slipped around the eastern edge of the Bluffs while another collected their bikes and wafted away in the direction of Old Town.

Sam's heart thumped, and not just from the quickly fading traces of his anger. After a week without word, he hadn't expected to see her again. He'd often reminded himself how clever and resourceful she was, though deep down he had started to believe the visions that swam through his head: Cassandra dying in an alley, her heart cooling in the bloody fist of Edgar Dritch; yet here she stood, a living rose in the wasteland of the Bluffs.

'Friends of yours?' he asked.

'The Bluffs Boyz?' Cassandra smiled. 'They're rather sweet, aren't they?'

'In a terrifying kinda way, I guess.' He raked fingers through his sweat-laced hair. 'Where've you been?'

'Everywhere. Nowhere,' she shrugged. 'Used a few techie tricks to lay a false trail so that Dritch would believe I'd gone back to the States. That took a while, and since then I've been moving around the country, just to be sure he couldn't psychically pinpoint me.'

'And are you safe now?'

'Safe as I can be, but it's not a good idea for us to talk out in the open.'

'Come on then, I know a place.'

Taking her hand, Sam led the way behind the crumbling high-rise.

'Are you OK?' She reached out to touch the dried tracks of his tears. 'Sam, what's happened?'

'Doesn't matter,' he said, turning his face away. 'It's nothing to do with the mirror.'

With the Bluffs behind them, they entered what had once been the hub of this community and which now stood as a sad reminder of its failure. Sam kicked through the long grass that grew like scraggy whiskers around the community centre's boarded mouth. Covered in creeping plants, the small square building was a mass of graffiti upon which even the birds had sprayed their distinctive yellow-black tags. Hard to believe that this place had once hosted tea parties, jumble sales and children's discos.

'Charming,' Cassandra smiled, as Sam swung back a loose plank from the door and led her into the musty shell. 'This where you bring all your dates?'

'You wanted somewhere out of the way.' He took a seat on an empty oil drum and fixed her with a direct gaze. 'So how come you're suddenly hanging with the Bluffs Boyz? Nearly getting blown up not exciting enough? Now you need a little pickpocketing on the side?'

'They were my eyes and ears while I was away. A grand well spent, I thought.'

'You gave that lot a thousand pounds?' Sam boggled. 'For what?'

'To keep an eye on my favourite Limey. Seems you've had an uneventful week.'

'Huh,' he snorted, 'I think you ought to hire yourself some better spies.'

He told her the tale of his investigations in the sewer network. In the silence that followed, Cass took a turn around the empty building, daylight from the busted roof dazzling against her smoothly freckled skin.

'He'll be away that night? You're sure that's what you heard?'

'Certain,' Sam confirmed. 'So what do we do? Break in and steal back the mirror?'

She shook her head. 'This isn't your fight, Sam.'

'Bollocks it isn't! My friends have been drawn into this and I . . .'

'Yes?' She looked at him curiously.

'Nothing,' he sighed. 'But look, I think it's time you told me what this mirror is exactly. It might be a good starting point for us to figure out what connects it with Project Hyde.'

'Some people call it "Jekyll's Mirror",' Cassandra began. 'Those few who know of its existence, anyway. Others have named it "the Stevenson Mirror" or "James' Gift". You've heard of the author Henry James?'

'Didn't he write that ghost story about the governess and the two kids?'

'*The Turn of the Screw*,' Cassandra nodded. 'James was a brilliant author in his own right but, for the purpose of our story, the most important thing about him was his friendship with Robert Louis Stevenson. In 1885, Stevenson moved with his wife Frances to the town of Bournemouth. He was a frail man and had been suffering from a chronic illness most of his life.'

'Right.' In the preface to his copy of *Jekyll and Hyde*, Sam had found a short biography of the author. 'Some kind of lung problem, wasn't it? I read he used to cough up blood and that he was on all kinds of weird drugs.'

'That's right. The drugs might even have inspired the nightmare that led to *Jekyll and Hyde*. He dreamed the transformation scene, you know: an ordinary man swallowing a potion and transforming into his darker self.'

'So what has this got to do with Henry James?'

'James was visiting his sister in Bournemouth when he heard that the Stevensons had bought a house nearby. He and Louis, as Stevenson preferred to be called, had been writing to each other for years, so James decided to pay a call. They soon became firm friends and James bought Louis a mirror to furnish his new home. Records my father unearthed suggest that the looking glass was purchased from an antique dealer on the Old Kent Road.'

'And?'

'Nothing. It was a circular mirror, thirty inches in diameter, with a convex surface which warped any reflection.'

'But it was some kind of supernatural object, right?'

Cassandra shrugged. 'To the best of our knowledge it was a perfectly ordinary mirror made by Boggs & Company of London.'

'Then how did it get its powers?'

'We don't know that it has any. Not for sure.'

'You're kidding! Then what's all the fuss about?'

Cass leaned forward, her palms pressed together. 'Edgar Dritch stays firmly in the shadows, Sam. He has agents to do his dirty work for him. But last Christmas he broke cover to go looking for Stevenson's Mirror, and he murdered my father and sister to get it. We don't know for sure what this mirror is, but if it's important to Dritch it must have power.'

'Someone has to have some kind of idea, though,' Sam argued.

'There are rumours,' Cassandra conceded. 'After the nightmare that inspired *Jekyll and Hyde*, Louis ordered that the mirror be boxed up immediately and placed in the vaults of his London bank. Years later, he had an urge to see it again and asked for it to be transported to his new home on the Pacific island of Upolo. There, in his tropical paradise, he opened the crate and looked into the dusty glass that, for almost a decade, had reflected nothing. He then turned to his wife and asked, 'Does my face look strange?' Those were the last words he ever spoke. He died a few hours later.'

'His face.' Sam shivered, thinking of the avatars from Project Hyde. 'Did it change?'

'That's one of the rumours, yes: that the mirror has the ability to change a person physically. To reflect the darkness pent up inside.'

'But how?'

'Well, again this is just rumour and legend, but it's based on a story Louis's wife told after his death.' Cassandra settled herself more comfortably on the barrel. 'On the night of the transformation dream, Louis woke in a terrified frenzy, the image of a man changing into his darker self still burning inside his mind. The first thing he saw when he opened his eyes was the mirror, his reflection warped in its curved surface. Some say that his incredible imagination somehow transmitted the theme of duality and the power to transform *into* the glass. Stories are strange things, Sam. They can change the lives of their readers, and *Jekyll and Hyde*? Well, it's one of the most potent stories ever written.

'After Louis's death, his wife had the mirror sent straight back to London. And there it remained for a hundred and twenty years. Six months ago, an auction of Stevenson memorabilia was held in New York and the mirror was part of a job lot. My father attended and bought it quite cheaply.'

'But if there were rumours then surely Dritch would've been there bidding for it.'

'The mirror was mislabelled by the auctioneers. My father didn't realize what he'd bought until he got it back to the store and did a little research. News of Edward Kane's purchase came to Dritch a few weeks later and he set off for the States.'

'And now he has the mirror. But what does he want to do with it?'

'That's the question,' Cassandra nodded. 'Now it's your turn to tell me what you know.'

Sam stumbled over his words. He outlined the story of Miss Crail's role-play game, gave brief character sketches of Doreen, Charlie and Martin, then explained how they'd been encouraged to vent their feelings against online personalities created by the program, the purpose of which was to demonstrate how anonymity could allow a person to show his true face to the world. He could feel shame licking inside as he thought back to the messages he'd posted.

'I guess it's like Dr Jekyll in the story,' he said. 'The mask of Hyde freed him from the rules of society and allowed him to become everything he really was.'

'Except that isn't quite the moral,' said Cass. 'Hyde became a monster because Jekyll was a hypocrite. If he'd lived more honestly, admitting to his friends and himself that he was a flawed man with natural urges, then Hyde wouldn't have been so violent and vicious. It was by denying his whole self that Jekyll was doomed.'

Sam shook his head. He didn't want to admit what the project had brought out of him, but it felt important to be honest with Cass. 'Some of the things I wrote on the forum, they were horrible. Things I'd never ... I don't know why I did it.'

'Don't you?' she murmured, and let the question hang.

'But I still can't see what the project has to do with the mirror,' Sam sighed. 'There's nothing in the program I've seen that mentions it. The players just post their messages and then the pictures they've uploaded start to change.'

'How?'

Again Sam couldn't quite put into words the deformity of Doreen's picture. 'But they've all changed in the past week,' he went on. 'They're on edge, they don't look like they've slept much, and they've all lost weight.'

'Almost as if they're being prepared ... ' Taking a mobile from her pocket, Cassandra's fingers danced over the keys. 'Sam, there's something you need to see.'

Twenty minutes later they were striding through the splendour of the city's upmarket shopping district. No broken windows here, no weeds foresting the pavements, no blood-tipped needles in the gutters, just the bright mask that the city wore over its festering face. Cassandra had been resolutely silent ever since they left the Bluffs. Only now, as they stepped into the Grand Metro Plaza, did she look up from her phone.

'I told you I was good with tech. After you mentioned Project Hyde, I managed to hack into the activity on the account of your friend Martin Gilbert, or "Joe Retched" as his Hyde avatar is known. What I discovered wasn't pretty. See that kid over there?' She pointed to a boy of about twelve standing alone outside an electronics store. 'Watch.'

In the great glass bowl of the open-air plaza schools of shoppers floated like fish from store to store, blinking vacantly through windows and fluttering in and out of doors. At the edge of this slowly spinning vortex, the boy rubbed his tired eyes and looked down at the phone in his hand.

'What am I supposed to be looking for?' Sam asked.

'Shhh.'

The whirlpool continued to gyrate around him while the boy stood stock still. And then suddenly his face twisted and tears spiked into his eyes. His hand shook and he started typing feverishly into his phone. There was a pause, then the kid rocked forward onto the tips of his trainers, a pose of silent anguish. He was waiting for something—a phone call, a text message—some communication that he both longed for and dreaded.

'Watch,' Cassandra whispered.

No one else heard the sound, or if they did they chose to ignore it. Focused so intently on the boy, Sam almost staggered back as a small but horrible wail reached his ears. The communication had been received and the phone fell from shaking fingers. The casing snapped and a passing shopper, busy with his own call, heeled the mobile into the ground. A moment later, the distraught child fled the plaza.

'Don't understand,' Sam murmured.

'I think you do. I've hacked into the kid's messages, Sam.' She held out her mobile phone for him to see. 'It's *real.*'

He watched the message flash on the small screen and knew that she was right. The project wasn't some lame educational tool designed to help students with their understanding of *Jekyll and Hyde*. Its purpose was dark and terrible, and it had the power to *change.*

Before Cassandra took back the phone, the flashing message burned itself into Sam's brain:

> Pathetic little Peter. You LOSER! Why don't you do the world a favour and
> KILL YOURSELF
> KILL YOURSELF
> KILL YOURSELF
> KILL YOURSELF
> KILL YOURSELF

Sender: Joe Retched

14
Dark Revelations

Sam wiped the last runner of vomit from his chin. Following Cassandra's revelation, he had fled the plaza and entered one of the side streets, where he doubled over and threw up his lunch. After quitting Project Hyde he had comforted himself that at least his victims were fictions created by the program. Now he knew they were real, he thought back to every snipe and barb. The worst of them might have had it coming, others had certainly not, and anyway, who was he to decide if someone deserved to be persecuted?

'It had to be real,' Cass said gently. 'There's no program on earth sophisticated enough to create so many fully rounded interactive characters. Instead it infiltrated social networking sites and selected people for the Project Hyde participants to victimize.'

'So I've been tormenting real people?'

'You didn't know.'

To Sam, that comfort seemed very small.

'It's called cyber bullying,' she went on, 'and, as you've seen with the kid in the plaza, the effects can be devastating. These messages are received on their normal

114

social networking site but the victims don't know who they're from, leading to a sense of isolation and fear.'

They walked in silence for a time, Sam's mind still reeling. A dark question occurred to him—would the spell of Project Hyde have worked had he known the truth? He'd like to think it wouldn't, but the obsession had soothed the Wrath and he couldn't be sure.

They returned to the courtyard below the Bluffs. Night was bedding its shadows around the tower as the sun finally dipped in the smouldering sky.

'Contact your friends and arrange a meeting for tomorrow,' said Cassandra. 'They don't know the harm they're doing, but kids like Peter shouldn't have to suffer like this.'

Turning away, she began to walk off in the direction of Old Town.

'Wait!' Sam shouted after her. 'What about tomorrow? How can I contact you?'

'I'll find *you*. G'night, Sammy.'

The snake tattooed on her arm rose in salute as she disappeared into the maze of streets surrounding the Bluffs. The sight of that sinuous serpent stirred a memory and Sam stood transfixed while something scratched at the back of his mind. Finally admitting defeat, he traipsed towards the lifts.

Inside the flat, he found Cora curled up on the sofa watching the evening news. Sam forced a cheerless smile and scratched the back of his bandaged hand.

'Itching's good,' she nodded. 'Shows that it's healing. You OK?'

'Yeah,' he sighed. 'Sorry for running off like that.'

'You had every right to be upset. The governor's given

me his personal assurance that you won't be getting any more letters from Stemist Moor.'

His heart lurched. That was good, right? 'Where's Lionel?'

'He's got a late shift.' Her gaze wandered back to the television where reporter Naval Bhasin stood under the pier on Balfour Beach. 'Now they're searching the hills and mountains around the town. Sam, whatever could have happened to those poor kids?'

*

He slept fitfully that night, sights and sounds tumbling through his dreams: a pencil sketch of a mother, father and son playing on the riverbank, the branches of a willow tree arching over their heads and red sap bleeding onto their upturned faces; a snake writhing across the fire girl's arm, appearing and vanishing; a body turning in the surf of an ink-black sea . . . Except that uncertain surface wasn't the sea, it was a mirror. And there, at the dead centre of its murky surface, a figure. The same figure that had invaded his earlier dream—a tall, rangy man with long arms and hair sprouting down past his shoulders.

A man with no face.

The dream's images were still shuffling through his head the next morning when he bumped into Cassandra outside the gates of Pendleton Grammar.

'You look tired,' she said.

'You look amazing.' The words were out before he could stop them. 'I mean . . . '

'Are you blushing, Sammy? Aw c'mon, don't frown, blushing suits you.'

He bristled. 'Want to see where we're meeting?'

116

'Sure. Are they all coming?'

'So they said, in their texts.'

He led her down the side of the school and through a rusted chain-link gate. Running behind some old outbuildings, a narrow path clotted with weeds brought them to a dilapidated tennis court. Surrounded by bramble bushes, the court provided a private oasis away from the eyes and ears of Pendleton. Since coming to the school, Sam had spent many hours here, wrapped in memories he never shared with Nurse Larry or Aunt Cora. Cassandra walked over to the net and ran her fingers through its mildewed mesh.

'Such a sad place, like that building behind the Bluffs. Why do you—?'

A shrill voice cut in. 'Sam? There you are! Now what's this all about?'

Doreen came striding into the court, her gaze switching from Sam to Cass. In the light that filtered through the bramble, she looked ever more sickly and wasted. The same was true of Charlie and Martin.

'Who's she?' Mould grunted suspiciously.

There was something rodent-like about them, their beady eyes blinking as if they'd been starved of daylight, their lips drawn back in an oddly threatening manner. Only Charlie seemed to have held onto some of his old carefree self.

'Party at my folk's place Monday night,' he said, sidling over and clapping Sam on the back. 'Why don't you bring your girlfriend?' He cast Cassandra an appreciative glance, yet to Sam it seemed an oddly hollow gesture. 'Kicks off at nine, bring beer.'

'Sam hasn't time to attend any parties,' Doreen said

117

tartly. 'I spoke with Miss Crail yesterday and it seems he's completely abandoned the project.'

'What?' Charlie's hand slipped from Sam's back. 'Dude, what's going on?'

'Who is she?' Martin repeated. 'You didn't say anything about *her* in your text.'

'I've put hours of work into this project,' Doreen persisted. 'I will not fail because my study partner can't be bothered to pull his weight.'

'Don't understand,' Chugger frowned. 'Why aren't you taking part?'

'Who *is* she?'

'I'll help you if you like. Get you started again.'

'Who. Is. She?'

'My grades won't suffer because—'

'Enough!' Sam's voice rang around the court and all three fell silent. 'This is Cassandra Kane. She came to me with suspicions about Project Hyde and—'

'Suspicions?' Doreen snorted. 'What suspicions?'

'There's something wrong with the program,' Sam said. 'It wasn't designed by Miss Crail and it has nothing to do with teaching us lessons about *Jekyll and Hyde*.'

Martin laughed. 'You're sounding like some kind of dumb conspiracy movie.'

'Mould has a point,' Charlie said. 'If it wasn't put together by Crail then who built it and why?'

'I can't go into specifics,' Sam admitted, 'but I can tell you the program's dangerous. But you already know that, don't you? You can see how it's started to change you. Doreen, you said it was addictive, compulsive. And Charlie, you told me about that private face gnawing at you and how this thing seems to let it out.' Chugger shuffled uncomfortably while Doreen stared at the ground. 'And Martin, look at how you behaved in the dining hall the other day, that wasn't you.'

'Maybe it *was*,' Martin said darkly. 'Maybe it was always me.'

'This is preposterous!' Doreen exclaimed. 'It's a game, that's all.'

'Except you don't really believe that,' Cassandra said, stepping forward. 'You're an intelligent girl, you know how this "game" has gotten under your skin. Literally.'

'What do you mean?' Charlie asked in a shaky voice.

'Just look at yourselves. You've changed.'

They glanced at each other, reluctantly examining haunted eyes, sagging skin, the bones poking at their flesh.

'No,' Doreen said at last, 'this is nonsense. Has to be. Anyway, I can't simply abandon the project, not without jeopardizing all the things Miss Crail promised us. I need to have this for my university application or my father—'

'You're scared of him, I know,' said Sam.

'You don't know anything,' she spat back. 'How could you?'

'Because I lived with a monster too . . . Look, I'm asking you to trust me on this. We have evidence that Miss Crail was blackmailed into using us as test subjects.'

'Subjects for what?' Charlie narrowed his eyes. 'You're going to have to give us a bit more than a few crazy theories, Sam.'

'Then I will. Cassandra?'

She turned to Martin, holding the screen of her phone an inch or two from his face.

'Last night you sent this message to one of the personalities created by the Hyde program. A kid called Peter. You told him he was a loser and that he ought to kill himself.'

Mould's already pale face blanched. 'How'd you know that?'

'Because we were with Peter when he received it.'

If Sam had expected a reaction he was to be disappointed. The three Hyde subjects stood in silence, their heads bowed. A moment passed, a tiny scrap of time in which Sam processed the truth.

'Did you work it out?' His voice quivered like a plucked harp. 'Did you realize before? The people you've been sending these messages to, you *know* they're real.'

'Don't be stupid,' Charlie laughed. It was a hollow thing, wan and weak.

'Why?' Sam whispered, his question addressed as much to himself as the others. 'You're good people, so *why?*'

Charlie came forward, palms outstretched, his voice pleading. 'Because—'

'Stop it!' Doreen grasped the hockey captain's wrist and dragged him away from Sam. 'You call us all here and expect us to swallow some half-baked theory, then accuse us of God knows what! I'm one golden key away from completing this task and I'll not be stopped now. We all know your history, Sam,' she sneered. 'Are you still seeing that psychiatric nurse once a week?'

'Yeah!' Martin pointed a trembling finger at Cassandra. 'And you never answered my question about who your girlfriend is. Some crazy hippie chick by the look of her. Bet they met at one of his therapy sessions!'

Cass sighed. 'Let's go, Sam. They don't want to see.'

'See what?' Martin called after them. 'That you're both a pair of certifiable freaks?'

Only Charlie remained silent. Looking back, Sam saw him shake off Doreen's hand and go stand by himself at the corner of the court. He looked so small, like a tiny child on its first day of school. Reaching the road outside Pendleton, Sam turned to Cassandra.

'I think I know why they're doing it, posting these cruel messages to people like Peter.' He shrugged. 'It's the same reason I did it. A simple thing really, no different from an angry man punching a wall. And doesn't everyone seem angry today? Disappointed, beaten down, frustrated people looking for something to vent their rage on. Except most of us keep it inside, screwed down and locked up tight . . . ' He swallowed. 'And some of us, well, we just push it down too far and wear the mask too well. *Jekyll and Hyde* was about hypocrisy, right? Dr Jekyll not admitting to himself who he really was. Well, that was just the kind of person Dritch needed for this project. Look at Doreen: bullied and pressurized at every turn, and what does she do? Soaks it all up and goes on playing the part of the good daughter.'

Cassandra nodded slowly. 'All the while keeping the anger and frustration hidden.'

'And then there's Martin, the butt of everyone's jokes since his first day at school. Never able to answer back because he's small and because maybe, deep down, part of him believes he's everything they say he is. Can you imagine the years of rage inside that kid?'

'What about your friend Charlie?'

'Hero of the hockey team, hit with the ladies?' Sam shook his head. 'I don't know about Charlie, but the rest fits. These were the perfect candidates for Project Hyde: pressure cookers just waiting for the opportunity to let out a little of their poisonous steam. It didn't matter who the victims were, and when they started they couldn't stop. I think the project might be a way to prepare them. They begin to show a little of their Hyde face, the face I saw on the avatar picture, and then they're ready for the mirror.'

'And what about you?' Cassandra said carefully. 'Why were you selected?'

She did not press him as they walked silently through the city streets, though privately Sam acknowledged that he too was a hypocrite who hid his true face behind forced smiles and a strict routine. At the courtyard of the Bluffs, he turned to her.

'Will you come up with me? I'm not sure I want to be alone right now.'

'Of course.'

The familiar stench of urine greeted them as the lift doors shuddered open. Sam had never felt embarrassed about living in the Bluffs, but then since coming here he hadn't felt much of anything. The house he'd shared with his parents had been a neat two-up two-down, the ugliness that lived there a slyly hidden thing. The Bluffs was different. The Bluffs wore its ugliness like a badge of pride.

Flat 3113 carried on the bleak theme. Cora did her best, hanging brightly coloured curtains over the flyblown windows and burning scented candles to disguise the smell of damp. Looking at it with fresh eyes, Sam saw how futile her efforts were. For years, the Bluffs had been rotting from the inside out and now the corruption had reached into every corner of its decrepit body, perhaps even infecting the people who lived here.

Before he knew it they were in his room, Cass standing in front of the drawing board where her likeness was neatly taped. Working from memory, Sam had congratulated himself on those startling eyes, the flaming hair, the delicious bump of her bowed lips. Now, in the presence of the real thing, all he could see was the inadequacy of his art.

'Do I really look like that?' Her fingers traced the tattooed snake from shoulder to hand. 'You've made me so . . . '

'It's just a rough sketch,' he said, peeling it from the board.

He was about to crumple the paper in his fist when she took it from him.

'You've made me look . . . ' She held the drawing to her chest. 'So much like her.'

'Your sister,' he said slowly. 'But of course you look like her, you were twins, weren't you? Identical.'

'Not identical,' she breathed. 'Not quite. Can I keep this?'

'Course.'

The slight puzzlement Sam felt was soon forgotten as she leaned in and kissed him gently on the lips. Close up, he could see the little details he had missed in the sketch: strands of almost white hair among her eyelashes, tiny acne scars on her cheeks: imperfections that perfected the whole. As they parted, Sam told himself it was a kiss of gratitude, nothing else.

'What's this?'

Confirming his suspicion, Cassandra was back at the drawing board as if nothing had happened. She was frowning at a sheet of paper which had been torn from his sketchpad. On it, the faceless figure from Sam's dream, its long arm trailing almost to its ankles.

'Just something I was working on for a comic book idea.' For some reason, it felt important to lie about that apelike figure, though Sam had no idea why.

Cass stood back from the board. 'There's something strange about it, don't you think? Like it's looking directly at us and smiling, as if it knows something we don't.'

'But it doesn't have a mouth.'

'Doesn't it? No, I guess not, but it has the *atmosphere* of a mouth, if you know what I mean. The idea of a mouth waiting to be born.'

'Let's get out here,' Sam said.

In the lounge they found Cora eating her lunch in front of the TV.

'What're you doing home?' Sam asked coldly. He was suddenly aware of two worlds colliding: his safe, sane home life represented by Cora and the madness of the Phantasmagorium which swirled around Cassandra Kane.

'I swapped shifts at the hospital. Come on,' Cora elbowed him gently in the stomach, 'you're not ashamed to introduce your old aunt to your girlfriend, are you?'

'She's not my girlfriend.'

'We're taking things slowly.' Cassandra drew him into a hug, and those lips which had pressed so warmly against his now whispered, 'Let's play along.'

Sam could see the sense of the lie. It would mean Cassandra could visit as often as she liked without arousing suspicion.

'Isn't this just terrible?' Cora said, breaking into their

fake embrace. 'I sometimes wonder what this world's coming to.'

They took a seat on either side of her as reporter Naval Bhasin began his midday bulletin. Once again he was standing in the shadows under the murder pier while a man in uniform, identified onscreen as Chief Inspector McMullan, hovered at his side.

'The small community of Balfour continues to reel from the murder of sixteen-year-old Lance Newton. At this stage, the police are keen to stress that they are not treating the twelve missing children as suspects. However, fresh evidence has come to light which raises questions about the children's involvement in Lance's death.' Bhasin turned to the policeman. 'Inspector, could you tell us about this strange development?'

McMullan shook his head as he spoke, as if he couldn't quite believe the turn his investigation had taken. 'Acting on information recovered from the children's computers, we've interviewed Melissa Drake, an English teacher at Balfour Academy. It seems that the only connection between these kids is that they were all working on the same project: a program designed by Miss Drake to highlight the themes of a book the students were studying. The program seems to have had a . . . ' McMullan's frown crumpled his entire face. 'A worrying effect on their behaviour.'

'How so?'

'It's rather early to go into details, but it seems the children may have started victimizing certain vulnerable students at the Academy.'

'Lance Newton included.'

'Yes.'

'And this program encouraged that behaviour? How?'

'We're not certain, although it does appear . . . '
McMullan coughed and spluttered, as if the impossible
words were choking him, 'that the program had some
kind of hypnotic effect. That the children were drawn
into what we can only describe as an almost cult-like
state where their personalities seemed to have been
altered.'

'That sounds incredible. And what about Miss Drake?'

'She claims that the program wasn't her idea. That
someone, she refuses to tell us who, forced her to
"experiment on the children".'

'One last question, Inspector: you said that this
mysterious program had been designed to help students
study a certain book. Which book?'

McMullan appeared more reluctant than ever to
answer the reporter's question. At last, his shoulders
sagged and he looked directly into the camera.

The Strange Case of Dr Jekyll and Mr Hyde.'

15
Sam Inside the Mirror

'Crazy, isn't it?' said Cora. 'Twelve school kids go berserk and kill one of their classmates then all vanish into the hills? And then there's that mother saying some weird-looking child broke into her house and dressed up in her son's clothes. Just bizarre!'

Cassandra stirred. 'I need to go. It was lovely meeting you, Mrs Kremper.'

'*Cora.*' Sam's aunt jumped up and gave her a hug. 'I hope we'll be seeing a lot more of you.'

At the door of the flat, Cass turned to Sam. 'I have to do some research. I thought Dritch was focusing on this city, specifically on Pendleton Grammar itself, but I guess his plans for the mirror are much more ambitious if they include Balfour.'

'Maybe it goes even further than that. Cassandra, do you think—?'

'No point speculating until I've managed to do some snooping . . .' she hesitated, 'but yes, it's entirely possible that other towns and cities are involved.'

'And Balfour is ahead of us,' Sam said. 'The kids there have changed, not just mentally but . . . ' he took a shivery breath, 'physically, if you believe the mother's story.'

'We still don't know the exact mechanics of this thing,' Cass nodded. They had left the flat and were waiting for the lift to haul its creaking carriage from the basement level. 'But I think you were right when you said the program's preparing them somehow, getting them to accept a little of their Hydes before it's time for the mirror. But something about the set-up's still bugging me.'

The lift doors grumbled open and Cassandra stepped inside.

'How does Dritch get them to look into the mirror? Maybe here he could kidnap Doreen and the others and drag them to the Phantasmagorium, but if this is happening all over the country . . . ?'

'Do you think it's time we had a little chat with Miss Crail?'

'Not yet. Let me investigate and we'll take it from there.'

'OK, but Cass?'

'Yes?'

'Why is he doing this? So he lures a few kids to the dark side, but what does he get out of it?'

'I guess we'll find out.'

She released the door hold button and the lift bore her away. Sam returned to 3113 and the lounge, where his aunt waited like an overexcited schoolgirl.

'Come sit down,' she wagged a playful finger, 'I want to know everything. She's American, isn't she? So what's she doing in England?'

'You wouldn't believe me if I told you.'

'All right,' Cora sighed, 'be mysterious. I'm just happy to see you smiling.'

'I'm always smiling.'

'I mean for real.' Her own grin faltered. 'Just now with Cassandra, that's the first time I've seen a smile reach your eyes since you came to live here.'

He wanted to tell her the truth: *It's just an act, Aunt Cor. I like her a lot, but why would someone like her be interested in a loser like me? And even if she was, I wouldn't try to get close to her. I wouldn't dare . . .*

The hours wore on and he did not see Cassandra again that day. With each passing minute, the old anxiety he had felt during Cass's previous absence started to resurface. Lionel came home at teatime and Sam tried to apologize for his earlier behaviour. As Cora was at the dining table, Lionel grunted his acceptance and went back to shovelling lasagne into his mouth. In the evening, they sat around the TV and watched the latest news from Balfour. There were no more details about the mysterious computer program but the story of an unfortunate adventurer made the hairs on Sam's neck bristle to attention.

'Scott Baker was an experienced mountaineer.' Naval had swapped his usual location under the pier for a windswept saddle between two lofty hills. In the valley below, the bewildered town huddled before a thrashing sea. 'Mr Baker set out yesterday from a nearby village with the intention of climbing these hills and reaching Balfour by late afternoon. This morning he was discovered at the base of this rise. At first it appeared he'd fallen from a great height, but later it was established that his injuries had resulted from being severely beaten with rocks

129

and sticks . . . ' Naval looked sternly into the camera. 'Mr Baker, who later died in hospital, was still conscious when Mountain Rescue found him. Before lapsing into a coma, he described his attackers. There were a dozen of them, he said, the size of children but with the faces of demons. They came at him out of the rocks, full of a mad animal fury. And so now we must ask ourselves . . . ' He looked up at the hills, their granite brows pocked and lined by the ages. 'What can possibly have happened to the children of Balfour and where are they hiding?'

'Drugs,' Lionel sniffed from the depths of his favourite chair. 'Because it happened in some nice little town in the middle of nowhere everyone's scratching their heads, but when kids around here go mental there's no mystery. S'always drugs.'

'What about the climber saying they looked like demons?' Cora asked. 'And that mother saying her son wasn't her son?'

'She's probably on something herself. What do *you* think, Samuel?'

'How should I know?'

'I've no idea,' Lionel smiled.

'I've got some homework to do,' Sam muttered. 'Night, Aunt Cor.'

Lying on his bed, he watched the sodium glare of the streetlights bulge into the blackening sky and thought about all those people he'd encountered on the forum. His victims. Had his comments caused them sleepless nights he wondered? Played on their minds and torn at their nerves? For a time they had satisfied his rage, but at what cost? He shivered and turned into the cold embrace of the blankets.

It took a long time for sleep to come, and when it finally descended he dreamed of demons dancing behind the mask of mountains. Both fascinated and repulsed, he watched their jig of freedom and felt a primitive terror reach out from the roots of his being. But there was something else mingled in with the horror, something he didn't want to admit, even in the privacy of his dreams. . . .

He longed to join them. Their delightful and disgusting, sickening and seductive, sane and senseless dance called to him like a siren song. In the gloom of their hideaway, he saw the hands of his brothers and sisters, gory with the blood of the mountaineer, reach out to him. *Come to us,* they called in their brutal voices, *join us and be liberated.*

We are waiting.

'No,' Sam whimpered in his sleep, 'I'm not . . . '

Waiting, Calamity Sam.

Waiting, Carrion Wrath.

Whatever name you choose, we are waiting.

' . . . Not like you.'

And they laughed and shrieked in their legion tongues.

'Our latest headline again: Melissa Drake, the teacher from Balfour Academy who was recently questioned by police, has been found dead. Early reports indicate that Miss Drake took her own life . . . '

Bleary-eyed, Sam pulled on his dressing gown and wandered into the lounge. Sunlight throbbed at the blinds and the morning heat seemed to pulse in time with the pain in his hand. Though the crust holding the torn skin together was a thin one, he'd thought the wound almost healed.

131

'Hello sleepyhead, that cut still bothering you?'

'It's fine,' he yawned.

Cora handed him a slice of toast from her plate. 'Heard the news? That teacher must have known something about what happened to those kids, don't you think?'

'Maybe Lionel was right.' Sam took an unenthusiastic bite. 'Maybe it was drugs.'

Cora looked towards the corridor and the bedroom she now rarely shared with her husband. 'Whatever he was suggesting last night, you know I don't believe a word of it.'

A strained smile, and suddenly she looked so much like her dead sister.

'So what're you doing with your Sunday? Seeing Cassandra?'

'Hope so.'

Just then his ringtone sounded from his bedroom. *Cass*. The brightness of the thought must have shown in his face.

'Go on, lover boy.' Cora waved a regal hand. 'You're dismissed.'

With the door shut behind him, Sam snatched the phone from his desk—a number he didn't recognize.

'Cassan—?'

'She's dead.'

At first he didn't recognize the voice. All he could sense was the world falling away from him. A line from *Othello*, the Shakespeare play they'd studied last term, sprang into his mind: *Put out the light, and then put out the light*. Was that how it had happened with the fire girl? Had the darkness of the Phantasmagorium extinguished her blazing light? If so then Edgar Dritch would answer with the snuffing out of his own dark flame.

'If you're there, please speak to me . . . '

'Doreen?' he swallowed. 'How'd you know Cassandra's dead?'

'Cassandra? Was that the girl you were with yesterday?' Fear had trampled over Doreen's usually prim tones, breaking her voice into jagged splinters. 'I didn't mean *her*.'

Later he would feel guilty for the relief that washed over him: Cass was safe. For now that was all that mattered.

'I needed to tell you . . . ' The broken voice rallied a little and Doreen managed a high-pitched giggle. 'Not that it has anything to do with *me*, of course, but I didn't want you seeing the news and getting any more crazy ideas about Project Hyde.'

'What're you talking about?'

'It's that girl from school, the one I saw you speaking to in the drama studio. It's been on the local news. Seems she took an overdose of her mother's sleeping tablets last night and . . . Well, they're saying she left a note.'

Why didn't I find her? Why didn't I look harder? I could've saved her . . .

'And why would I think this has anything to do with Project Hyde?' Sam said, breaking into his own bleak thoughts. 'Unless Cass was right about you victimizing people in the real world. Gail Matthews was scared to death that day. She told me it was "someone out there" tormenting her, and then you showed up and mentioned the name of your Hyde avatar . . . It was you, wasn't it? You killed her.'

'Are you mad?!'

'Not with your own hands, I don't think our Project Hyde has advanced as quickly as the one in Balfour, but we're on the cusp. Gail committed suicide but you drove her to it.'

'That's slander! You can't possibly prove I had anything to do with this.'

'No, I can't. But if you don't feel responsible then why call me?'

A long, brittle silence followed.

'It's just a harmless game, Sam.' Pulling together her last shreds of defiance, Doreen laughed again. 'And I'm so close now to finishing. So close . . . '

The line went dead, and immediately a horrible possibility occurred to Sam. Who was to say that his own twisted work on Project Hyde hadn't resulted in a similar tragedy? He dropped into the seat behind his desk like a puppet whose strings had been cut. Was someone out there hurt or grieving because of him? He felt bile rise in his throat and it was all he could do to keep it down. The only comfort Sam took was that he hadn't known his targets were real people, yet such a crumb tasted bitter in his mouth.

This had to stop.

Short of getting the bus over to Merridown House, abducting Doreen and tying her up in the community centre, Sam was at a loss. He couldn't force the Project Hyde participants to stop using the program, Cassandra had forbidden him from confronting Miss Crail, and alerting the police to a possible connection with the Balfour case seemed like a last resort. Then again, maybe after the murder of the mountaineer and the death of the teacher, they might take his story seriously.

Before making any calls he decided to check on the Project Hyde site, just to ensure he still had access so that he had something to show the police. Sam opened his laptop and input the web address. The animated lamppost glowed on the black screen as Mr Utterson appeared out of pixelated shadows.

'There you are!' the moderator's voice sounded tinny through the little speakers. 'I thought we'd lost you for good, but I guess you couldn't stay away.'

I'm only doing this to get evidence, Sam told himself . . . and wondered if that was entirely true.

The old man strode forward until his dead-eyed face filled the screen.

'Despite your recent reluctance, you remain Mr Dritch's especial favourite.'

Sam shuddered. For the first time the program was admitting what it was.

'Now, you have already allowed a little of your *other* face to show, thereby admitting the existence of . . . ' A sly, computer-generated smile. 'What is it you call your true self? Ah yes, "the Wrath". Your soul is a leaky pipe, Samuel, and the Wrath is seeping out. Why not give in to the flood?'

It was like the siren song of the demons from his dream. The screen switched to his Hyde homepage and, with a click of Utterson's digital fingers, the bank at the top of screen jingled with twelve golden keys.

'Your final reward,' the moderator winked.

The screen changed again: now a simple wooden door, its cracked surface tongued with peeling paint. This didn't look like an animated image but a live video feed from a real location. The Phantasmagorium. He was seeing the inside of Dritch's lair at last.

'You have the keys. All you have to do now is click and the door will open.'

The cursor hovered over the warped woodwork.

'Just push and all your questions will be answered.'

We are waiting, Calamity Sam . . .

'A simple push . . .'

Waiting, Carrion Wrath.

' . . . and there will be no more doubt.'

Waiting, Samuel Stillhouse.

'No more need to hide.'

Waiting, whatever your name may be.

Sam slammed down the screen and pushed the laptop to the back of the desk.

'We're off now, love! See you this evening!'

The front door clicked shut behind his aunt and uncle. Alone, Sam moved silently through the flat, vacuuming, washing up, arranging his pencils in HB order, drawing random images in his sketch pad, anything to keep his mind from Utterson's coaxing voice. Still, he returned often to the bedroom and ran his graphite-grey fingertips over the laptop. It was like a digital Pandora's Box, and he knew he should not open it, but the temptation remained.

Hours passed. No communication from Cassandra, no let-up in the pounding heat, no easing of the desire to open the laptop. He ate breakfast. Lunch. An early dinner. When he wasn't hovering by the bedroom he was at the lounge window, scanning the courtyard below. People moved from shadow to shadow, scuttling like half-mad ants trapped under a bully's magnifying glass. When the air rumbled around them they turned to the sky, eyes full of hope.

Behind the city's gleaming skyscrapers, a host of titanic clouds lifted their tumorous heads and roared.

It was coming at last—the heaven-sent fury that would smash the heat wave. The TV, which had been on all day, started to stutter as static from the storm interfered with its signal. For the first time in hours, Sam focused on the screen.

'We are now receiving stories that suggest the murders and disappearances in Balfour might not be an isolated case.' Sam stood thunderstruck as the storm gathered behind him. 'Reports are coming in from around the country, all detailing similar instances of children going missing in strange and violent circumstances. On an East London estate an unconnected gang of youths joined together to set fire to a residential care home. Meanwhile a group of teenagers in a village outside Bristol is being blamed for a spate of animal cruelty. Child experts are at a loss to explain this sudden and widespread eruption of violence. Stranger still, many of those who have witnessed attacks report that the children's faces are somehow deformed or distorted.'

Sam walked slowly to the open bedroom door.

The lights flickered.

The TV froze.

Stammered.

'Isolated riots . . . police mystified . . . enhanced strength linked to physical transfor— . . . entire family seriously injured . . . father claims it was no longer his daughter . . .'

Lightning flashed around him, threw his shadow into the bedroom and then snatched it back out again. At last, Sam made his decision. It wasn't giving in to the Wrath (*do you really believe that?*), he needed to act now or the madness of the mirror would spread.

He went to the laptop. On opening, he saw that the

video feed from antique shop was still streaming. A large bluebottle had landed on the scabby skin of the door and sat there like a mole clinging to a decayed face. Utterson's tempting voice did not return. There was no need. The very sight of the door was all the temptation that was required.

Sam clicked the cursor.

The light in the Phantasmagorium's corridor wavered as the door swung slowly inwards and the camera tracked into the room. Whatever he had expected—a vast cavern, perhaps, with the grand, imposing mirror resting on an elaborately carved plinth—it wasn't this. The place of honour for the Jekyll Mirror appeared to be some kind of storage cupboard. Ugly brown paper clung to the walls, its bumpy surface illuminated by a single bare bulb. Then the camera tracked left and its eye fell upon the mirror.

Sam almost laughed. Was this sad little circle of convex glass what all the fuss was about? Had this mildewed antique really inspired children all over the country to maim and murder? He did laugh, and yet the laughter did not sound like his own.

Then, very slowly, the bulging surface of the mirror began to move . . . to turn . . . to twist. Sam tried to prise his gaze away but the glass held him as surely as if it had snared fishhooks in his eyes. It pulled him closer, closer, until his face was practically against the laptop screen. Inside the Phantasmagorium, the camera zoomed in, blocking out the rest of the tiny room and focusing solely on the mirror in its bloated mahogany frame. One question reeled through his mind as Sam stared into that whirling vortex: *how can it see* me? The camera on the laptop wasn't working, and so could not project an image of Sam into the cupboard, yet the hazy reflection of his face was there, trapped inside the mirror.

The Wrath stirred. He could feel its hideous brilliance respond to the pull of the glass. The tug of his caged-self came as a physical jerk that lurched into his chest and sent out whips of pain into his neck and jaw. The heat of these phantom strikes was staggering, like strips of molten wire locking around the bones of his lower face and melting slowly through the soft, yielding tissue.

I've always known it was there, he thought. *My other face.*

And now . . .

He found his scream.

The scream of transformation.

Now I'm going to see it.

Pain razored its way through the thin organic glue which held Sam's skin to his skull. Sharp electrical charges fizzed there and, at their prompting, muscles spasmed and his appearance began to change. He saw it all in the mirror: the chipping back of his nose until it became a foreshortened snout, the nostrils shaped like ragged teardrops; the horrible crack of his jaw as it lunged forward into a simian underbite; the pigment of his blue-green eyes darkening until they were almost as black as the pupil. When he opened his mouth to scream, a snowfall of teeth fell from his bloated lips and in their place he saw new teeth, brown and blunt, rise up out of bleeding gums.

'No!' he cried in a voice that was not his own.

'Yes,' his reflection answered. 'Yes, yes, *yessssssss*.'

And the face in the mirror smiled.

16
The Face of Something New

The screen snapped shut and the mirror vanished. Adrenalin still kicking at his heart, Sam grasped his face. He found no jutting jaw, no snoutish nose, no missing teeth. He looked up from the hand that had just slammed down the laptop lid to find Cassandra standing over him.

'I changed,' he panicked. 'My face, my eyes, it wasn't me any more. It'll happen again, won't it? Like in the story, my Hyde will get stronger and stronger until—'

The slap made his senses reel. Before he could recover himself, Cassandra dragged him from the chair and into the bathroom. A shock of cold water stung his skin and then that surprisingly strong hand was thrusting his face at the bathroom mirror.

'What do you see?'

'I don't—'

'*What do you see?*'

'Me.'

'And who are you?'

'Sam. Sam Stillhouse.'

'That's right. For better or worse, *this*—' Her finger

pointed at the pale dripping face, 'is who you are. Don't ever forget it.'

When at last he turned from that frightened reflection, he found Cass slumped on the edge of the bathtub, head in her hands. Tumbles of red hair fell through her fingers so that it appeared that the tattooed snake was writhing in a nest of flames.

'When you came in, was I . . . ?'

'You were screaming, like you were trapped in the worst kind of nightmare. And the mirror was transmitting, I guess from the Phantasmagorium.'

'Must be how Dritch has worked the project all over the country,' he nodded, the jackhammer beat of his heart starting to settle. 'In Balfour, in London—'

'I've seen the news.' Cassandra looked up at him. 'It's like you said, those kids were probably introduced to the program by teachers who were blackmailed by Dritch. Then they're prepared for the mirror by the moderator, who encourages them to expose their anger and frustrations. And now, thanks to your brainless experiment, we know what happens in the final stage—a virtual door is opened to the mirror.'

'Then they change.'

'You didn't change, Sam.'

'What?'

'There must be a delay when the mirror's powers are accessed from a distance. Your reflection had transformed but you hadn't actually started the process yourself. When I came into the room you were screaming, that's all.'

'But it felt so real.'

'Must be a kind of sympathetic reaction: the horror of

what you were seeing onscreen manifesting as physical pain. Still, you were probably only seconds away from the real thing.'

'I'm sorry,' he sighed. 'I wanted to understand what was happening to these kids, maybe find a way to stop it.'

'Was that all?' Cass posed the question bluntly, then in a softer tone, 'It was a brave thing to do, and it tells us something important about Dritch's plan for the mirror.'

'Which is?'

'That the mirror is accessible to anyone, anywhere.'

'Which could mean thousands of transformations,' Sam said grimly. 'Thousands of disappearances, assaults and murders, just like in Balfour.'

'A country infested with Hydes,' Cassandra nodded.

'So how do we stop it?'

'At this stage? I've no idea. Once we've retrieved the mirror, we *might* be able to reverse its effect.'

'But we can't get into the Phantasmagorium until Tuesday. A lot of crap could go down in the next forty-eight hours . . . Maybe if we launched a surprise attack—'

Cass shook her head. 'We can't storm Dritch's headquarters, they're too well protected. We have to wait until our chance on Tuesday night. In the meantime, I've been in touch with some contacts in the occult world. A man like Edgar Dritch has many enemies: rival magicians, necromancers, warlocks, shamans. They've agreed to use their powers and resources to help round up the Hydes and keep them contained.' She smiled bleakly. 'Your mission, Sam Stillhouse, should you choose to accept it, is to help me deal with the Pendleton Grammar Hydes.'

'Doreen, Charlie and Martin . . . OK, so who's first?'

'Come with me.'

Cass led the way to the kitchen where she spread out a detailed map of the city.

'Just before I arrived here, I checked a trace I'd put on your friends' computers. It's detected a Hyde account accessing the Phantasmagorium camera. The IP address of the computer takes us to this location.' She made a circle around a rural area to the northwest. 'Recognize it?'

Sam pointed to a hatched rectangle hemmed in by woodland. 'That's Doreen Lackland's house.'

'Then we have our first mission.'

They were inside the lift and rattling down the tower when Sam, finally shaking off the last traces of bewildered terror, turned to the fire girl.

'How exactly did you get into the flat?'

Cass ferreted in her pocket. 'I took this from the pegboard in the hall yesterday.'

'You stole Lionel's key?'

'Thought it would come in handy.'

'I guess it did. But look, how are we supposed to get out to Doreen's? Your car's trashed and the bus'll take ages.'

'I've got some friends on the case.'

The lift juddered to a stop and they headed out to the courtyard.

Wisps of dark cloud reached down like the legs of some monstrous insect and seemed to propel the strobing storm over the city. Though not a drop of rain had fallen, the promise of a deluge had cleared the streets of everyone except that wily crew known as the Bluffs Boyz. The tattoos on Weevil's face crinkled with delight and he slapped his massive palm against a Mercedes' gleaming bonnet.

'Like the ride I rustled up for you, Red?'

Parked in the middle of the pedestrians-only court-yard, the banana-yellow roadster roared into life, its powerful halogen headlights splashing against the face of the tower. Grin transformed to fury, Weevil ducked into the car and yanked a squeaking twelve-year-old out of the driver's seat.

'You got a licence, Toolboy? Then what you doin' behind the wheel of a car?'

Considering the Mercedes was obviously stolen, Weevil's respect for the laws of the road struck Sam as almost comical. The leader of the gang dropped his wayward follower gently to the ground and a sullen Toolboy melted into the Bluffs Boyz ranks.

'I asked for something inconspicuous,' Cassandra said, taking the driver's seat.

'Did my best,' Weevil pouted. 'Still get my money, right?'

Cass handed over a fat envelope and Weevil's grin returned.

'I won't count it, I trust you.'

'Better men than you have lived to regret those words. Hop in, Sammy.'

'A house key's one thing,' Sam protested, slipping into the passenger seat. 'But this?'

'Needs must. Now, hold tight.'

She rolled the steering wheel with the heel of her hand and the Mercedes squealed in a tight circuit. As the roadster bumped off the pavement, its lights flashed over a figure approaching the Bluffs, his pencil-thin frame wrapped in a ridiculous plastic poncho. Lionel Kremper blinked in the glare and Sam ducked into the footwell.

'Someone you know?'

'You could say that.'

'Well, I think you got away with it.' She pulled away from a side street and onto the main road that led out of the city. 'You can get up now.'

Sam slid back into the cool leather seat. On the electronic noticeboards strung over the carriageway signs flashed warning of 'SEVERE WEATHER—POSSIBLE FLOODS', yet the black clouds had still not broken.

'So what are we going to do when we get to Doreen's?'

'I've texted the coordinates of the house to certain friends. We'll try to contain the situation until they get there.' Cassandra's bangles clacked as she accelerated into the fast lane. 'If the transformation's already happened, well, then things might get messy.'

'But Doreen's such a little thing.'

'Remember the story, Sam. Mr Hyde was no giant.'

He directed her into the suburbs that ringed the metropolis, then into country lanes where streetlights became ever rarer until the only illumination came from the Mercedes' twin beam and the occasional burst of lightning. After five weeks of fiery dawns and burnt orange sunsets, Sam now looked out on a world drained of colour. Even the trees at Catchpole Corner appeared to have pulled on the dead hues of winter.

'Next left takes you to the house.'

The Mercedes shrieked around the bend and plunged into the throat of the tree-tunnelled lane. Cassandra pushed the speedometer to fifty and gravel spat like shrapnel against the body of the stolen car. Splashing down the path, the headlights picked out the shapes of storm-startled creatures burrowed in the bracken.

'You should see the gate any minute n—*STOP!*'

Another shape had appeared out of the shadows: a man careering down the lane, his face drawn long with terror, his eyes horribly round in the flash of the headlights. As Cassandra slammed the brakes and the car came to a lurching halt, Mr Lackland fell forward onto the gravel. He stayed there, legs drawn up to his chest, his entire body twitching as if a finger of lightning had stroked his spine. Sam was halfway out the door when Cass pressed a short-nosed revolver into his palm.

'Safety's off. Try not to shoot yourself.'

'What? I'm not going to shoot *anyone*!'

'Brits.' She rolled her eyes, and taking a similar weapon from her pocket, cocked and loaded. 'If Doreen attacks, you shoot to maim. If she gets busy ripping your throat out, pull the trigger and hope for the best. It's the American way.'

She left the motor running and they went to check on the shivering figure. Dressed in silk pyjamas with his initials embroidered on the breast, Mr Lackland groaned as he was turned gently onto his back. His gaze was wild, darting between Sam and Cassandra then pitching back into his head. Cass opened his mouth and a dilution of red drool bubbled from his lips.

'Scared witless. Bitten clean through his tongue.' She checked his wrists. 'He seems to have been tied down.'

Sam ran back to the Mercedes and found a tartan blanket in the boot. He draped it around the man's quivering shoulders.

'*Wuh-wasn't.*' Bloody spittle foamed through Mr Lackland's teeth. '*Wuh-wasn't hu-her.*'

'It wasn't your daughter,' Cassandra nodded. 'Yes, we know.'

Lackland looked desperately at Sam. *'Nuh-o. Don't under-st-stand. It wuh-was her. Tuh-tied me up. Muh-made me suh-see. Sh-she chuh-changed.'* A fresh shudder rocked its way along his spine. *'Trans-fuh-ormed.'*

'We should call an ambulance,' Sam whispered, his hand on Mr Lackland's heaving back.

'We can't involve the authorities yet,' Cass said. 'But we do need to get into that house. Are you ready?'

Propping Doreen's father in a sitting position against the car, Sam used a wad of bandages from the first aid kit in the Mercedes' boot to wipe Mr Lackland's blood-smeared lips. Then he picked up his revolver and they set off down the avenue. Behind them, the man with the shattered mind whined like a maltreated dog. Despite the horror of what Doreen had forced her father to witness, that part of Sam which had revelled in Project Hyde couldn't help but approve—that mewling little monster would think twice before bullying her again.

Lightning blazed as they broke out of the tree tunnel and into the courtyard. Striking like a twisted silver root, it reached down and touched the conductor attached to the side of the house. Suddenly, the acrid scent of ozone transformed the sultry air and Sam felt his skin ripple into gooseflesh. The lead-framed windows of the house flashed white, and in the lightning's after-image those sandstone bricks seemed to burn with a light of their own. The black clouds rumbled, rain finally began to patter, and Sam pointed to the huge oak door.

'There.'

They were within a hundred metres of the porch when another fork sizzled from cloud to cloud. In that instant, Sam saw the great door swung wide and, in the deepest shadows of the porch, the thing that had once been Doreen Lackland emerged.

The face was the one he had seen on the Project Hyde profile, except now it was even more distorted. Sam felt certain that Doreen's persecution of Gail Matthews and its tragic consequences had added a final stamp of horror to the indefinably hideous mask of Mary Merridown. He shuddered. How easily *he* might have ended up like this; all it would've taken was a few more days in the virtual torture garden of Project Hyde for his spirit to have tipped into utter darkness.

'He sent her mad, you know . . . ' All of Doreen's fear and frustration now made itself heard in Mary Merridown's strange, rumbling voice. 'My mother. With his slaps and pinches, his jokes and cruel comments, his little bullying games. He took away her self-worth, her dignity. Stripped it from her as easily as he might strip the skin from an orange, until all that was left was the raw, weeping flesh beneath. He sent her mad, and now . . . '

Deep, hooting laughter echoed out of the house.

'Now I've done the same to him!'

With apish grace, she stepped back into the hall and beckoned them to enter.

'No more slaps, no more pinches, not from him, not from anyone.'

The clouds burst at last. Silvered with lightning, rain chattered into the doorway and touched the face of something new.

'Won't you come in?' it grinned. 'You're very welcome here.'

17
Hyde Unbound

'Do you like what I've done with the old place?' That odd animalistic hoot echoed around the medieval hall as Mary spun on the spot, her long arms spread wide. 'Daddy never allowed me to decorate my own room, but I think he's going to be a little less finger-wagging from now on.'

The hall was a ruin, the once beautiful staircase pulled to pieces, great chunks of banister ripped out by hand and smashed to kindling. The historical weapons in which Mr Lackland had taken such pride had been torn down from the walls while the portraits of his ancestors were covered in painted profanities; swear words that Sam was surprised the prim and proper Doreen had ever known.

Gun in hand, Cassandra took a step forward.

'We can help you, Doreen.'

The girl cocked her oversized head to one side. 'That's not my name, you stupid bitch.'

'Just listen to her,' Sam pleaded, following Cass's steady progress into the hall. 'This isn't you.'

'Oh, but it *is*,' the creature smiled. 'That little girl you knew, trapped by the ambitions of her father, always bowing to his whims, *she* was the fake and I am her soul set free.'

149

'But this isn't freedom.' Sam reached out a shaky hand. 'I know you're still in there, Doreen. You have to be.'

They were now within a few metres of the changeling. Under the almost constant flicker of lightning it was possible to pick out some of those disturbing new features, though the whole continued to defy proper description. Gone was the plain face of the overachiever, replaced by a swollen head in which murky-blue eyes and a long, spongy nose seemed to swim. Mary was dressed in one of Doreen's knee-length skirts, her tattered blouse straining against a muscular, lumpy body.

'You should've read the story more closely, Sam,' Mary sneered. 'Hyde won because Jekyll was weak.'

'Get ready,' Cassandra whispered, and raised her revolver.

'Doreen no longer exists.' Mary threw her words at them. 'Because she was WEAK!'

Three sharp stabs of lightning illuminated the frenzy of raging limbs as the creature hurtled towards them, a primal chunter breaking through her lips. Her knees were bent and her hairy arms trailed almost to the floor. Reaching the heavy oak chair in which she must have bound her father so that he could witness the horror of her transformation, her bare feet slipped on the highly polished floor. With Mary momentarily unbalanced, Cassandra took aim. Sam watched the fire girl's practised hand and steady eye line up the shot, then heard the little firearm bark out an imitation of the thunder.

Mary grunted, blood flowered, and her huge hand swung up to cradle her right shoulder. The impact would have been enough to throw the tiny Doreen halfway down the hall but, as Mary had reminded them, Doreen was little more than a memory.

'Gonna pay for that,' she grunted. 'Dare try to kill *me*?'

'If I'd meant to kill you, you'd be dead,' said Cass, refocusing her aim. 'Now stay still, help's on its way.'

'Help?' Mary lunged forward. 'It's you that's gonna need help!'

The floorboards quaked under heavy feet and Cass pulled the trigger again. Instead of the gun's thunderclap there came a pitiful click. The revolver had jammed. Before Sam could think about the cold steel in his own hand, the mirror-conjured creature was on them. A powerful blow struck him under the jaw, snapping his teeth together and sending him crashing to the floor. Cast into the wreckage of a suit of medieval armour, he tried to regain his feet, but the blow had disoriented him and the best he could do was reel onto his knees. He hadn't experienced a skull-shaker like that since his father . . .

LOVE

He whipped his head from side to side, trying to shake the image loose, but the letters hovered before him as if they'd been tattooed onto his eyeballs. Beyond them, he saw Mary grab Cassandra around the throat and toss her idly to one side. The fire girl struck the wall a metre above the wainscot and dropped onto the hard floor. Impossibly, she still had hold of her gun. Shame flooded through him as Sam realized that his own weapon had been abandoned during his flight through the air.

HATE

Mary made a victorious circuit of her fallen foe. When Cassandra tried to lift the revolver it was dashed from her hand.

'You're the kind of pretty girl who used to make fun of dowdy Doreen.' Mary's bare foot slammed into Cass's stomach and the fire girl groaned. 'Not laughing now, are you?'

The creature bent down and picked up a piece of broken banister. Still swaying on his knees, Sam saw that it was in fact the newel post, the thick beam from the foot of the stairs.

'Beauty's only skin deep they say.' Mary raised the post over her head. 'Let's see if that's true, shall we?'

Cassandra closed her eyes.

Rain lashed the windows.

Thunder boomed.

And Sam saw a gleam of metal.

'Stop!'

Mary turned towards him. 'And what do you think you're going to do with that little toy?'

Sam's revolver trembled in his fist.

'Let her go or . . . or I'll shoot.'

'Oh Sam, but why would I ever take your threats seriously? We all know your story: you couldn't save your mother then and you can't save your girlfriend now. You're just too ch-ch-ch-chicken.'

His rage stirred. It pulsed through his body and Sam felt his sinews stiffen and the trembling subside. This was a new kind of anger, cold as the steel in his palm and as focused as the aim of the gun. He had always associated the Wrath with that flash-point fury of his father, but this felt different.

'Step away,' he said, his voice level, 'or I'll put you down.'

That horribly ballooned head turned back to him. 'You do make me laugh, Sammy!'

'Don't call me that. Only she . . . '

In the lightning flash Cassandra's green eyes shone brighter than ever. There was a message there, a pleading, but the Wrath did not understand.

'Sammy, Sammy, Sammy.' Mary pranced around Cass's head, each heavy step enough to crush the fire girl's skull. 'Sammy the orphan, Sammy the little lost boy, Sammy the coward who wouldn't look into the magic mirror and see the nature of the beast.' Her murky-blue eyes suddenly became focused and she lifted the newel post again. 'If you have the guts you better do it, otherwise it's gonna end bloody . . . for both of you.'

'No,' said Sam. 'For all of us.'

He pulled the trigger.

The bullet flew wide and shattered a pane of beautiful stained glass in the dining room door. Multi-coloured shards rained down on Mary and Cassandra, a hail made dazzling by an eruption of light through the hall windows. At first Sam thought that it was another lightning strike but the rumble of engines told a different story. While metal doors slammed and boots scraped gravel, Mary Merridown staggered towards the ruined staircase, her big hands clawing at her throat. Meanwhile, Cass rolled onto her front and slithered away from her misshapen attacker. Dropping the gun, Sam rushed to help her.

'Are you OK?'

'I'll survive.'

'We should really get that printed on some T-shirts,' he panted. 'What about her?'

The creature writhed on the steps, a vicious splinter embedded in the goitre-like folds of her neck. Before Cassandra could answer, the oak door swung wide and an army of men rushed into the hall. Gloved and helmeted, they appeared to be dressed in anti-riot gear, their arms, legs and torsos protected by thick padded plates. If Sam hadn't just experienced the power of a Hyde, he might have thought the collection of guns, knives and ammunition buckled around their waists and shoulders a little excessive. As it was, he felt glad that they had come prepared.

Twenty or more fanned out, checking rooms and shouting '*Clear!*' through the crackling radios built into their helmets. Meanwhile, six of the largest men approached the monster on the stairs. Mary now lay still, her hooded eyes tightly shut.

'Be careful,' Sam advised, 'she might be—'

His warning came too late. A man built like a grizzly bear had bent down to check her pulse when Mary's colossal fist smashed into the side of his head. The helmet's reinforced shell cracked like an overcooked egg and the man toppled senselessly onto his back. Radios fizzed into life—'*Man down! Hostile is active!*'—and the sound of safety catches being disengaged echoed like the snapping of tiny bones. A sea of black bodies surged forward and surrounded their flailing target.

Sam and Cass raced around the private army to the side of the stairs. Through staves of broken bannister, they saw red rifle sights floating against the creature's new-born body. The glass splinter was still staked into her neck and Mary's sudden movements had caused a fresh spout of blood to gush from the wound. Still she tried to lift herself, her wordless mouth snarling as her murderous hands grasped the air. The only one not among the gunmen was a military medic tending his fallen comrade.

'Flanagan's dead!' he cried. 'She caved his skull in!'

Sam noticed how they all stiffened, fingers tensing in their trigger guards.

'Steady!' said a man at the heart of the pack. 'We're only here to extract the target.'

'But sarge, she killed Flanagan!'

'Not *she*,' another voice barked. '*It*. That thing ain't human.'

'Which means this ain't murder.' A soldier stepped forward and thrust the nose of his rifle into Mary's growling face.

'Stand down, private,' commanded the sergeant. 'We have our orders.'

'All due respect, sir, those orders come from civilians. They're not seeing the carnage these things are leaving in their wake.'

'And they're not having to guard 'em day and night,' another voice broke out. 'Jesus, the way they look at you, like they want to tear out your heart and eat it!'

'They need to be put down!' shouted the man with the muzzle in Mary's face.

Sam saw his chance. Gingerly, he reached out and unclipped the taser attached to one of the soldiers' belts. Cassandra nodded her approval and ran to a corner of the hall where she let loose an ear-splitting scream. Clearly well-trained, most of the soldiers did not fall for the ruse, but enough twisted around to make a gap in their ranks.

Though they tried to catch him, Sam slipped through each gloved fist until he reached the stairs. The gunman's visor snapped round and, through tinted plastic, a pair of hard eyes narrowed in anger. Sam didn't hesitate. He depressed the trigger and two wire-trailing probes leapt from the weapon's cartridge and thunked into Mary Merridown's chest. Spittle fizzed as fifty thousand volts zapped through the creature's ponderous body, arching Mary onto her heels.

'That's enough.'

The sergeant came forward and took the taser from Sam. With the wires released the charge was cut and Mary sank into a groaning state of semi-consciousness. Meanwhile Cassandra elbowed her way through the soldiers and came to stand in front of the leader of this special ops unit.

'Remove your helmet.'

The sergeant obeyed, revealing a scarred and sunburned face.

'You're Olaf Mankowitz, a mercenary currently in the employ of the necromancer Dakshata Singh? Sergeant, your men were given clear instructions to assist in the capture of these children.' Her gaze swept the mercenaries. '*Children*, gentlemen.'

'These ain't kids!' spat the gunman who'd been intent on terminating Mary Merridown. 'They're killers, plain and simple.'

'Take him away,' Mankowitz ordered.

'No need.' The man threw down his rifle and stalked towards the door. 'I quit.'

Eyeing Cassandra, Mankowitz gave a reluctant nod and three of his soldiers set off in pursuit of the deserter. Over the rain still drumming the courtyard, they heard a scuffle and the sound of the man being bundled into a truck.

'We can't risk loose tongues,' Cass explained to Sam. 'I discussed it with those enemies of Dritch that were willing to help us. If news of the clean-up operations get

156

back to the Phantasmagorium it'll put our enemy on his guard.'

'So you'll keep the Hydes and any deserters out of sight, for how long?'

'Until we retrieve the mirror, and maybe come up with some way of reversing its effects.'

'Can't we just smash it?' Sam wondered.

'Something tells me it won't be that easy.'

'So where are you keeping all these prisoners in the meantime?'

'That's classified,' Mankowitz interjected.

'He's one of us,' said Cassandra. 'Like I told you, Sam, there are many people in the occult world with a grudge against Edgar Dritch. Wealthy necromancers like Miss Singh are providing private armies and secret containment facilities. The Hydes'll be looked after until we can figure out what to do with them.'

During this exchange, a medical officer had extracted the shard of glass from Mary's throat and bandaged the gaping wound. The sight of blood reminded Sam of the man they had left behind in the tree tunnel, and he asked Mankowitz if his unit had found Mr Lackland.

'He's been taken to hospital,' the sergeant nodded. 'There was no point in us detaining him, not with the stories from Balfour already out there. He was unconscious when my boys dumped him in A&E, but he'll be up and about soon enough. We need to clear out.'

Mankowitz made a gesture with his fist and the securely strapped Mary was carried out of the hall. Sam, Cassandra and the sergeant followed. Under the glare of lightning, the creature was placed into one of the four black vans parked in the courtyard.

'We found your car in the driveway,' Mankowitz grunted as the back doors slammed shut and the van sped away into the trees. 'Nice little roadster, but perhaps too eye-catching a ride for an eighteen-year-old. We've taken the liberty of providing alternative transport.' He handed her a set of keys. 'You'll find it where you left the Merc.'

Mankowitz's men had piled into the remaining vans and were awaiting their commanding officer.

'Where to now, sergeant?' Cassandra asked.

'Edinburgh. I don't suppose you've seen the news, but around twenty kids from that city have gone missing. Eight fatalities so far.'

'You know we still have two possible Hydes here. Can we expect any help if they get access to the mirror?'

'You have my number,' Mankowitz shrugged, 'we'll be there if we can. Better yet, stop them looking into the bloody thing in the first place. Good luck.'

With that, he hauled himself into the driver's seat and the mercenaries disappeared in a spume of gravel. Sam looked back at the Lackland house, its great door gaping like an astonished mouth. For seventeen years it had held within its walls a tormented child, just as Doreen had held within herself the frustrations of her secret life.

'That shard of glass,' he murmured, 'it was just blind luck.'

'You're not kidding,' Cass laughed. 'That was some fortunate warning shot!'

'It wasn't a warning shot. I think . . .' He turned his face to the gently weeping sky. It was difficult to remember just what he'd been thinking in that split second, when his fear for Cassandra and his own pent-up rage had collided. 'I think I wanted to kill her.'

'But you didn't.'

'Only because I'm a bad shot.'

She pulled his face away from the thunderheads and forced him to look at her.

'That thing was the width of quarterback and you were standing within spitting distance. I saw the focus in your eyes, Sammy. If you'd really wanted to kill her, you would've. It was a warning shot, understand?'

He wanted to believe it, but the words still felt hollow. 'Yes, I understand.'

'Good. Now I think we better look in on those other friends of yours.'

18
Secrets Told, Secrets Kept

The Gilbert residence was in darkness when they arrived. When no one answered the door, Cassandra stepped back from the house and checked her mobile.

'Nothing from my trace suggests that Martin's accessed the mirror. Maybe we should wait and see if he turns up at school tomorrow.'

They walked to the kerb and the decidedly inconspicuous Ford Mondeo left for them by Mankowitz's men.

'So where to now?'

Sam directed her out of the estate and into the suburbs at the southern tip of the city. He had been to Charlie's once or twice for parties, all part of the routine to convince Cora that he was making friends. Not that it was difficult to get on with the easy-going Chugger. In fact, that was what made his involvement so puzzling: Doreen, Martin, Sam himself were all obvious candidates for transformation, their suppressed frustrations so clear it hardly needed Edgar Dritch's psychic abilities to pick them out as ideal mirror material, but Charlie was different. Though aggressive on the playing field, the captain of the hockey team was so laid back he practically defined horizontal.

They were soon driving into one of the leafy cul-de-sacs in that exclusive area of the city known as the Meadows. At the end of a quiet street stood a modern house of steel and glass; a sparkling geometric puzzle of a building, as far removed from the concrete ugliness of the Bluffs as it was possible to imagine. While Cassandra parked outside the huge gates, Sam tried Charlie's mobile.

'Huh-hello,' a sleepy voice answered.

'Charlie, we need to talk. Now.'

'Sam, is that you?'

'Yeah. Can you meet me down by the gate?'

'You're here? OK. Sure, I guess.'

Sam nodded and they got out of the car. With the storm swept aside, a galaxy of stars shone in the puddled pavements, their brilliance distorted by the fog of pollution that capped the city.

'God, it's already Monday morning.' Sam flexed his fingers, feeling the dull ache of his wounded hand. 'For better or worse, this could all be over in the next forty-eight hours, though I suppose it won't be up to us any more.'

Cass frowned. 'What do you mean?'

'Well, now people like Mankowitz are on board I guess it'll be their job to go to the Phantasmagorium and steal back the mirror . . . Cass, what is it?'

She shook her head. 'Mankowitz and the others are mercenaries in the employ of very wealthy magicians and necromancers. This joint operation is working on the fragile basis that all those donating time, troops and money have one thing in common: they hate Edgar

Dritch. But don't let that fool you, these people are dangerous in their own right. Once the mission is over they'll all be scrabbling to get their dirty mitts on the mirror. And it isn't just that.'

'What then?'

'I've been in touch with a psychic I trust. She said . . .' Cass twisted her hands together and the snake on her arm seemed to writhe. 'Sam, you need see this thing through, for your own sake.'

'What does that mean?'

'I don't know, she couldn't tell me.'

'Why?' he laughed nervously. 'Does she get off on being cryptic?'

'It's not that. Predicting the future's a tricky business, even for psychics. All she could tell me was that every sign is pointing to the fact that you have to be there when the curtain falls. Otherwise . . . '

'What?'

'Something terrible is going to happen to you.' She took a deep breath. 'You might not believe in prophecies, Sam, but I do, and this one scares me.'

'You don't have to worry about me,' he muttered. 'I'll survive, I always do.'

The fire girl's smile failed to reach her eyes. 'There's more to life than just surviving, Sammy.'

The gates behind them clanked and began to open automatically. Dressed in pyjama bottoms and a Pendleton Panthers team shirt, Charlie came jogging barefoot down the drive. To Sam's surprise, the fullback ran right up to him and threw his muscular arms around him.

'Dude, I'm so pleased to see you, even if it is the middle of the night!'

Struggling to catch his breath, Sam managed to squeeze out of the bear hug. Miraculously, Charlie seemed back to his old self. Gone were the haunted eyes of yesterday, replaced by Chugger's infectious smile and rosy-cheeked robustness.

'Hello again,' he beamed, taking Cassandra's hand and twirling her on the spot. 'Sorry if I was a bit odd the other day, but everything's OK now, thanks to Sam.'

'What do you mean?' Sam put a calming hand on his friend's shoulder. 'Charlie, tell us what's happened.'

'Right. Sure. Well, it was after that weird telling-off you gave us all yesterday.' The light dulled in Charlie's eyes and his gaze dropped to the ground. 'You were right, Sam. I'm not sure about the others, but I knew those messages I was sending over the Hyde program were going to real people. I've never bullied anyone before . . . '

'I know.' Sam gripped his friend's arm. 'You've got a good heart, Charlie.'

Chugger shook his head. 'I can't believe some of the things I wrote. But it was like the program was teasing out all the anger I'd been building up over the years and gave me a way to vent. You've no idea how seductive cruelty can become.'

'Oh, I think I do . . . ' Again, Sam felt a shameful flame burning inside. Then he swept his gaze over the glass mansion Charlie Ridley called home. 'But why were *you* angry? You're the most popular kid in school, you've got this great life.'

'Because I couldn't be all that I am,' Chugger sighed. 'Putting on the act, never showing my true self, that was what gnawed at me. If you live a lie then the anger you

163

have at your own dishonesty grows inside like a cancer. The program gave me a way to let that anger out while still wearing the same old mask. But after you spoke to us yesterday, I knew I had to stop. You were right, something was wrong with the program, but worse than that, something was wrong with the way I was living my life. If I wanted to break the hold Project Hyde had over me I needed to face myself. So I told my parents.'

'Told them what?'

Charlie shrugged. 'I'm gay.'

'What?' Sam's mouth dropped open. 'But . . . but the girls and the—'

'They were my mask. I'm ashamed to say I used them, just like I used the program to redirect my anger onto people who didn't deserve it. It wasn't being gay that made me say those horrible things but the rage I had for my own dishonesty. Soon as I told my folks, the anger was gone and just like that,' he snapped his fingers, 'I never wanted to go near Project Hyde again.'

'And your parents?'

'That was the weirdest part! I'd been so scared about how they'd react, because my dad's this real alpha male type, but they were both really cool about it.'

'That's great, Charlie,' Cass smiled.

'I know.' His beam widened and he turned to Sam. 'I'm not sure why you've turned up here at one in the morning, but I just want to say thanks. It was you who made me face up to it at last.' He looped a big arm around his friend. 'For the first time in my life, I'm *me*.'

Returning his friend's hug, Sam found himself smiling a rare, genuine smile. After a time, they separated and Chugger yawned and stretched.

'So you're both still coming tomorrow night?' he asked. 'The hockey guys are trying to get me to change the theme to a Coming out Party. Should be a laugh.'

'I'm not sure,' Sam began. 'Cass and me, we've got to—'

'Of course we'll be there,' Cassandra interrupted. 'Wouldn't miss it.'

Chugger accompanied them to the car, his huge feet kicking through pavement puddles.

'You still haven't told me why you're here,' he said, his tone darkening as they got into the Mondeo. 'Has something happened to Doreen and Martin?'

'Why'd you say that?'

'It doesn't take Sherlock Holmes to figure it out.' He squatted down and poked his head through Sam's passenger window. 'Something weird was going on with the program and we were changing. Not just becoming meaner but physically changing, like it was sucking the life out of us. And now here you are checking up on me, so something must have happened.'

'It's Doreen,' Sam said when Cassandra gave him the nod. 'Tomorrow you'll hear that she's gone missing and that her father's been attacked. She'll be fine, I swear, but for now we need you to keep everything you know about Project Hyde to yourself.'

'You made it sound like we were being used as subjects in some kind of experiment,' Charlie said. 'That it wasn't Miss Crail who designed the program. Sam, what's happening?'

'We can't tell you,' said Cassandra. 'Please, just keep quiet for the next forty-eight hours, after that you're free to go to the authorities.'

165

'All right,' Charlie sighed. 'But what about Mould?'

'We've been to his house, couldn't get an answer.'

'It's just him and his dad at home,' Chugger nodded, 'and his old man works night shifts. I'll go round in the morning.'

'No,' the word came from Sam like an order. 'Leave him to us.'

Cass had started the engine when Charlie reached into the car and grasped Sam's shoulder.

'We weren't the only ones selected for this project. You were on the list, too. I just want to say, whatever you have to face, go right ahead and face it. Soon as you do you'll take away its power to hurt you. Good luck, mate.'

As they turned out of the cul-de-sac, Sam thought he saw a figure lurking in the trees that bordered the Ridley property. It was a fleeting impression, the vaguest hint of a shape in the darkness. He might have mentioned it to Cass but for the echo of Charlie's words circling inside his head. Chugger had faced the source of his frustrations and had emerged stronger and happier, no longer needing the dark release Project Hyde had given him. That was all well and good, Chugger coming out was something to be celebrated, but the Wrath had no other side to it, no acceptable face, no understandable root. Sam could no more show it to the world than he could cut out his heart and go on living.

City lights passed in a blur, and the next time he looked up they were under the shadow of the Bluffs.

'What now?' he asked.

'I head back to my little hideout,' said Cass. 'I'll see you in the morning.'

'Wait.' He reached out and took her hand from the wheel. 'What you said earlier about us having to be the

166

ones to take back the mirror. Well, I guess we better do it. I'm not sure I believe all that stuff you were saying about prophecies, but something needs to be done. We can't leave Doreen the way she is, and if the mirror holds the answers, then count me in.'

She kissed him. Not a light touching of lips this time but a full, deep kiss. Sam's fingers moved gently along her serpent-sketched arm and lost themselves in the burning folds of her hair. In that moment, his anger had never seemed so distant.

'I'm sorry.' She took a sharp breath and pulled away. 'We can't.'

'Cass—'

'No. We haven't been honest with each other, Sam, and this is too important to let our feelings get in the way. I'll see you tomorrow.'

Stunned, he got out of the Mondeo and watched silently as she drove away. It had all happened so fast he'd barely had time to process what she'd said. Now, trudging across the courtyard and summoning the lift, he tried his best to understand. She had to have known that he was living a lie—why else would he have been selected for Project Hyde?—but in what possible sense had *she* been dishonest with him?

Exiting the lift, he took the flat key from his pocket. About to slip it into the door, he stopped dead. The picture he'd found on the internet, the one attached to the report about the murder of Cass's family, flickered inside his mind. He saw her again, beautiful, vulnerable, turning towards the paparazzo's lens. Something was wrong with that image. Something true and yet at the same time dishonest . . .

The door of 3113 swung open.

'Where've you been?' Cora brushed tears from her cheeks and slapped her hand against the jamb. 'Where. Have. You. Been!'

'I've—'

'Get inside. Now.'

He felt her at his back, a fuming presence made all the scarier by the fact that he had never seen her angry before. Lionel sat like a Cheshire cat on the sofa, tired but triumphant. He patted the cushion next to him, and his face fell as Cora remained at the lounge door.

'I need you to be honest with me, Sam, I think you owe me that.'

I owe you much, much more. 'I'll try,' he murmured.

'Are you in a gang?'

'No.'

'Are you on drugs?'

'No.' Not even the anti-depressants Nurse Larry had tried to prescribe him.

'Are you still going to your therapy sessions?' Tears formed and fell. 'Why not?'

'It isn't doing me any good.'

'Did you hit your uncle? No? But you pushed him, right? That's not acceptable, Sam, no matter what he says to you.'

'Cora!' Lionel exclaimed. 'I've never once provoked him.'

'Shut up,' she ordered, her eyes never leaving her nephew. 'Why've you been staying out so late? Is it this new girlfriend?'

'It's not Cassandra's fault.'

'All right, but Lionel's made some pretty wild

168

accusations and I want you to tell me if there's any truth to them. Were you involved in the burning of that café where the waitress died?'

Sam stared at Lionel Kremper. He must have seen the news reports the next day and remembered the smell of smoke on Sam's clothes.

'I don't know anything about that.'

'Well maybe you know something about a stolen car, Mr Whiter-than-white!' Lionel growled. 'Didn't you and this new bird of yours go driving off in a brand-new Mercedes tonight, or was that just my paranoid imagination?'

What could he do? What could he say? 'Yes, we took the car.'

'See! I told you what he was, but you wouldn't have it!' The Cheshire cat leapt from the sofa, his thin legs twitching as if desperate to perform a dance of victory. 'Now open your eyes and see this kid for what he is.'

'He's troubled,' Cora snapped. 'Who wouldn't be after what he's gone through?'

'Making excuses again? It's just the same old pattern over and over: *him* grinding us into the dirt while you sit there with your bleeding heart. Well, I'm not having it any more. This is my house and I say he goes.'

Cora rose wearily to her feet.

'Both our names are on the council papers,' she said, 'and I say he stays.'

'Pathetic!' Lionel snapped. 'You couldn't save your sister and so you're trying to make amends with her son, whatever the cost to yourself, to our marriage. Well, I refuse to stand idly by while he gradually builds himself up to it.'

'Up to *what*, for crying out loud?'

Lionel jabbed a finger at Sam's face, the dirty nail almost touching the point between his eyes. 'I've told you before, it's *in* him. He's Samuel Stillhouse, a killer in the mak—*aarrgghhh*!'

Seething ever since he had abandoned Project Hyde, the Wrath now broke against Sam's mind. It swept his other senses aside as it tripped synapses and flooded power into his hands. The grip around his uncle's neck felt strong, true, and he could barely hear Lionel's wheezing nor feel Cora tugging at his wrists . . .

But something struck him as wrong. In this instant of ultimate release, of unparalleled completeness, he felt neither complete nor free. That secret he had refused to share with Nurse Larry, the truth which terrified him more than any other, was still locked inside. The Wrath was its child, but the Wrath was not itself the secret. With a swell of courage, he tried to grasp it but that terrible, delicate knowledge slipped through his fingers as surely as Lionel's scraggy throat.

Sam stared down at his empty hands, then at his aunt and uncle huddled together on the floor.

'I'm sorry . . . ' He felt the Wrath slip smoothly back into its box. 'Lionel, I'm so—'

'Get out.' Cora looked up at him in anguished wonder. 'Get out and don't ever come back.'

19
A Curious Confession

From his park bench bed, Sam watched the sun cast its blistering gaze upon the city. A new dawn, a new life. The Bluffs was lost to him now, his security and routine utterly destroyed. Perhaps it was for the best. Tomorrow night he had an appointment at the Phantasmagorium, a date with destiny from which he and Cassandra might never return. Better to part ways now than to disappear and leave Cora wondering why he had never come home.

Still, he couldn't shake the guilt of that parting. Strapping his sleeping bag to his backpack, he went over the scene again in his mind: the scorpion sting of anger, his hands around Lionel's throat, but what had been the prompt for the Wrath? If only he could make sense of it, articulate it, perhaps he'd never need the kind of release Project Hyde had once offered him. He would be free.

In a filthy cubicle in the park's rancid public toilets, he changed his clothes. It was a delicate operation, hopping into his school trousers while trying not to let the fabric touch the suspiciously sloppy floor. A quick brush of his teeth in the tobacco-brown sink and he hurried back to the park. Never had the city's fume-filled air smelled so sweet.

Sam's stomach grumbled and, fishing in his pocket, he found enough change to buy breakfast from the Parkside Café. Waiting for his order, his gaze drifted to the greasy television over the counter. Though the volume was muted, a headline ticker crawled across the screen:

CAVE FOUND IN BALFOUR HILLS—EVIDENCE OF
RECENT OCCUPATION—CHILDREN STILL MISSING

(Sam wondered if a unit like Sergeant Mankowitz's had got there ahead of the police)

HOME SECRETARY DESCRIBES CONTINUING CRIMEWAVE
AS 'BAFFLING'—MURDER RATE UP 179%—EXPERTS NOW
CONSIDERING A TERRORIST VIRUS THAT TARGETS THE
NERVE CENTRE OF TEENAGERS AND MAY HAVE A
DISFIGURING EFFECT—PHOTOGRAPH TAKEN BY
TEACHER SHOCKS NATION ...

The screen switched from the newsroom to a shaky photo caught on a mobile phone. The café's early-morning hubbub lapsed into silence as all eyes were drawn to the bloodied face of something warped and strange. The ticker rolled on:

POLICE NAME THIS 'PERSON' PRIME SUSPECT IN
SECONDARY SCHOOL MASSACRE.

His appetite forgotten, Sam picked up his backpack and left the café. It seemed that the subjects of Project Hyde were now claiming real-world victims as well as those they'd persecuted online. His thoughts returned to those *he* had bullied during those mad days and nights, and he felt sickened all over again. He couldn't apologize to them or make things right, but perhaps thwarting Edgar Dritch might go same way to easing his conscience.

With no way to contact Cassandra, he decided to head straight to school, hoping that when she failed to find him at the Bluffs, Pendleton would be her next logical port of call. Twenty minutes later he was walking through the front entrance and following the deserted corridors to the library. His surprise at finding the school open so early evaporated at the door of the drama studio, where he paused for a moment, his thoughts suddenly full of Gail Matthews.

'Sam, is that you?' a thin voice called out. 'What are you doing?'

'What am I doing?' Bitterness flavoured his echo as he turned to face the teacher. 'I'm thinking about an innocent girl who died because of *you*, Miss Crail.'

She had not transformed like those children who had looked into the Stevenson mirror, but the change in Miss Crail was dramatic in its own way. Exhaustion had bent her back and bowed her shoulders while despair radiated from her like a physical force.

'Come with me,' she whispered.

Blinds down, the windows of her office glowed like a swatch of dawn cut from the canvas of the sky. From the table around which the project participants had first gathered, Sam picked up a battered copy of *Dr Jekyll and Mr Hyde*.

'Robert Louis Stevenson was always obsessed with duality.' He turned the slim volume over in his hands. 'I've been reading about him, you see? When he was little he was tormented by waking nightmares. To keep him calm, his father had to play along with the delusions. He'd stand outside his son's room and pretend to be all these different people—innkeepers, coachmen, butlers—constantly swapping identities. Maybe we all do that: change who we are so that we can survive. Is that what you did, Miss Crail? Transform so you could sell us to Edgar Dritch.'

The shuffling teacher went to the wall behind her computer and unhooked the portrait of her daughter. She passed him the gilt frame, then clicked the button on a travel kettle and brought out two chipped mugs from the cupboard.

'We look alike, don't we?' Her chuckle was dry as book dust. 'Lorna was never going to win any beauty contests, but her soul, her spirit, her mind, in those things she was the most beautiful person I've ever known.'

'You're speaking in the past tense,' Sam murmured. 'Has Dritch—?'

'No, not yet.'

She took back the portrait and placed a mug of tea in his hands. Despite tasting a little gritty, the drink was warm and sweet and helped to ease his parched throat.

'Lorna was at university when she got involved in the supernatural.' Miss Crail blew brown ripples into her tea. 'At first it was just academic research, but soon she became convinced that there was more to the paranormal world than mere myth. She began to develop a special interest in the art of scrying.'

'The art of what?' His thirst slaked, Sam put the grainy drink aside.

'A magical practice that involves focusing on water, fire, or glass in order to foretell the future. She'd come home during the holidays, lock herself in her room and stare into her crystal ball for hours. Little did I know then that her visions were real and that their source was the Phantasmagorium. You're aware of Edgar Dritch's emporium of wonders?' Her lip curled over the final word. 'He'd been supplying my daughter with free visions for months. Then, when she was hooked, he started charging for his wares. I now believe he has similar rackets running all over the world. Not only a dark magician, you see, but the mastermind behind a vast supernatural empire.'

Sam felt a shiver work into the hinges of his jaw. 'What happened to Lorna?'

'When she could no longer pay her debts, Mr Dritch turned up on my doorstep. He took me to that hellish place, showed me things that prove there's a world beyond the one we know.'

'And he offered you a deal? What were the terms?'

'Lorna would be held prisoner at the Phantasmagorium until her debt was paid. I told him I had no money but he brushed that aside. My payment would take this form: I was to select a number of students who, I felt, had unresolved issues of conflict and anger in their lives. It's funny, you know, but teachers often develop a deep knowledge of their students that even the children's parents cannot match. It's all down to years of experience, I suppose. Anyway, I would introduce these pupils to a computer program devised by Dritch and . . . Well, you know the rest. Once the project was complete my daughter would be released.'

Sam guessed that similar arrangements must have been made with teachers all over the country. He asked, 'Why are you telling me this now?'

'Because of Doreen. The police have been in touch with the school. It seems that she's gone missing and that her father's been hospitalized. It won't take the authorities long to see the pattern started in Balfour repeated here.' She tipped back the mug and finished her tea. 'So tell me, how do you know so much about Edgar Dritch?'

Should he trust the apparently remorseful Miss Crail? Even without Cassandra to advise him, the answer was obvious. Sam changed the subject.

'You know what happened to the teacher in Balfour?'

'She killed herself.'

'Apparently.'

'I don't care what happens to me,' Crail said defiantly, 'as long as Lorna's OK.'

'And that matters more than the lives of three innocent kids?'

'Only three? Aren't you innocent, too?' She looked at him closely for a moment. 'It was a terrible choice I had to make, Sam.'

He nodded. 'You should be careful, Miss Crail. I don't think Edgar Dritch would like it if he found out we'd been talking like this.'

In the empty hallway with the door closed behind him, Sam felt increasingly uneasy. Had Doreen's transformation really prompted this confession? With Lorna still the prisoner of the Phantasmagorium it seemed highly unlikely. But then what was the purpose of Miss Crail's revelations? Sam's train of thought was interrupted by the voicemail alert from his phone. Heart in his mouth, he listened to the message:

'Sam, I . . . I hope you're OK and that you . . .' Cora's voice almost broke, 'you found somewhere to sleep.

176

I came looking for you, walked the streets for hours. I'm
sorry I shut you out like that . . . Look, just please come
home and let's talk about this. I love . . . '

The message cut off.

Sam's mind reeled. He needed to clear his head.

Beyond the main school building lay the art block,
the top floor of which had been set aside as an exhibition
space for students' work. With lessons not starting for
at least another hour the gallery would be empty. Sam
trudged up three flights of stairs, his legs heavy as lead.
Since leaving Crail's office, his sleepless night on the park
bench seemed to be catching up with him; every muscle
ached, his throat felt raw, his eyes scratchy.

He half-walked, half-stumbled through the avenue of
plinths and easels, his gaze so hazy now that watercolour
landscapes, oil-trowelled impastos, and jagged cubist,
sculpture melted into a single chaotic palette. Halfway
through the room, he staggered against a taboret and
drawers flew open, spewing oils, acrylics, and pastels,
over the floor. Everything around him was running: the
ceiling, the walls, the floor, as if he had stepped into
a Jackson Pollock painting. He staggered to a drawing
board and hauled himself onto the stool. Before letting
his backpack slip to the floor, he took out a 4H pencil
from one of the pockets.

The heel of his hand brushed the page, the familiar
grain of paper and the smell of graphite a comfort in this
wheeling world. His first colouring pencils had been a gift
from the good man, Samuel Stillhouse senior, who hadn't
understood books and libraries but whose strong fingers
had rarely destroyed Sam's artwork. Only a year ago, he had
seen his father alone in a room just like this. He hadn't been

to so much as a parents' evening before, and yet there he stood in the school's exhibition space, staring at a portrait Sam had painted of his mother. Were those tears in his red-rimmed eyes? Surely not. And yet . . .

'Proud of you, son,' he'd whispered. 'Proud of you.'

The secret of the Wrath: it was there, glimmering, hideous . . .

Gone.

The pencil scraped the page, sketching a rough oval. Features would fill it soon, the horror of the face he had glimpsed in the mirror, but first Sam must go somewhere, feel something. He tried to speak and the words were taken from him . . .

He was falling, tumbling, cascading into darkness. Fear began to creep from the corners of his mind and when pain, dazzling and white-hot, exploded through every nerve, his terror became absolute. Sam's short life had been punctuated with pain—the pinch, the punch, the slap, the kick—but he had never experienced agony like this. He could see it as a colour, sickly green at its centre, biting lime at its serrated edge. Like a blade, it cut through him, chewing along the highway of his spine and sinking its rabid teeth into the soft tissue of his brain. In this unending night, his real or imagined body bucked and sawed as the bright torment continued. He felt his flesh peeling away until his body was nothing but a raw chalice for his soul. Hands reached out of the darkness—**LOVE**, **HATE**—picked him up and drank from him until . . .

'Sam! Sam, can you hear me?'

Red-etched light glared behind his closed lids. He blinked, and the pain was gone.

'Cass?'

'Don't talk. Drink.'

She held a bottle of water to his lips. He swallowed, choked, swallowed again. Lying where he had fallen, Sam luxuriated in the feel of the hard floor under his back and the harsh light beating into the gallery. This was solid, this was real, the pain only a dream.

'What happened?'

'Not sure,' he said, his voice rough as sandpaper. 'When I came here I was dizzy, exhausted . . . ' Backtracking, he told her about his uncle seeing them in the stolen Mercedes, then how he'd been kicked out of the flat and had spent the night on a park bench. The only part he left out was his attack on Lionel. 'Guess I was just suffering after a sleepless night. How did you find me, by the way?'

'I ran into Charlie at the gate. He thought he'd seen you leaving school, but then this caretaker comes over and says he saw you going into the art block. Think you can stand up now?'

Her scent, a delicious mix of vanilla and anise, overwhelmed his senses as she helped him to his feet. In the awkward intimacy of the moment, he remembered their kiss from the night before and that crisis of doubt in which she had suggested they weren't being honest with one another. He saw the same memory reflected in her eyes and she drew away.

'So what were you doing here so early?' she asked.

'I'm homeless, remember? I had no place else to go. By the way, something weird happened this morning.'

He told her about Miss Crail's confession. Echoing his earlier thoughts, Cass posed the question, 'Why would she be saying all this when her daughter's still Edgar

Dritch's prisoner?' She shook her head. 'Come on, we've work to do.'

'Wait a minute . . . ' Sam cast his gaze around the gallery. 'My bag, it's gone.'

'Maybe someone came in while you were out cold and stole it,' Cass suggested.

'Damn,' he groaned. 'All my stuff was in that bag. I'll have to go back to the Bluffs.'

He needed to return Cora's call anyway. Maybe if Lionel was at work she'd let him into the flat to collect a few things.

'First things first,' Cassandra said. 'We need to find Martin Gilbert.'

28
The Talented Mr Tooms

Mr Tooms blinked in the light, his dark-adapted pupils pained by the slightest glimmer. These baking streets and dazzling shop fronts made him tetchy, and for someone like Tooms that was a very dangerous thing indeed. Emerging into the morning glare, he had found himself hungry but without the funds to feed his ravenous appetite. He would need money soon, lots of it, and so the idea of visiting the Phantasmagorium had struck him. Yes, Edgar Dritch would pay handsomely for his knowledge and expertise . . .

Everywhere he looked people were filling their faces with sandwiches, crisps, sweets, cakes, hotdogs, and burgers. His big hands curled into fists as he moved among them, ignoring their startled glances and suspicious stares. The Phantasmagorium lay in a side street away from this busy thoroughfare, and so Tooms lumbered east, following his memories.

Cutting through an avenue of terraced houses, he came across a child playing in her garden. She was a girl of about five years, her red hair tied in a nauseating pink bow. Tooms pitched up to the gate and, making sure that they were entirely alone, whispered—

'What you got there?'

The little girl looked up at him in that frank way small children have. She sensed the same wrongness as the people in the street but seemed curious rather than afraid.

'What's up with your face?'

Tooms regarded his reflection in one of the windows of the house. 'What d'you mean?'

The people had shuddered on an instinctive level, for there was nothing outwardly amiss with Mr Tooms. In fact, he might even be considered handsome.

'It just doesn't look *right*,' the girl insisted, the pink bow bobbing in time as she shook her delicate, crushable head. 'Even Smudges thinks so, don't you, pretty boy?'

She lifted the twitching, white-tailed rabbit so that Smudges could get a proper look at the stranger.

'Shame that thing doesn't come with a crust,' Tooms smiled. 'I do enjoy a bit of rabbit pie . . . '

He left the little girl in her garden, screaming but unharmed. The same could not be said for Smudges, whose blood Tooms now wiped from his chin. After breaking the bunny's neck he had used his strong fingers to rip away the fur and had eaten most of the good flesh before tossing the carcass into a dumpster.

With a spring in his step and a whistle on his lips, he continued east until he reached that dull little street with its dull little shop. He marched straight up to the door and executed a jaunty *rat-a-tat-tat* on the peeling woodwork. While he waited, Tooms let his tongue roam the gaps between his teeth and suck out any trace of Smudges he found there.

He got through three verses of Run, Rabbit, Run before the door was opened.

'Hello?' he called to the darkness. 'Anyone home?'

There was no answer, and so Tooms stepped into the long, flesh-grey corridor.

From those first few steps, he began to thrill to the atmosphere of the Phantasmagorium. His own distorted nature reached out to the building's twisted soul and from there to the black heart of its master. Tooms sensed him—a desiccated spider in his web, an ancient viper in his hole, waiting patiently for the strands of his grand design to come together. *Here is a man I can do business with*, he thought, *and I have such interesting things to tell him. I'll do whatever he asks, and I have the oddest feeling that I'll enjoy my work. Then, when my task is done, he'll help me take what is rightfully mine. He must, for we are like twins, the magician and I.*

A faint red light showed up ahead.

'Hello! Sorry to disturb, but my name is Mr Tooms.' He spelled it out: 'M-i-s-t-e-r T-double-o-m-s.'

And he chuckled, as if at some private joke.

21
They Are Here

Sam and Cass were ushered into the Gilberts' lounge. Still in his security guard uniform, Mr Gilbert grazed an unsteady hand along his bristled cheek.

'When did you notice Martin was gone?' Sam asked.

'When I got in from work this morning. I didn't call the police, not until lunchtime when I saw the news about that Doreen girl. Seemed a bit of a coincidence, two kids from the same school going missing.' He let out a long breath. 'I don't know. It's been hard for us ever since Martin's mum left, and I know some of the kids at Pendleton tease him about his clothes and stuff. Maybe if I worked harder, gave him nicer things.'

Cass shook her head. 'None of this is your fault, Mr Gilbert.'

They had no other words of comfort and so slipped quietly away. With disturbing rumours spreading like wildfire most neighbourhoods were deserted. The only people Sam noticed were the gangs of would-be vigilantes, drinking beer on street corners and tugging the leashes of half-savage dogs.

'I'm not sure what scares me most,' he said as they drove past a particularly intimidating group, 'the Hydes or the way people will respond to them.'

'They both feed off the same poison,' said Cassandra. 'That was part of Stevenson's message: humanity wears this mask of civilization, but it doesn't matter how much we progress, underneath the same old monsters are always waiting to break free.'

'And we've made those monster so much stronger lately,' Sam said. 'The things we tell ourselves we must have and must be—rich, famous, idolized, desired—just to get some sense that we're worth something. That we matter. And if we don't get everything, right here, right now, we see ourselves as failures and all we're left with is frustration, anger, rage. The DNA of Jekyll and Hyde.'

They left the estate behind and swept through abandoned streets, the Mondeo's wipers thunking to clear a skin of summer dust.

'Have you thought any more about why Miss Crail decided to spill her guts to me this morning?' he asked. There was no stir of the Wrath, yet still he thumped his fist against the dashboard. 'God, why doesn't any of this make sense?'

'You mean magic mirrors that transform kids into monsters?' She gave him a playful shove. 'It's your own fault really.'

'My fault?'

'You're seeing the wonders behind the looking glass, Sammy, but it was your choice to follow the red rabbit, remember?'

He smiled. In the impossible days since their first meeting, the world had flipped upon its side and shown him the thinness of reality, while paradoxically the fire girl had become ever more solid and tangible. Although thoughts of her had dimmed during his obsession with Project Hyde, Sam had often found himself reaching for her reassuring light and, in turn, had sensed her own serpent-sketched hand reaching for him. Only that strange allegation kept them apart: *We haven't been honest with each other . . .*

He had been dishonest, was still being dishonest, with Cass, with Cora, with himself. The Wrath which had delivered him to Project Hyde was a child of something hateful and diseased, a monstrous secret he could never face, but she had confessed dishonesty, too. He looked at her now, the jade serpent coiling down her right arm, the rainbow bangles ticking in time to the engine. What secret could be hiding behind such beauty?

'Maybe we'll get some answers tomorrow night,' she said quietly.

'Terrific,' he nodded. 'I didn't have any plans for the rest of my life, did you?'

Though he had meant it as a joke there was no laughter in Cass's eyes. 'You're sure you want to do this? I have to go, but you—'

'Why do you *have* to go? The man who murdered your family won't be there, Cass.'

'Taking the mirror from under his nose will be enough payback. For now.' She gripped the steering wheel. 'But what about you? This isn't your fight.'

'Of course it is.' His fingertips moved uncertainly across his stomach and chest, tracing the memory of old scars and vanished bruises. 'You have to make a stand some time, don't you? Can't keep hiding forever . . . '

'Sam—'

A hand tapped Cass's window. 'Toll please!'

They had reached the Pickman Tunnel, a two-kilometre subterranean dual carriageway that ran under the city's main river. Like a sludge-brown scar, the River Dunwich divided the city between the splendour of the commercial district and those shunned estates like the Bluffs. Before dipping into the communication black hole of the tunnel, Sam tried his aunt again. She was probably pulling a double shift at the hospital, and so he left a message, saying he was going back to the flat to pick up some clothes and would call again later.

Despite the relatively empty streets, the route under the Dunwich was already jammed, both with nervous commuters hurrying home and those that lived in the city scurrying back to their luxury flats and dank high-rises. Creeping steadily forward, Cass switched on the radio:

' . . . eyewitnesses have described pitched battles in which armed officers have taken on mobs of . . . ' The announcer cleared her throat. '"Hydes": the controversial term now being used after the discovery of the computer program in Balfour.

'Figures are being updated by the hour with current estimates suggesting that over four hundred children are missing, six hundred people injured and forty confirmed dead. Theories as to the cause of this inexplicable crime-wave remain sketchy, with some blaming violent films and video games while others point to the widening gap between rich and poor. What no one seems able to explain is the strange physical appearance of the criminals, the whereabouts of the missing children, and how a computer program could have played a part. While chaos reigns only one thing is certain: the sales of *Dr Jekyll and Mr Hyde* have gone through the roof.'

Cass chewed her lip. 'Even the armies sent out by Dritch's enemies can't hope to keep a lid on this any more.'

'Then what can we do?'

'We begin by finding Martin Gilbert. He's out there somewhere, we just have to—'

Magnified by the throat of the tunnel, a string of hideous screams cut her short. They rang in the fume-fogged air and made even the drone of idling lorries sound muted and small. Sam and Cass exchanged glances and stepped out of the car. Having edged slowly down a long incline, the Mondeo had just passed the centre point of the tunnel. Before them, a line of gridlocked vehicles rose gently upwards while a little way behind the parade ascended again like the trembling segments of a strange metallic caterpillar. A sign on the curved walls told them that they were standing eight metres below the riverbed. Strip lights glared overhead but there was not a glimmer of daylight in either direction to indicate the tunnel mouths.

The screams had stopped. With the traffic at a standstill other people were getting out of their vehicles.

'Please return to your cars,' Cassandra called. 'It's not safe on the carriageway.'

'Who are you to tell us what to do?' asked a lorry driver ambling between the lanes. He thumbed back the peak of his greasy baseball cap and spat a gob of chewing tobacco onto the tarmac. 'I heard a woman screamin', and Buffalo Bob don't like it when there's a little lady in distress.'

By this time a small group of motorists had gathered around the Mondeo. There was a young couple dressed in identical Van Halen T-shirts, their kohl-heavy eyes wide with shock; a flustered mother fretting about the effect of the fumes on the baby clamped to her chest; a loud-mouthed banker telling anyone who would listen how much money he was losing every second they were stuck in this hole; an elderly couple clearly enjoying their underground adventure immensely; and Buffalo Bob, shoving another plug of tobacco into his mouth and working it around like a cow chewing the cud.

Other groups were assembling up and down the tunnel. One bright spark clambered onto the raised walkway that ran against the northbound wall and accessed the emergency telephone mounted there. Conversations fell to a murmur as eyes turned to the man—'Yes, I understand. You . . . you say they're coming this way?' Silence now, but for the grumble of engines and the *tuck-tuck-tuck* of Buffalo Bob's jaw. Sam watched the man on the walkway replace the telephone with exaggerated care, take a deep breath and turn to the waiting crowd.

'There's been an incident at the north end of the tunnel. Someone's been injured and the police are on their way. In the meantime we're to do as this young lady suggested.' He indicated Cassandra. 'Get back into our cars and lock the doors.'

'But what's happened?' shouted the boy in the Van Halen T-shirt.

'That scream,' his girlfriend shuddered, 'it was—'

'Terrible,' the mother nodded. She was already

heading back to her car, baby clasped tighter than ever. 'I've never heard a scream like it, and I'm a nurse on an emergency ward.'

'Come on, Professor, tell us the whole tale.' Sam had to admit that Buffalo Bob had a point—with his wild white hair and little round glasses the man on the walkway did look rather professorial. 'Whoever you were talking to said "they". *They* are coming this way.'

'Isn't it awful!' the old woman tittered gleefully. 'I'm quite frightened now.'

Her husband beamed and helped the old girl back to their Citroén Sedan.

'I'm not waiting down here all night!' The sharp-suited banker strode over to the walkway and, with a little help from the professor, pulled himself over the handrail. 'Give me that thing here.' Emergency phone in hand, he nodded confidently at the crowd. 'Bit of leadership, that's what's required. Kind of leadership we bankers have shown throughout the economic cri— Ah yes, to whom am I speaking?'

The professor had now descended the walkway and was hurrying back to his vintage Aston Martin DB6. Cass called after him, echoing Bob's earlier question, 'Who are *they*?' He glanced over his shoulder, his face almost as pale as his hair.

'The children. The Hydes . . .' He swallowed. 'Whatever the hell they are, they're coming.'

The strip lights flickered and another scream broke out. The professor dived behind the wheel of his car and slammed his hand against the lock. Sam was about to advise the Van Halens to beat a hasty retreat to their camper van when a shadow caught his eye: a long scrap of darkness stretching over the smoke-tainted tiles of the curved wall and slipping onto the walkway.

'D'you know who you're talking to?' the red-faced banker fumed. 'My name is Sir Fred—'

The snap of his neck crackled down the tunnel. As the body of the financier sank like a bad investment, the thing which had cast its shadow over him leapt onto the handrail. Bare toes curling with monkey-like agility around the railing, it looked down on the crowd, a ravenous joy in its yellow eyes. The Van Halens shrieked in unison. Sam reached out and took Cass's hand. Buffalo Bob's bottom lip dropped and an idiotic brown mush slopped down his checked shirt.

People started running to their cars.

But it was too late.

They were here.

22
Down Among the Monsters

They came like giant rats, skittering down the carriageway, tumbling over cars, swinging from the electronic signs suspended from the roof. By Sam's rough estimate there were thirty, although many more might be advancing out of the shadows. The thought of escaping back the way they had come was soon wiped from his mind; a dozen creatures swarmed down the southbound lane and cut off any hope of retreat. Meanwhile, the Hyde on the handrail licked its slobbery lips and pointed a stubby finger at the horror-struck Van Halens.

Sam was looking around for a weapon when Cass pulled the gun from her jacket and fired. The Hyde's hungry grin transformed into an expression of agony and he tumbled back onto the walkway. Following Cass's lead, Sam hauled himself over the rail to where the creature had fallen beside the body of the banker.

'Right leg shattered,' Cass said, pointing to a grisly mess of blood and bone. 'He's not going anywhere.'

Like his fellow creatures, this snarling Hyde possessed that inexplicable air of deformity. The hair sprouting from his narrow head was perhaps a little too coarse to be human, the lower jaw too prominent, the teeth too sharp, but with his hoodie pulled down he might have passed unnoticed through the city's teeming streets. How many had he victimized online to end up like this, Sam wondered? What hateful comments had twisted his body and mind until breaking a man's neck had seemed as easy to him as snapping a twig? And, if Sam had continued with Project Hyde and looked long into that mirror, would *his* monster have behaved any differently?

He looked back to the carriageway and the creatures on the bonnets of cars, smashing their fists with simian frenzy against rooftops and windscreens while inside the people cowered.

'Where have they all come from?' he asked.

'Dritch must've involved other schools in the city, not just Pendleton,' Cass said, snapping the chamber of her gun and checking the tally of bullets.

Sam nodded. 'I think you better give me one of those.'

'You're asking me to trust *your* shooting skills in a confined cylindrical space?' She raised an eyebrow. 'Forget it. If a bullet ricocheted off these walls there's no telling where it could end up.'

'Fine.'

Leaving the monster clutching his injured leg and spitting swear words at the ceiling, Sam headed back to the car. He popped the Mondeo's boot, wrestled the wheel brace from under the spare tyre and tested the weight of the weapon in his hand. Rejoining their little group, Cass pulled open the back door and instructed the Van Halens and Buffalo Bob to get inside. A thread of brown drool continued to wind its way out of the trucker's mouth as he stared at the transformed child on the walkway.

Meanwhile, Cass eyed the creatures all around them. The Hydes had seen what had happened to their brother and, for the time being, had decided to give the red-haired girl and her companions a wide berth. Nevertheless, they were the only accessible prey. One creature in particular appeared to focus on them. Her hands bloody from a stubborn windscreen, she dropped to the ground and began pacing cautiously towards the Mondeo. Noting the impending danger, Cass struck Bob hard across the face. The shell-shocked trucker looked at her blankly, muttered a few indiscernible words, and started running back to his lorry.

'Stop!' Cass called after him. Opening the passenger door, she threw the keys to the Van Halens. 'Lock yourselves in. Sam, we have to move.'

A backward glance showed that the Hyde's attention was glued on the fleeing figure of Buffalo Bob. She moved with a sideways lope, back hunched, long arms almost to the ground. She was dressed in the shredded uniform of St Bede's Academy, a posh girls' school on the other side of town where the hunting of humans would certainly be frowned upon. Cleverly, she kept herself close to the cars so that Cassandra, who was tracking her, couldn't hope to get off a shot without endangering the people trapped in their vehicles. Sam took a fresh grip on the wheel brace. If he timed it right, he could intercept the Hyde en route between the Mondeo and the neighbouring Citroën Sedan, the car that housed the excitable elderly couple. Only now they didn't look quite so bubbly.

'He's almost at the truck,' Cass hissed. 'If you take

out her legs from under her, he should have time to get into the cab.'

The other monsters had ceased their crash and hammer and, like a parliament of freakish owls, turned their disturbing heads towards Sam and their sister. Their cries of warning were not needed. The Hyde saw the danger and altered her trajectory, pouncing over the swiping wheel brace and continuing on her way. A horn sounded, and Sam caught sight of the professor in his Aston Martin pointing at a row of newly emboldened creatures creeping towards them.

'I've got to take the shot!' Cass called. 'If I don't then—'

With a single decisive blink, the strip lights died and the whirr of the ventilation system chattered to a stop. Now only the faintest of glimmers came from the distant tunnel mouths, while in between a gradation of shadows led to the pitch blackness of the bowed centre point. Stock still, Sam and Cass listened to the sound of approaching feet.

'Lights!' the voice of the professor called through a crack in his driver window. 'Turn on your headlights! The girl needs to see!'

The professor's beam cut the darkness and fell upon the heavily muscled back of the schoolgirl Hyde. A second, this time provided by the elderly couple, shone against Buffalo Bob as he clambered up the steps of his lorry. A third, fourth and fifth came together, forming a patch of light into which the horde began to press. Reaching the lorry, the schoolgirl stretched out her long arm and plucked the trucker down from his cab as easily as a parent might lift a child from a climbing frame.

'Can't risk it,' Cass cried. 'They're too close.'

They were now standing back to back, Sam facing the oncoming Hydes while Cass struggled to get a fix on her target. A horrible snapping sound echoed down the tunnel and Buffalo Bob screamed.

'You have to try,' Sam called back, 'otherwise he *will* die.'

Cass swore, acknowledging that he was right. 'Then I need to get closer.'

'OK, let's do this.'

Footfalls echoing off the curved walls, they streaked down an avenue of cars and towards the lorry where a horrific scene was playing out. Having broken Bob's arm, the thing in schoolgirl uniform now held him up like a ventriloquist working a loose-limbed doll.

'Let him go or I'll shoot,' Cass cried as they skidded to a stop.

'Do you dare?' the girl giggled. Shielded by the hanging trucker, she popped her distorted face out from behind his shoulder. 'Now you see me, now you don't!'

She jerked him this way and that while her brothers and sisters crept slowly onward.

'Need to do something soon,' Sam shouted. 'They're almost . . . '

A figure bursting at the seams of a Man United football kit landed in front of him and dashed the wheel brace out of his hand. Ducking the creature's meaty arm, Sam twisted round to face Cass, who was still trying to get a clear shot.

'I'm sorry,' she whispered, and squeezed the trigger.

The muzzle flared and Buffalo Bob screamed again as the bullet puffed through his left shoulder and both he and his tormentor fell to the tarmac. Sam and Cass raced forward and dragged the injured trucker away from the snarling, shrieking Hyde. Blood bloomed against Bob's shirt, but Sam could see through the torn material and, by some mixture of skill and miracle, Cass had only clipped his shoulder. The Hyde had been more seriously wounded, the bullet having smashed her collarbone.

'I'll get him into the cab,' Sam said.

A tricky hoist and Buffalo Bob was returned to his saddle. Sam told the trucker to keep his hand pressed firmly against the sopping wound and Bob nodded his understanding. By the time he joined Cass again, the Hydes had regrouped and were pressing forward.

'We need to draw them away from the people,' Sam panted. 'Those doors and windscreens won't hold for ever.'

Cass lifted the gun shoulder-high. 'Then we better haul ass.'

She fired three shots over their heads and, though the Hydes shrank back among the cars, they soon stirred again when they heard the click of an empty chamber. Cass threw the revolver at the first deformed face that dared to peek from its hiding place.

'Run, Sam!'

The professor's plea for people to spark their headlights had not reached beyond Buffalo Bob's lorry, and so Sam and Cass were soon enveloped by darkness. They ran blindly, smashing their stomachs into motorbike handlebars and cracking their fingers against glass and metal. Meanwhile, Sam could hear the flat thump of Hydes leaping from car to car and baying like a pack of hungry wolves.

'The walkway.' Cass found his hand. 'It's our only chance.'

It was as they groped their way around the blunt nose of a large vehicle, probably a bus, that powerful fingers latched onto Sam's collar and pulled him back. His hand slipped out of Cass's and his school shirt hitched tight around his neck. The collar twisted like a garotte and Sam's tongue lapped thickly against the roof of his mouth. He tried to reach back, to claw at those murderous fingers, but his arms were like dead weights. For the first time in his life, he prayed that the Wrath would rage through his veins and give him the strength to fight off this mirror-born monster . . .

'*Ccarrrrgghhhh!*'

He snatched at the air like a newborn. The top button of his shirt had broken and the collar had snapped away from his throat. Quick as a flash, he ripped the shirt from his back and followed Cass's panic-stricken cries to the walkway.

'Here,' he croaked, catching her wrist. In the darkness, she wrapped him in a rough hug. 'I'm OK, keep moving.'

Though the space between the handrail and tunnel wall was narrow, they made much quicker progress than they had running the gauntlet of wing mirrors and handlebars. Sam could feel the angle of the walkway beginning to rise and the first wisps of fresh air breaking against his bare chest. Most of the cars here had been abandoned and, with their doors open, the interior lights shone like candles in the gloom. From some came the crackle of radios—classical music, pop and rock interspersed with news bulletins:

' . . . killing spree in Liverpool continues . . . '

'Police have cornered the group and opened fire . . . '

'Church attendances are skyrocketing.'

'Is this the next stage in human evolution, or are we in fact *de*volving into a more primitive species?'

Sam was beginning to despair of the darkness (was this the same Pickman Tunnel he had journeyed through a hundred times or had they stepped into a twilight dimension where the chase of the Hydes would never end?), when a blade of light sliced into his retinas. Less than a quarter of a mile ahead, where the road banked at a steeper gradient to complete its climb to the surface, a phalanx of uniformed figures was stretched from wall to wall. To their rear, the cars, lorries, and motorbikes had been cleared and row after row of blue-haloed vehicles had taken their place.

'This is the police!' a voice boomed down the tunnel. 'Please stay in your cars.'

The fume-flavoured air caught in Sam's throat. Under blue lights, he saw hundreds of bodies littering the floor, crushed and thrown aside like the toys of a troublesome toddler. All this the work of children whose grasping fingertips now brushed the beads of sweat rolling down his back. Up ahead, an officer with a megaphone stood at the centre of the police line, her eyes widening at the sight rushing towards her.

'Hurry!' she called to Sam and Cass. 'You need to get to us before . . . '

Shaking her head, she dropped the megaphone and spoke through her radio—'Gasmasks on!'—and the barrier of officers reached for the breathing equipment strapped around their necks. With his mask secured, a policeman emerged from the line and took up a kneeling position, a belt of canisters cinched around his waist and a wide-barrelled rifle tucked into the crook of his arm.

'Cover your face!' Sam shouted.

A second later they heard the soft pop of a tear gas grenade being discharged. Trailing a comet tail of white smoke the canister landed a few metres short of Sam and Cass, then tripped on its merry way under the abandoned cars. The gas cloud billowed behind them and, although they had cleared the bulk of its toxic body, a few poisonous whiffs were enough to set a fire in their skulls. Tears streaked from Sam's eyes and strands of vomit-mingled snot burst through the fingers masking his mouth.

'C-Cassss . . .'

It was no good. The combination of the gas attack and almost being choked to death had robbed him of speech. Through straining slits, he saw a dazzle of blue, a cruel wisp of white, then the black leather of a glove reaching out and dragging him behind the police lines.

'Bottle,' a voice demanded.

He felt the blessing of warm water in his eyes, his nose, his mouth. His vision came slowly into focus and he saw the policewoman who had been at the centre of the ranks.

'How many were chasing you?'

'Th-thirty. I think.' He spat thick phlegm onto the ground. 'Cass?'

'She's being seen to.'

'There're people still alive in there,' Sam panted. 'The professor, Buffalo Bob, the Van Halens.' He shook his head. 'Sorry, I'm not crazy—'

'It's the gas,' the policewoman nodded. 'Count yourself lucky you only caught a whiff, those ugly swines sucked down half the canister. We're rounding them up now.'

Sam caught her sleeve. 'Be careful. They're not human.'

'We know.' She looked back into the tunnel where torches flashed and monsters shrieked. 'By God, we know.'

A little while later another officer came forward and guided Sam into the daylight. It was chaos at the tunnel mouth. Stretchers zipped to and fro and fed the dead and dying into the bellies of ambulances. Draped in orange blankets, survivors stood around in huddles calling out the names of the missing or simply wandering in dazed circles. Someone came up to Sam, took his blanket and handed him a plain white hoodie. Still tearing, his eyes raked the crowd, moving beyond the toll booths to where a police cordon kept back a host of TV cameras.

He stopped dead. He'd seen something: a face plucked from his nightmares, a vision so impossible that at first he'd dismissed it as a mirage conjured by stress or the chemical after-effect of the gas. Now he backtracked, searching desperately among the throng, examining each onlooker while his heart galloped and his blood ran cold . . .

'Sam?'

He spun round and caught Cass in a tight hug. 'Are you OK?'

'Think so,' she smiled. 'Although I haven't cried like that since I was eight years old and me and Dad buried my cat Tigger behind the store . . . ' She hesitated. She'd meant the comment as joke but now a wary look tightened her features. 'We need to get out of here.'

Amid the confusion, it was relatively easy to cross the police line. Secure in the crowd, Sam looked back to where officers were escorting groups of shaken survivors out of the tunnel. He guessed that, for the time being, they were keeping the Hydes locked in police transport and would bring them out once the journalists and gawpers had dispersed. He was happy to see the young mother with her baby walk into the sunshine unaided, then the Van Halens and the excitable elderly couple. The professor walked beside Buffalo Bob's stretcher and patted the trucker's trembling arm.

'We saved them.'

Cass nodded. 'Guess it makes up for all those times in life when we've screwed up.'

Sam's smile died. *No*, he thought, *it doesn't make up for anything*. His gaze switched back to the cordon, where he half-expected to see the face again, that fulsome smile on those familiar lips. But what Sam had seen in the crowd was just an illusion. His father was over two hundred miles away, serving out his sentence behind the bars of Stemist Moor Prison. And yet . . .

The face had seemed so real.

23
Chaos Swarms

Moving warily through the estates that led to the Bluffs, it quickly became apparent that the monsters in the Pickman Tunnel were only part of a much larger picture. Everywhere the air vibrated to the tune of sirens as gallons of water were discharged into burning buildings and paramedics pumped chests, pricked veins, and bandaged wounds. Sam saw injured children being tended to in the streets and the blackened skeletons of cars, some with smoking bodies still inside.

They walked on through increasing havoc and, though they never glimpsed a Hyde, suspicious eyes watched their progress. Sam caught sight of baseball bat-wielding gangs rubbing shoulders with the elderly residents of the tower blocks, the youths who had once terrorized these neighbourhoods now mobilized into protection squads. One such guardian angel broke away from his posse and came sauntering up to Cass.

'S'up, Red?'

She nodded at the grinning Weevil. 'Glad to see someone's having fun.'

'Fun? My boys've been risking their lives out here.

One of them things smashed up Toolboy pretty bad.'

Sam remembered the skinny twelve-year-old who'd wanted to drive the stolen Mercedes. 'Will he be OK?'

'He'll live,' Weevil shrugged, trying to hide the catch in his voice. 'You know this thing's spread right across the city? All the gangs are patrolling their areas, putting these evil-faced mothers down if they can.'

'Leave that to the police,' Cass advised.

'The pigs?' The tattoos around Weevil's mouth spread wide as he laughed. 'Nah, we protect our own.'

'But these things aren't monsters. They're people underneath, kids like Toolboy.'

He stared at her. 'You lyin'.'

'I wouldn't, not about this. Something's happened to change them. If you're cornered and you've got no choice, then kill them, but if you can trap them somehow . . . ' She handed the gang leader a slip of paper. 'This man Mankowitz can take any Hyde off your hands.'

Weevil ran his tongue over gold-capped teeth. 'All right, Red, I'll spread the word.' He then glanced at Sam. 'You live in the Bluffs with your aunt and uncle, true?'

Sam felt a flutter of panic. 'Are they all right?'

'Not seen the woman, but the guy: he the skinny dude who works at the CostLow on Draybo Road?'

'What's happened to him?'

'Draybo crew phoned me an hour ago and said the CostLow's been firebombed. They found your uncle in the alley behind the shop, roughed up by one of these Hyde things. They tried to help him but he just started screaming and—Hey!'

Sam took off through the devastated streets, skirting tragedy and mayhem until he reached the courtyard of the Bluffs. Having summoned the lift, he doubled over and tried to catch his breath. His throat continued to ache and a sandy sensation rasped in his windpipe. He was reaching for the call button again when his phone rang.

'Hey Sam, just checking you're still on for the party later.'

'Charlie?' Sam panted, incredulous. 'D'you know what's going down in the city?'

'End of the world? Yeah, I heard. Maybe we should call it Chugger's Apocalypse Party!'

'You realize this is all connected to Project Hyde,' Sam exclaimed. 'For God's sake, we haven't even found Martin yet, and Doreen—'

'Do you think I don't care about them?' Charlie snapped, then his tone softened. 'Look, my parents are out of the country. I'm on my own at the house, and my thinking is there's safety in numbers, so please be here. Later, mate.'

Sam swore and stabbed his finger at the lift button. The wound on the back of his right hand, that cut never seemed to heal, started weeping just as Cass arrived and the doors juddered open. Before they stepped into the car, Sam's phone bleeped again.

'Cora,' he said breathlessly. 'Did you get my message? I'm sorry about last night, I never meant to—'

'I know,' she sighed. 'Look, I can't talk right now. What with the massacre in the tunnel, the hospital's going into meltdown. I want you to head straight home and lock yourself in the flat. If Lionel's there tell him I said it was OK for you to stay until this madness blows over. I love you, Sam.'

'Cora wait!' He tried redialling but the call went straight to voicemail.

'Chugger's going ahead with the party,' Sam grunted, as they stepped into the lift and Cass took his bleeding hand in hers. 'Can you believe that?'

'Dancing while the world burns?' she nodded. 'I like his style.'

Sam burst out laughing. 'You're as crazy as he is.'

'Well, there's very little we can do until our date at the Phantasmagorium tomorrow night. This could be our last chance to party before Edgar Dritch hangs our pretty corpses from his battlements.'

The lift deposited them outside 3113 and Sam slipped Cass's stolen key into the lock.

'What do you think the police will do with the Hydes?' he asked.

'I've no idea.' She shuddered as they moved into the gloomy hall. 'Such strange and powerful creatures could be worth millions to the right people. This could get seriously ugly before—Sam, look out!'

He moved just in time. Ducking under the kitchen knife, Sam left the blood from his injured hand smeared against the wallpaper. Lionel, who had burst through the lounge door, was dressed in a scarlet-stained CostLow uniform, his face cut and badly bruised.

'Get out!' he shrieked. 'Please, just leave me alone.'

His body crumpled like a deflating concertina and he dropped the knife. Sam picked up the weapon and placed it on the hallstand out of his uncle's reach.

'You're hurt.' He took an uncertain step forward. 'Let me—'

'No!' Completing his slump to the floor, Lionel sat with his back against the wall. 'I told her, *told her*: it's not up to us to take the kid in, there are social services and foster homes, but she's just like your mother—too soft-hearted to recognize evil.' His laughter was half-giggle, half-sob. 'You can't help it, I suppose, it's just in you.'

In you, Sam's mind echoed, and suddenly that face in the crowd seemed more real than ever.

'But I won't suffer any more because of you and your friends. All my life I've been the butt of jokes, the little man it was OK to ridicule and bully.' Lionel spread his hands. 'This was my only safe haven and now even that's gone. Was it because I took the money, Samuel? Is that why you hate me so much?'

'What money?' Sam asked, but his uncle's disjointed train of thought had moved on.

'Your friends attacked me in the alley behind the shop; the ones whose faces are all wrong. They beat and cut and kicked.' His gaze switched to Cass and he laughed again. 'Samuel was with them. He didn't hurt me but I saw him watching, enjoying every minute.'

Cass shook her head. 'Sam's been with me all day.'

'He was *there*,' Lionel insisted. 'He's dangerous, you know? Just like his old man.'

Looking down on this shrunken wreck, Sam now understood that Lionel's mind was like a china vase that had been smashed and mended once too often. Broken by every slight, real or imagined, he had done his best to glue the fragments back together until today's assault had finally shattered it to dust. Now, like Sam, he was seeing faces that weren't there.

'Do you want to kill me, boy?' Lionel used his shoulders to slither up the wall. 'I know you do, I can see it in those baby blue eyes. His eyes. *His.*'

'No!'

Sam wrenched at the door and pulled Cass out onto the landing. Alarmed by the crazed laughter coming from 3113, several of the Krempers' neighbours had emerged into the open-air walkway. Sam pushed them roughly aside as he made for the lift.

'He wants to kill me!' Lionel trilled after him. 'And he will. He *will!*'

Faces he saw every morning, people he had smiled at and waved to as part of his old routine, now looked at Sam as if he were a stranger. Cass said nothing as they entered the lift, just squeezed his hand and tucked her head against his shoulder. In the courtyard, he took out his phone and dialled Cora. Again, it went to messages.

'Hi. It's me. I . . . I've seen Uncle Lionel and something's wrong. Please call me before you go home, I don't want you to see him like that and . . . Well, just call.'

He felt Cass pulling him on. 'Come with me.'

He remembered very little of their walk out of the estate and towards the old industrial section of the city. At times he sensed the prickle of the sun against his neck and that persistent scrape of grit at the back of his mouth. For the most part he floated beside her, content for once to surrender all control. He barely noticed the continuing signs of a city in turmoil: cars aflame, smoke scratching at the sky, a disembowelled dog hanging by its neck from a lamppost. Only when they reached a sprawl of tumbledown factories did he stir.

'Where are we?'

'Home.'

She pulled back a sheet of corrugated metal from a boarded doorway and they squeezed through into the vast stone belly of a Victorian foundry. Like the rest of the buildings in this forgotten district, Collier Bros Steelworks had lain empty for more than forty years. In the flagged floor indentations showed the places in which gigantic machinery had once stood, while across the walls towering scorch marks haunted the brickwork like the ghosts of industry.

'You've been living *here*?'

'Since last night, yes. I needed to keep moving from place to place to keep ahead of Dritch's psychic tracking. It's not so bad, once you get used to the rats.'

She led him up a flight of stairs to a second level where he immediately encountered one of her hairy housemates. Cass shooed the rodent through the door, then cleared her sleeping bag from a battered couch in the centre of the room. With its viewing window overlooking the foundry floor, this had clearly been some kind of manager's office. While Cass busied herself at a table by the window, Sam slumped onto her surprisingly comfortable bed.

'Maybe I should call the police,' he said. 'Lionel was pretty out of it, he might try to hurt someone.'

After waiting a few minutes for the emergency number to connect, he explained the situation to a harassed dispatcher who promised to send the first available officer to the Bluffs. With the city going up in flames, Sam doubted that a middle-aged man having a nervous breakdown would be their top priority.

'Eat,' Cass urged, handing him a sandwich and a bottle of water.

'I'm not hungry.'

'Don't make me force-feed you. You need your strength, Sammy.'

'I asked you to stop calling me that.'

'Why? Because your dad liked the name? Your mom liked it, too.'

'And you know that because ... ? Ah right, your research.' He felt as if he ought to be angry but the Wrath remained silent.

'Whatever your uncle thinks, you are *not* defined by your father,' Cass said. 'You have the right to move on with your life, free from fear and guilt. I want that for you ... ' Her phone buzzed and she glanced at the caller display. 'Sorry, I need to take this.'

She vanished through a door at the back of the office, leaving Sam to his thoughts. The damp air of the foundry possessed a metallic, almost bloodlike tang, and when he looked down at his palms and saw the stains there, he very nearly screamed. It took a moment for him to understand that the blood had come from his wounded hand, that he was here in the ruined foundry and not in the hall back home, his mother dead in his arms. Still, he rubbed his palms together, as if removing a memory.

His seesawing elbow brushed sharply against something buried in the couch cushions, and reaching down he pulled a framed photograph from its hiding place. It was a picture of Cassandra and her father. Edward Kane had a warm, open face with a band of freckles peppering his nose. Cass's arm was draped loosely around his shoulder and she was smiling in a carefree way that, until now, Sam had never seen. Just like the photo he'd found in the newspaper, something about this happy scene struck him as wrong. It wasn't anything to do with Mr Kane, but a nagging sense that the fire girl herself wasn't quite right ... Again, Sam

210

admitted defeat and tucked the frame back between the cushions.

'Martin Gilbert has accessed the mirror,' Cass announced as she emerged from the back room. 'I just got an alert from the surveillance bug I have on his computer. But that's not all. You remember I told you about my friend the psychic? Well, she's picked up something she's never sensed before: it seems that a new player's entered the game.'

The dull light which throbbed through the grimy office window faded, as if a cloud had passed over the face of the sun.

'Who is it?'

'A man called Tooms. She can't get a clear picture of him in her mind, but she senses a great darkness clinging to him. He's brought Dritch some kind of valuable information and the magician has taken him on as a kind of henchman. Whoever he is, the psychic fears him. She says he's unique, strong, cruel.'

'Maybe he's a Hyde.'

Cass shook her head. 'She says he's *preternatural*: something outside the normal laws of nature but still rooted in this world. All she really knows is that Mr Tooms is something new.' She made a spyhole in the dirty window and a wash of sunset reddened the room. 'And one more thing—she senses that *we* are now Tooms' focus. From here on out, we'll have to be more careful than ever.'

'OK,' he breathed, 'so what about Mould?'

'He must have transformed by now,' said Cass, 'but the worst part is—'

Sam's phone echoed through the cavernous spaces of the old foundry.

'I should get that, it might be Cora.'

He activated the loudspeaker and a chaos of shouts and screams sliced through the rustling radio waves. Over the cacophony, Charlie's frightened voice wavered.

'Sam? Sam, he's here. Martin Gilbert. I think it's him anyway, but he . . . he's changed. Oh God, he's hurting people!'

Sam and Cass looked at each other as the last of the light fell to darkness.

'He says he's going to . . . '

'Charlie! Are you still there? Talk to me!'

But the line was dead.

24
Retched Ratrace

Cass led the way into the street where half a dozen cars had been abandoned, one zippy little Mini with its key still in the ignition. The only problem lay in getting it out of the city. Every major route was blocked by looters taking advantage of an over-stretched police force and, at one of the main exit roads, the smoking remnants of a fuel tanker. Seconds earlier they had felt the explosion shudder through the Mini's chassis; now, pulling up a few kilometres short of the wreck, they witnessed a mob of Hydes dancing around the flames like the crazed worshippers of some ancient god.

Cass slammed the car into reverse and they were away before the creatures had chance to notice them. With the benefit of some dextrous driving, a series of back roads eventually brought them to their destination, where Sam was surprised to find the exclusive Meadows almost as badly affected as the estates. There was no reason why the Hydes would be limited to any particular area, he supposed, but the Bluffs was so used to seeing the darker side of life it seemed a more natural setting for murder and mayhem.

They parked the car and walked through the Ridleys' yawning gates. Not a trace of illumination shone from the angular body of the house and the inky gardens seemed still and at peace.

'Do you feel it?' Cass whispered.

Sam moistened his lips and recalled the blood odour of the foundry.

'Yes. It smells like death.'

It was only when they reached the glazed front door that their intuition was confirmed. A huge puddle of blood spread out before them, its surface almost black in the moonlight. There was no sign of a corpse, and yet the amount of blood was horribly suggestive.

'People have died here,' Sam said quietly. 'How could Martin do something like this?'

'We're all a balance of light and dark,' Cass whispered. 'And if you take all the checks away—morality, conscience, empathy—then I think *any* of us could do this.'

Could I? Sam wondered, and he thought again of the bodies in the Pickman Tunnel.

The door opened at Cass's touch and sighed softly shut behind them. Like the grounds, the house was thick with silence, although the stillness here seemed to hold an air of expectation.

From the grand entrance hall, with its mirrored walls and intricate mosaic floor, they moved from room to room, finally reaching the library, an immense space furnished with comfortable reading chairs and fragrant with the papery scent of books. Sam's eye was drawn to the floor-to-ceiling shelves and the carefully arranged volumes housed there. His mother, who had found islands of peace between the covers of her favourite books, would have loved this place.

Cass picked a plastic cup from the floor and swirled the alcoholic dregs. They had seen the signs of flight in every room they'd visited: broken bottles, overturned tables, smashed windows with traces of blood and torn clothing on the glass. Despite the chaos, they'd found no bodies, and Sam wondered if all those killed had been hidden somewhere, as if even now a small part of Martin was ashamed of what he had done.

'There were a lot of people here,' he said, his fingertips tracing leathery spines as he paced through the library. 'I guess most of them must have got out. I only hope Charlie . . . '

He stopped at the window, his gaze hooked by the pair of figures caught in the moonlight. The fear which had been tingling beneath his skin ever since that silent walk up the drive suddenly intensified.

'Sam, what is it?'

Waving her back, he kept his face turned to the window. In spite of the adrenalin pumping through his veins, Sam had already started to form a rough plan. He was the one who'd received the phone call from Chugger; he was the one standing in full view of the creature outside: as far as Martin Gilbert knew, Sam was alone in the house.

'They're by the swimming pool,' he said, trying to move his lips as little as possible. 'He has Charlie. But listen, he doesn't know you're here. I'll keep his attention focused on me while you cut round the back of the garden. You'll need a weapon.'

'Understood.'

He heard the whisper of her feet as she slipped into the hall.

'Don't just stand there, you bloody little coward!' Martin Gilbert's Hyde had a piercing, hysterical voice, like the squeal of an electric saw. 'Come down and join the party!'

Sam went to the sliding door that opened onto the garden. It was warm outside, the heat of the day rising from the grass and forming a dewy mist which covered the path to the pool. This part of the property was enclosed by an inner wall trellised with pungent tropical flowers. Approaching the poolside, Sam felt an almost irresistible urge to glance to his right—there was an arched doorway through which he might catch a glimpse of Cassandra . . .

'Come closer,' Martin ordered.

Apart from Charlie's frantic breathing and the gurgle of the pool's filtration unit, only the distant cries of the city disturbed the stillness. Martin was kneeling on the coping at the pool edge, his strong fingers locked around a clump of Charlie's hair. The captain of the hockey team was in the water, his mouth striving just above the surface. From his torn forehead, veins of blood stretched into the pool like the sinewy tentacles of a scarlet jellyfish.

'Suh-Sam,' Charlie choked. 'Help *muuhhhhh.*'

Martin thrust down, plunging his plaything under the water. Sam watched from the shallow end as his friend struggled and thrashed.

'Stay put or I'll break his neck.'

Sam's hands curled into fists as the Hyde's laughter rang around the walled enclosure. Then, with the smallest of efforts, Martin pulled Charlie clear of the surface. Shaken to his core, the half-drowned boy disgorged a glut of mucus from both mouth and nose. His face had been washed clean in the frothing water, but as soon as he emerged a flap of skin fell back from his forehead and blood flowed again.

'Martin, just stop!' Sam pleaded.

'Martin?' the monster echoed. 'Oh, I'm afraid Martin's not at home.'

'So what do I call you?'

'"Ratface" will do.' He grasped Charlie's hair at the roots and shook his screaming prey. 'It was my first nickname at primary school, the first of many: Retched Ratface.'

'But Charlie's never hurt you. Why don't you let him go and we can—'

'Talk it over?' he laughed. 'Do you know what I've done here tonight? Can you guess? And you want to *talk?*' He grunted and pushed Charlie back under the water. 'I heard you the other night—you, that bitch girlfriend of yours and this proud little poof. The mirror was calling to me even then, and after you warned us about the computer program, I decided to keep an eye on you. You could've ruined the project, got it shut down somehow, and I couldn't allow that.'

Sam remembered the figure hiding in the trees at the edge of the Ridley house. As paranoid as any addict, Martin had been spying on those who threatened to end his cruel pleasures.

'Let him up.'

'I don't take orders from cowards,' the distorted boy sneered. 'This time he stays down.'

'But why?'

'Because I can! Because *I* have the power.' With each word he thrust Charlie deeper into the water. 'Not the teachers, not the tormentors, *me.*'

A shadow formed in one of the doorways of the wall. A figure creeping silently behind the Hyde . . .

'And you think killing Charlie proves something?' Sam called. 'All it proves is that Martin Gilbert isn't strong enough to live without misery in his life.' Used to making his laughter sound natural, Sam chuckled. 'It's pathetic.'

Martin's new face contorted with rage.

'When I'm finished with him, I'm gonna tear out your entrails. Gonna smash your skull to a pulp!'

The shadow behind him grew into a solid shape, the fire girl's hair flaming out of the darkness. Meanwhile, Charlie's feeble squirming had stopped and the frenzy of bubbles that had frothed the surface began to settle. Cass raised her weapon high.

'I'll scoop out your eyeballs and tear them apart with my teeth. I'll cut out your heart and crush your spine. I'll—'

Though the whistle of air caught his attention, Martin had barely begun to turn when the hockey stick cracked against the back of his skull. Immediately, the creature released its death-hold and Charlie bobbed to the surface, face-down and unmoving. Sam gave Martin a quick glance (the heavily-muscled monster had toppled sideways in a dead faint, one hand trailing in the pink water) and dived into the pool. Seconds later, he was hauling Charlie over the side. Cass dropped to her knees and started CPR.

Under the moon's cool glare, neither Charlie nor the Hyde was stirring. While Cass pumped Charlie's chest and blew air into his mouth, blood from the heads of both monster and victim trickled across the tiles and snaked into the pool. Sam was beginning to despair when Charlie's eyes snapped open and he rolled onto his side, water gushing from his lips.

'See to him,' Cass said, and went to check on the creature.

Sam helped his friend into a sitting position, then took Charlie's hand and moved it to his wounded forehead.

'Keep pressing and the bleeding should ease.'

'Can't stop shaking,' Charlie said, his voice tremulous. 'D-did you realize?'

'Realize what?'

'How unhappy he was.' Charlie hugged his knees to his chest and stared at the moon-mirrored walls of his house. 'Course you didn't. None of us really see each other, do we? Not until it's too late.'

Crouched over the Hyde, Cass looked back. 'It's no good. I think he's—'

The creature roared and caught her by the throat. With his demonic grin reborn, Martin Gilbert squeezed and squeezed. Charlie was the first to react. Leaping to his feet, he grabbed the hockey stick from where Cass had dropped it and, with practised poise, delivered another shattering blow to the monster's skull. Again, the Hyde released its victim and sank to the tiles, only this time it stayed down.

Sam helped Cass to one of the poolside deckchairs; she was shaken but not seriously hurt. Meanwhile, Charlie ran to the house, reappearing moments later with rope, chains and a couple of sturdy padlocks. Before setting to work, he placed a compact mirror against Martin's crusted lips. The glass fogged.

'He's alive.'

With the final fist-sized lock clicked into place, Sam and Charlie stood back from the beast.

'Think it'll hold him?'

'That would hold a wild bear.' Despite his confidence, Charlie took a fresh grip of his hockey stick. 'So what next? Do we call the police?'

'They've got enough on their plate,' Cass said, and took out her mobile. 'Hello? Yes, I need a squad ASAP . . . I'll text you the address. One Hyde and a number of possible fatalities . . . Yeah, I'll wait.' She nodded to Sam. 'Some soldiers are en route. They'll take Martin to a containment facility then, once they've found any victims, they'll arrange for the dead to be discovered at another location. There shouldn't be anything to connect Charlie with what's happened here tonight.'

'Nothing to connect me?' Charlie's face cracked and tears flooded down his cheeks. 'Am I supposed to forget everything I've heard and seen?' He gestured towards Martin. 'This could've been any of us, couldn't it? All we needed was a little push and the darkness would come spilling out.'

Sam put his arms around his friend. He was still holding on to Charlie when his phone rang, the caller ID flashing 'HOME'.

'Cora,' he said, picking up, 'did you get my message? Have you seen Lionel?'

The pain-cracked voice of his uncle whispered in his ear. 'Sam. Yuh-your aunt . . . c-can't reach her. Need to tell her. Tell her before . . . '

'Tell her what?' Sam panicked. 'Speak to me.'

'Tell huh-her I love her. Always did.'

'What's happened, Lionel? Has someone hurt you?'

'Too late to pl-play act,' Lionel gurgled. 'I forgive you, Sam. Th-that's why I called. It was never your fault. Not really.' There came a shuffling sound, like a body shifting itself into a more comfortable position. 'It's in you, that's all there is t-to it.'

'Lionel, can you hear me?' Silence at the other end. 'Say something!'

Cass took the phone from him. 'Line's dead.'

'OK,' Sam took a sharp breath. 'I need to go.'

'Can you drive?'

'Yeah.'

'Sam, are you sure?'

'I haven't passed my test if that's what you mean,' he snapped, 'but I don't think there'll be too many traffic cops on the road tonight, do you?'

'I only meant that I could come with you.'

'No,' he sighed. 'No, you should stay here. I can handle this by myself.'

After a quick hug from Charlie, Sam and Cass set off down the drive.

'You'll need this.' She handed him the spare key she'd stolen from the flat. 'I'll get one of the soldiers to drop me off after they've secured the Hyde. Be careful.'

'You too.'

Sam opened the door and dropped behind the wheel. In the heat of the night, his clothes had almost dried, though it still felt like he had half the swimming pool sloshing around in his shoes. Gear stick into first, push down on the accelerator, release the handbrake, check mirrors: he was pretty sure that wasn't the correct procedure, but it got him turned around and out of the cul-de-sac. In the rear-view mirror, he watched the girl on the pavement getting smaller and smaller. For the first time in days, Sam felt the ache of his lonely heart and, driving back towards the burning city, he suddenly understood.

Amid madness and death and horror, he had fallen in love with the fire girl.

25
Tooms' Gift

Sam closed the door on the roar of destruction and the joyous cries from souls remade. The switch in the hall clicked uselessly. It had been the same story down most of the streets he had driven: very few properties still had light, and most of those were in the better parts of town. As usual, places like the Bluffs were the first to be abandoned to darkness.

'Lionel?'

No answer. On the hall table, the base unit of the portable telephone stood empty, a crust of blood on its plastic casing. Sam went to the kitchen (floor and surfaces clean, not a hint of red), the lounge (curtains drawn, TV black, furniture neat and tidy), bathroom (sink and tub dry to the touch), Cora and Lionel's bedroom (closet empty, nothing lurking behind the door), and finally his own room. The city's inferno throbbed through the thin curtains and cast its hell-light on the drawing board.

A crumpled sketch was taped there, the picture of the figure from his nightmare, that long-armed, loose-legged man with the blank oval for a face. Fear began to scrape its ragged nails along Sam's nerves. Although he knew this was the same sketch he had discarded, still he checked the waste basket to be sure. Empty. Someone had taken it out, smoothed down the creased edges and taped the paper back to the board.

Fingers shaking, he peeled it away from the smooth, angled surface. The sudden glare of a distant explosion shone darkly along the pencil strokes and illuminated a patch of writing on the other side. Sam turned the page.

YOU'RE WELCOME—MISTER TOOMS

His mobile rang.

'Hello?' His voice sounded small, guilty.

'Sam, are you at the flat?'

'Yes, Cora, I'm here.'

'I got your voicemail. Has Lionel said something to you? Look, I should be home within the next hour or so. Wait for me, yeah?'

'Yeah.'

Without thinking, he slipped the sketch into his pocket. Edgar Dritch's henchman had been here, and suddenly the already ominous atmosphere of the flat thickened. He moved slowly into the hall where his gaze was drawn again to the table and the empty base unit.

'Damn it,' he whispered. '*The phone.*'

The battery-powered unit possessed a 'find' feature to locate the portable handset if it went missing. Sam pressed the button. The answering tone was so muffled that at first he didn't hear it. He pressed again and, opening all the doors in the hall, swept quickly in and out of each room. The soft *de-deep-de-deep-de-deep* seemed to be coming from the lounge. Sam upturned the sofa, pushed over the coffee table, even pulled the old TV back from the wall. Still the phone sang its mocking song.

'Lionel, where are—?'

A firework spread its spider-fingers across the sky and lit up the lounge window. For one brilliant second the silhouette of a man strobed against the drawn curtains, head lolling, arms sunk at his sides. Then the flare died and darkness reclaimed him. Stamping down his fear, Sam crossed the room and pulled back the drape.

Lionel Kremper stood upright, his scarecrow body lashed to the balcony rail with a length of washing line. From somewhere in the city, a klaxon screeched and suddenly it seemed as if a scream had broken through the dead man's lips. Sam staggered back from the window, his gaze focusing on the bleeping telephone that had been dropped in a great pool of blood. Tooms must have given Lionel the phone as he was dying, but why? To call an ambulance? To speak one last time to the woman he loved? No. The sketch gave the reason: Lionel's killer had wanted him to call Sam, the second direct dial number saved in the handset, so that he would return to the flat and see this . . . *Offering*, Sam thought. A strange word, yet somehow it felt right. *He thought I wanted this*.

Horror suddenly gave way to grief and Sam wept; for his aunt, for the uncle he had resented, for himself. He was still weeping almost an hour later when Cass slipped her hand gently into his. He showed her the drawing, explained about the handset, jabbered on about things that didn't matter. When he was finished, she said, 'We need to get out of here.'

'But Cora's coming back. I have to do something, cut him down, warn her.'

'Listen to me, Sam: they'll think *you* did this.'

'What?' He stared at her. 'Cora would never—'

225

'Maybe not, but think how it looks. All those people, your neighbours, they heard him accuse you of wanting to kill him, and now he's dead.'

'But if I run it'll look even worse.'

She sighed. 'If you don't come with me now then the cops will be the least of your worries. Remember what the psychic told me: you have to see this thing through to the end. If you don't, something terrible is going to happen.'

'Jesus, Cass, something terrible already has!'

'To *you*, Sammy.' She smoothed the tears from his cheeks. 'To you.'

Moments later, they were climbing into the Mini. Sam noticed how Cass kept checking her mirrors as if she believed someone might be following them. For his part, he saw no one in the garbage-strewn streets leading to the steelworks. Before stepping into the abandoned foundry, Cass asked if she could see his phone. He handed it over and she promptly crushed it underfoot.

'What the hell!'

'The police could use it to trace us. Anyway, it'll be safer for Cora if you don't contact her.'

Dumbfounded, he followed her into the echoing vastness and up the iron stair to the manager's office. Once there, she insisted he take a seat on the battered couch while she used a paraffin stove to heat up some soup. Night birds cooed softly in the rafters while rats honed their teeth against the wooden walls. The sound of those sharp incisors clicked in his head like a frantic clock counting down the seconds until Cora's dreadful discovery. *Tick-tick-tick* . . .

'No!'

His hand shot out and knocked the bowl from

Cassandra's grasp. Like a shock of pale blood, tomato soup splattered against the wall while the bonelike crack of china sent Sam scurrying to the end of the couch.

'I'm sorry. I didn't mean to. It was an accident.'

'Sammy.' She dropped her own bowl to the floor and went to him. 'It's OK, I'm here.'

She perched beside him, her gentle fingers easing his stubborn hands apart. They were close now. So close he could lose himself in that comforting aroma of vanilla and anise. The fire girl's hair fell against his downturned face, an incandescent cascade that both warmed and thrilled. He closed his eyes . . .

Her kiss was deep and liberating, and in the tumble of the moment Sam sensed, but did not quite understand, the sympathy of a kindred soul and the darkness of a life which, like his own, had been shattered by tragedy. His heart surged, terrified by the words he was about to speak.

'Cass, I . . . '

She put a finger to his lips and smiled. 'I know.'

He beamed. Happiness was such an uncommon emotion, Sam had never really been sure how to handle it. He had always thought of it as a fragile and sickly thing, like a wounded bird he must bear carefully in the cup of his hands. Too often, it withered and died.

'I love you,' he laughed. 'I love you, Cassandra.'

Her own smile died then.

'Love demands honesty.' She disentangled their hands and went to stand by the moon-grey window where her fingers teased the bracelets on her wrist. 'Honesty from both sides. If I tell you my secret, Sammy, you must promise to tell me yours. Will you try?'

The moment was coming. The time to strip away the mask of routine and to confess to the existence of the Wrath.

'All right,' he whispered.

She looked at him long and hard, and even before she said the words, he understood.

'I am not Cassandra Kane.'

26
The Truth of Flames and Serpents

'You're Cassidy,' he said. 'You took your sister's name.'

'How did you know?'

'A couple of photos and a cat named Tigger.' Sam slipped his hand between the cushions and brought forth the framed photograph of Edward Kane and his daughter. 'I thought it was odd, having this memento of you and your dad but no picture of Cassidy. But of course this *is* a keepsake of your father and sister. I think your story about how you grew up is true; only *you* were the one who stayed in New York while Cassandra went to live in Louisiana with your mum. She was the wild one, disappearing off on road trips while you were on West 57th helping out at your dad's antique business.'

Cassidy nodded and heeled the tears from her eyes.

'You told me that you and your dad buried Tigger behind the shop. But was it likely that a Louisiana cat would be buried in New York? Even if Cassandra had come up for a visit, surely she wouldn't have dragged a pet all that way. Wasn't it more likely that the cat was Cassidy's? And then there was the snake.'

Cass' fingers traced the serpent from shoulder to wrist.

'In this picture the tattoo looks a little faded, like it's been on the girl's arm for a year or two. Yours is more vibrant. How long have you had it?'

'Four months.' She took the photograph and held it against her chest. 'This was taken a week before they were killed . . . You said something about a picture in a newspaper?'

'I found a report online,' Sam nodded. 'A few days after the killings, there was a paparazzi shot taken of you through the antique store window. At first I couldn't understand what was bugging me about it. The clue only came to me a second ago, and it was the tattoo again. In the newspaper photo your left arm was bare and your right was in the sleeve of your cardigan, so the snake would've been hidden. Except that was the wrong way round. The photographer had caught your reflection in that big mirror behind the counter, so everything was in reverse. Your left arm was in fact your right, and the right didn't have a tattoo.'

It was dark in the room; so dark it was impossible make out the expression on Cassan— *Cassidy's* face.

'I lived very happily in her shadow,' she murmured. 'Friends, family, neighbours, teachers, everyone was bewitched by her while I stood in the crowd, cheering as loud as any. She was the most daring kid you could ever meet, the first to leap off a high wall or run into a haunted house. Where Cassandra led, I followed.

'Then our parents split and she was taken from me. The morning she was due to leave for Louisiana, we ran and hid in the alley behind the store. We clung to each other fierce and it took both our parents to separate us. After she left, I cried for three solid days.

'We called each other almost every night, and although I could feel her spirit racing towards me down a thousand miles of telephone line, it wasn't the same. She missed me too, I'm sure . . . ' The words hitched in Cassidy's throat. 'In the end, we grew apart. I continued to idolize her, but now I worshipped my sister like some kind of distant and unpredictable god. I was the good twin, doing well at school, studying an advanced course in computer science and helping out at dad's store in the evenings and at weekends. Meanwhile, Cassandra wasn't being challenged academically, so out of boredom she got involved with a bad crowd and ended up spending a month in juvenile detention. After mom passed away, she packed some clothes and just disappeared . . .

'Then, one cold night last December, she turned up at the store. Almost two years without a word, and the moment she walked through the door all the hurt was forgotten and forgiven.'

'Where had she been?'

'She didn't want to tell us. She attracted people to her, you see? The good, the bad, and each wanted to take away a little piece of her flame to keep for themselves. At eighteen years old, my sister was tired of life . . .

'A few days after her arrival, I had to head up to New Jersey on business. Cassandra was still in bed when I left and my dad was in the back office, wrapping up the Stevenson mirror. He'd sold it the week before to a collector of oddities in Cumberland County.

'Dad said how good it was to have her home, but despite his smile, there was sadness in my father's voice. He drew me into a hug and whispered, "Don't you go vanishing just because she's come back." "You think I'd take off?" I said. "Dad, I'm not like Cassandra. Even if I had reason to, I wouldn't have the guts to run away." He kissed the top of my head. "I mean disappear inside *yourself*. She still shines bright, Cassidy, but you've got your own fire and one day you might need it."

'Those were the last words he ever spoke to me. It was late when I got back, snowing hard and blowing a gale. The back door of the store had been left open, something my security-obsessed father would never have allowed, and there were strange footprints in the snow.'

'Strange?'

'Tiny. Almost like a child's. And they were . . . ' She narrowed her eyes. 'Joyful. As if the thing that had made them was dancing. I ran inside, shouted their names . . . '

Sam stirred. 'You don't have to talk about it.'

She shook her head. 'All I knew as I looked down on their bodies was that I couldn't face the future without them. And so, when the cops came, I told them my name was Cassandra Kane and that my father Edward and sister Cassidy had been murdered. I even put on Cassandra's Louisiana drawl and, in time, began the physical transformation into my sister. I threaded my hair with beads and covered my arms with her bangles.'

'Why?'

'Because Cassidy wasn't strong enough to take vengeance, but Cassandra? Oh, she had the strength to hunt this murderer to the ends of the earth.'

'You changed identities as easily as that?'

Cassidy shrugged. 'Identity can be a shadow on the wall, Sammy, always moving, always changing.' She turned to face him, the fragile Cassidy reabsorbed into the forthright Cassandra. 'So I lied to you. Do you forgive me?'

The night birds called, the rats ticked, and beyond the window, the city shrieked from every quarter of its ravaged body.

'Who am I to judge?' he whispered. 'I've been hiding all my life. At school they called me "Calamity Sam" because I always seemed to be walking into doors and getting black eyes. Calamity Sam was my mask right up until my mother died. After that, I became the miracle boy, who'd lived a nightmare and yet still managed to smile through every dark day.'

'Why are your days so dark, Sam?' Cassidy asked. 'It isn't just the grief, is it?'

He took a deep breath.

'Because it's *in* me. *His* cruelty and rage and evil. He had these letters tattooed onto his knuckles—H, A, T, E—and it's that word I keep hearing in my dreams: hate, hate, hate. It's his hate I felt when I came out of the kitchen and saw my mother's body on the floor of the hall. He'd struck her hard in the face, something he'd done a hundred times before, only this time she'd lost her balance and hit her head against the banister. He just stood there watching the pool of blood get bigger and bigger while I cradled her in my arms. He told me he was sorry. *Sorry*—' Sam spat the apology, 'and then he ran, leaving us alone together. Sorry,' he murmured it now, 'and with that word I felt the Wrath for the first time.'

'The Wrath?'

'My father's rage.'

'It's natural for you to feel angry, Sam.'

'This isn't just anger. This is *his* legacy. It's why I wrote those terrible things on the Hyde forum, to appease it somehow.'

'Then you must face it,' she said. 'I know you're keeping something back. I can see it in your eyes. Confront the source of your anger, Sam, and you'll take away its power to hurt you.' Though he tried to look down she held his gaze. 'You *and* others.'

The source of the Wrath was a simple thing: three brutal, hateful words, but speaking them would expose the most loathsome corner of his soul. That was why he hadn't been able to admit it to Nurse Larry and especially not to Cora. They would hear his confession and their once sympathetic faces would twist with revulsion and he would be cast out.

'You won't tell me, will you?' Cassidy smiled sadly. 'Then I think we need to put some distance between us.'

'What do you mean?' Sam's heart lurched. 'Are you leaving?'

'No. We'll see this thing out together. But afterwards, if we're still upright and breathing, we go our separate ways.'

'Cass—'

'No.' She wrenched her hand from his and the tower of bracelets cascaded to the floor, circles of onyx, jade, and, burnished gold rolling away into spidery corners. 'We should take it in turns to keep watch tonight,' she said, the practical mask of Cassandra Kane back in place. 'I'll go first.'

She didn't wait for an answer, but headed down the iron stair and into the screaming night.

27
Into Madness

'Although military authorities have detained several "Hydes", the government is still refusing to confirm that these creatures and the missing children are, in fact . . . ' the local news anchor tried to keep the incredulity out of his voice, 'one and the same. That the children have somehow . . . transformed.'

Sam turned down the volume on the looted TV set they'd found abandoned in the street. 'Everything's falling apart out there,' he muttered. 'We need to do something.'

While the presenter enumerated horrifying statistics of casualty rates nationwide, Cass paced up and down the dimly lit room.

'There's nothing we can do. Not until tonight.'

'And after that?' Sam said, not wanting to pose the question but hungry for an answer.

'If we're successful, I'll examine the mirror and try to reverse its effects. My psychic friend in New York might be able to help.'

'And us?' he asked. 'What about us?'

'There is no us.'

Ever since he'd woken her at 6 a.m., Cass had slipped back into her cool, professional rhythms. The confessions of the night before seemed to have been forgotten and she had not once referred to Sam's refusal to acknowledge the truth of the Wrath.

'We get the job done and we go our separate ways.' She looked as if she was about to say more when the television caught her eye. 'Sam . . . '

A picture of Lionel had appeared onscreen behind the newscaster.

'Not all the lives taken last night have been laid at the door of these Hyde children,' said the announcer. 'In the early hours of the morning, the body of local shop worker Lionel Kremper was discovered by his wife, Cora. A violent argument between Mr Kremper and his nephew, Samuel Stillhouse, was witnessed by neighbours a few short hours before the murder. A bloodied handprint, which the authorities believe belongs to Mr Stillhouse, was also discovered at the flat. Police are appealing for witnesses, but caution that the public should not approach Samuel, who must be considered dangerous . . . '

Sam pitched forward in his seat, hands clamped together. What must Cora be thinking right now? Did she really believe that he had murdered Lionel? He longed to talk to her, to explain, but what story could he tell that she would ever believe? Sam shook his head. Cora and his old life was lost to him now . . .

The day wore on. They ate beans and buttered toast for lunch, the same for dinner. Noise from the city ebbed and flowed: the now familiar shouts and screams, an occasional explosion rending the air, and once the unmistakable chatter of automatic gunfire. Had the Hydes got their hands on firearms, Sam wondered, or had the government authorized lethal force to be used against these demonic children? His question was answered on the six o'clock news where shaky phone footage showed a battalion of armed police opening fire on a kettled crowd. A horrified reporter described how panicked officers had fired on both Hydes and civilians alike.

Cass received occasional updates from the enemies of Edgar Dritch: fatality numbers, patterns of attack, the success or otherwise of containment operations. At one point she stopped mid-pace and shot Sam a stricken glance. Sergeant Mankowitz and his men had fallen to a Hyde ambush under the gatehouse of Edinburgh Castle. None of the unit had survived.

By 9 p.m. they were finally ready to move out.

'So I guess your contacts will be sending us guns and bulletproof vests?' Sam said. 'All your basic breaking-into-a-villain's-lair equipment.'

For the first time that day, Cass smiled. 'An entire arsenal wouldn't do us any good against the magician.'

'Do we know if he made that flight to Munich?'

'A man called Dritch boarded the plane half an hour ago.' She took hold of the metal sheeting at the foundry doorway. 'Are you ready?'

Although the sun would only just be dipping over the horizon, the smoke of a thousand fires had already snuffed out the day, and so the Mini trundled through ashen streets and Sam watched the reflection of flame lighting up the underside of clouds, its terrible luminescence both chilling and beautiful.

Soon enough, they were weaving into the little backstreet in which he had first met the fire girl. Apart from a half-starved dog nosing for scraps among the overturned bins and a stately black bird standing sentinel on a telephone wire, the road was empty.

'Those animals.' Cass narrowed her eyes. 'Do they look normal to you?'

'I guess,' Sam murmured, though his skin crawled at the creatures' eerie watchfulness.

'They look like scavengers waiting for a corpse to pick clean,' said Cass. 'And there's something else. Look . . . '

Like most other streets in the city, every building here had at least one of its glass eyes put out. Only the tinted windows of the antique shop had been left untouched. Sam remembered the back of the building where even the boldest graffiti artist had not dared to leave his tag, and wondered if, for all their murderous violence, the Hydes were also afraid of the Phantasmagorium. It was an unnerving thought.

Cass got out of the car and mounted the shallow step to the Phantasmagorium's flaking front door. Taking a large leather satchel from the back seat, Sam joined her. An anxious moment passed while the fire girl went to work on the lock with a grip from her hair and a long, sturdy pin.

'Where'd you learn how to do that?' Sam whispered.

'One of the advantages of having a badass sister.' Cass twisted the grip and they heard the lock's yielding click. 'You pick up a lot of neat tricks.'

'Think the place'll be alarmed?' Sam asked, and received a shrug in response. 'OK, then,' he breathed, 'here goes.'

Cold as ice in his grasp, he turned the metal handle and the door to the Phantasmagorium swung smoothly inwards. Sam wondered how the handle could be so frosty when the air that billowed from inside was like a furnace blast. Cass took a torch from her pocket and spread its beam into the sulphurous corridor.

'Oh God,' she murmured. 'Is that—?'

'I think so.' His stomach cramped as he watched the tiny light illuminate swatches of human skin, hanging like grey wallpaper down the long, dismal corridor. 'Is this guy insane?'

'Very possibly.' Cass nodded. 'So, shall we?'

Wondering if this was the last time he'd see the sky, Sam looked back. Before reaching the polluted heavens, his eye was snagged by the black bird now sitting statue-still upon a chimney. It blinked down at him, and a fragment from a haunting poem once read to him by his mother flitted through Sam's head.

'*And his eyes have all the seeming of a demon's that is dreaming.*'

'What's that?' Cass asked, turning from the doorway.

'It's from "The Raven",' he said, 'a poem by Edgar Allan P—' but when he looked back, the bird was gone.

28
His Hellish Game

Beyond the long, flesh-papered corridor, beyond the small red door at its end, beyond reason and reality, Sam and Cass entered the impossible heart of the Phantasmagorium. A vast dimension that extended well beyond the physical limits of the tiny shop, it took the shape of a kind of warehouse, plain brick walls stretching out to a vanishing point while overhead a medieval stone ceiling reached into shadow-strewn darkness.

'How's this possible?' Sam murmured.

Cass said simply, 'Magic.'

High above, among ancient rafters, a host of dead-eyed, leather-winged creatures looked down on the newcomers. It was difficult to make out their exact form but their distant chitter reminded Sam of the hungry gnaw of the foundry rats.

'Go slowly,' Cass advised, and together they moved forward into the warehouse.

Stacked before them in shelved walls ten metres high was Edgar Dritch's incredible collection of cursed and mystic objects. Six separate pathways weaved among these treasures and snaked off into the dim reaches of the warehouse. With no clue as to the whereabouts of the mirror, they chose at random and took the second path.

As soon as they turned the first corner, the horrors and marvels came thick and fast. Sam saw a huge wall hung with beautiful ivory masks, each with bleeding eyes and a thick black tongue slurping from its rigid mouth; a doll's house in which lights burned and stiff-limbed silhouettes danced past the windows; the charred painting of a boy in blue, his vacant stare enough to conjure the sensation of fire on your skin; a large glass box containing what appeared to be a hunched child ferociously combing its balding head, but which on closer examination proved to be the prison of something raddled and elfish.

Hearts thundering, Sam and Cass moved on: past an old-fashioned gramophone which played the blood-curdling confessions of long-dead murderers; into an avenue stacked with mummified corpses whose withered chests heaved and whose toothless mouths intoned an ancient song; past a wooden-framed window hovering in mid-air, the thin pane of which appeared to hold back the awesome power of an imploding star.

At last, they turned a final corner and found themselves at the centre of the maze. Bathed in that red light which touched every surface and seemed to have no source, this roughly circular space was about the size of the courtyard at the Bluffs. On entering, the first thing they saw was the girl chained to the floor. Dressed in rags, she was kneeling as if in prayer, her bare legs manacled to a large metal grate through which an evil odour seeped. Wincing at the stench, Sam knelt beside her and asked her name.

'Lorna.' She shifted her stick-thin body and the chain binding her to the grate made a hollow clank. 'Are you one of my dreams?' she asked in a wavering voice. 'I dream a lot. Mostly about my scrying ball. Mr Dritch has promised to give it back one day . . . one day . . . '

'It's Miss Crail's daughter,' Sam said.

Cass frowned. 'Why is she the only one here?'

'What do you mean?'

'Dritch must have blackmailed hundreds of teachers all around the country, using their family members as leverage, but Lorna's the one we find. Doesn't that seem odd?'

'I guess. But look, we don't have time to figure it out right now.' He tested the manacles which had cut so deeply into the girl's weeping skin. 'No good. We'd need a blowtorch to get these off.'

'Or a key.'

'Yeah, but Dritch isn't likely to have left something that convenient lying around.'

'You don't know him.' Cass smiled bitterly. 'He's a sadist, Sam. Just look at how her knees have been cut by the rough concrete, her fingers scraped to the bone. When she was first chained here she was given hope.' Cass turned and followed the scuffs of old blood across the centre of the maze. Her eyes lit up and she pointed to a dull bronze object at the mouth of the third pathway. 'There!'

From the bloodstains it was clear that Lorna had made it to within a few cruel centimetres of freedom. Cass scooted across the floor and returned with the tarnished key.

'Thank you,' Lorna trilled, as Sam helped her to her feet. 'Are you here for the magic mirror?'

'Yes,' he said, surprised. 'Do you know where it is?'

'There.' She pointed to an area near the mouth of the sixth pathway. 'In there.'

'Go,' Cass said. 'I'll look after her. And Sam? Be careful.'

As gently as he could, Sam passed the skeletal Lorna into Cass's strong arms, hoisted the satchel onto his shoulder and set off. Overhead, those half-seen creatures continued to chitter among the rafters, as if impatient for some direction or command.

Close to the pathway's opening, a dark nook or grotto had been made in the wall of strange treasures and, as he stepped near it, Sam could feel the pull of the mirror. For some reason, that lure to his dark self didn't seem as powerful as it had when he'd used the webcam to look into the glass. When his eyes adjusted to the grotto's dimness, he understood why. Propped on a small easel, the mirror's surface was covered with a black velvet cloth.

Despite its diminished hold over him, he could still sense the power of the glass reaching out. He grasped the rounded edges in shaking hands and lifted its veiled face from the easel. The cursed object felt surprisingly light. Crouched over, he was backing carefully out of the grotto when his foot slipped and the mirror lurched against his chest. Invisible hooks seemed to reach inside him and latch onto that terrible secret buried in his heart. He wasn't even aware of crying out until Cass wrenched him from the grotto.

'Get it in the bag,' she said breathlessly. Then, 'Wait. Let me see.'

In the confused tumble, the black drape had become

243

caught and a portion of mirror unveiled. Cass now ran her finger over a scrap of glass close to the edge.

'See this tiny chip? That wasn't there when my father purchased the mirror.'

'Maybe it got banged about in transit from New York,' Sam suggested. Though Cass looked dissatisfied with this explanation, they recovered the glass and headed back to the second pathway where Lorna Crail waited.

'Are we going home now?' she asked in her singsong voice. 'Am I going to see my mum? Can I look into my scrying ball? Are you . . . ' She smiled at Sam, her addict's gaze drifting and unfocused. 'Are you an angel?'

A high, mocking voice rang around the walls.

'No, my dear, he most certainly is *not*.'

The red light dimmed until the warehouse was plunged into near darkness. In the shadows, Sam reached for Cass and found the fire girl's hand groping for his. Footsteps clicking on concrete: the approach of Edgar Dritch, dread master of the Phantasmagorium. Only why did those footfalls seem so light and airy? Almost as if the man was skipping towards them like . . .

'A child,' Cass whispered.

Yes, a child. A boy of no more than twelve years, dressed in torn black jeans, scuffed Nike trainers and a faded Mickey Mouse T-shirt, rubber charity bracelets around his thin wrist and his short blond hair spiked back from his forehead. He looked at each of them in turn, innocent eyes staring out of an alabaster face. Then he made a gun of his fingers and, grinning broadly, pointed at Lorna Crail.

'*Bang.*'

The girl screamed and the child burst into a fit of giggles.

'Who are you?' Sam challenged.

The boy spread his short arms. 'Who d'you think?'

'The child's footprints in the snow outside my father's store,' Cass murmured.

The boy locked his hands behind his back and stared down at his feet like a chastised infant. 'Didn't need to kill them, I suppose . . . ' Then he looked up, the wide grin back in place. 'But it was just *so* tempting.'

Sam had to hold the furious Cass back. 'So you're Edgar Dritch,' he breathed. 'How's that possible?'

'Oh, I have quite a collection of different faces, old and young, pretty and . . . well, not so much. Think of them as projections of my true self. Avatars, if you like. My real form I keep locked away where no enemy will ever find it.'

'So what is this all about?' Sam asked. 'The mirror, Project Hyde, the kids you've turned into monsters? What's in it for you?'

Dritch laughed until the echo of his amusement filled the warehouse. 'Fun, of course. What else?'

'What?' Cass said, incredulous.

'Oh, you expected some grand Machiavellian scheme?' the boy chuckled. 'No, no, I was just bored, that's all. Can you imagine the dull routine of eternity? A being who has lived for centuries must have his little games and diversions, you know.'

'You murdered my family for the sake of a game!'

'You, you, you,' Dritch waved an airy hand. 'There are hundreds of people dying out there right now, and all you can think about is that father and sister of yours.'

'What about the Project Hyde kids then?' Sam spat. 'Watching them tear their souls apart is just part of the fun, is it?'

'No one forced them or *you* to type those messages, Sam. No one made them look into the mirror. They just couldn't resist. You see, Mr Stevenson was on to something with that little book of his: underneath all the trappings of evolved society, human beings are really only one step up from Neanderthals. Take it from one who has watched the history of your species for thousands of years . . . ' The devilish grin returned. 'Maiming, murder, warfare and genocide: *that* is the true art perfected by the human race.'

'You talk as if you're different from us,' Cass snapped.

'Goodness, but I admire you, my dear! But it's true, I'm not one of you. I am forever.' Dritch clucked his tongue against the roof of his mouth. 'Oh, I suppose it was rather a lot of planning—stealing the looking glass, blackmailing the educators, engineering the game so that the right children were precisely primed for the mirror's attentions, but I have *so* much time on my hands, and you must understand that, after a century or two of boredom, one is perfectly willing to devote a little effort to something utterly unique. And think of what I've achieved: the mass production of Mr Hyde and the world burning at my feet.' The boyish smile faded. 'And now I believe it's time you handed back my property.'

'Just a minute,' Sam said, desperately trying to think of a way to stall the magician. 'How did you know we'd be here? I heard you on the phone, you were going to Munich.'

Dritch looked at him curiously. 'A new friend informed me about your plans.'

'Was it Tooms? You sent him to kill my uncle, why?'

'That had nothing to do with me. Mr Tooms did, however, pay a visit to the Phantasmagorium and offered his services.'

'What did he tell you?'

'Everything. And now . . . '

Dritch glanced up at the rafters and, placing his fingers between his lips, whistled. From high above, the flap of wings and the scrape of released talons answered him. Fixated by the oncoming flock, the magician paid no attention to Sam's urgent whisper.

'We need some kind of distraction.'

'You've got a plan?' Cass asked.

'"Plan" is stretching it.'

She nodded and, from her coat, drew out a small glass bottle. He had glimpsed it during their passage through Dritch's strange treasury—a miniature blue phial containing what appeared to be a perpetual flame but he'd had no idea that Cass had pocketed it.

'My psychic friend,' she explained. 'She told me to be on the lookout for something like this. Said we might need it. So what now?'

It was that familiar primordial stench that had alerted Sam to the possibility of escape. Now he looked from the slimy grating that had held Lorna Crail to the horror sweeping down from above. Confident that his trap was foolproof, Dritch had turned away from them and, throwing his hands into the air, encouraged his pets in their descent. Meanwhile, Sam and Cass began to edge silently towards the grate. Lorna came with them, her glassy eyes wide as saucers. Suddenly, she pointed upwards and hissed.

'Look! The shadows are coming!'

Sam laid the satchel containing the mirror carefully on the floor and slipped his hands through the huge grating. Moving the iron cover a couple of millimetres was enough to produce a tell-tale squeak, but again they were lucky. The sound was masked by the creatures' first screams.

Sam looked up and all thought of escape was momentarily wiped from his mind. Shadows, Lorna had called them, and shadows was as good a description as any. Aside from a pair of razor-tipped horns, shining black eyes, and a slash of molten red that served as a mouth, the dog-sized monsters were entirely featureless.

'Now,' he hissed.

Several things then happened at once: Sam heaved with all his might and the rusted grate shifted from its recess; alerted by that metallic rasp, Edgar Dritch turned towards them; and Cass lifted the glass bottle to her lips, spoke some whispered prayer, and threw it hard at the feet of the magician.

Sam had just managed to get the grating upright when the phial broke and the eternal flame sparked against the ground. From that single flash, a wall of fire four metres tall erupted across the centre of the maze, cutting them off from Dritch. Through the carnival of flames, they saw the face of the magical child contort into an expression of ancient fury while the ravenous creatures beat their wings against the conflagration.

Sam tore his gaze away and, with a belly-deep grunt, overturned the grate. The light from the flames licked into the circular blackness below and showed the slick rungs of a ladder clamped to the wall.

'You first,' Cass said, thrusting the satchel into his arms.

'No,' he protested. 'You or Lorna should—'

'You argue, we die!'

Reluctantly, he hoisted the bag onto his shoulder and started down the ladder. With the mirror bumping at his back and his elbows slipping against the moist brickwork, the hole was a tight fit. Twenty rungs down, he glanced up and saw the girls framed against the firelight, Cass urging Lorna to hurry while Miss Crail's daughter took each step as if they had all the time in the world. A moment later, the magical flames began to fade and the red light started to reclaim its hold on the warehouse. Sam was about to call out to them when his leg plunged downward and he realized he'd reached the foot of the ladder.

Opening into the arched ceiling of a large underground tunnel, the hole had come to an end ten metres above a channel of churning sewage. Sam saw his shadow flicker on the crawling brown surface, the satchel on his back like a hideous hump. He called up to Cass, warning her of the drop, then took a deep breath of fetid air and let go of the ladder.

He reeled through toxic vapours, hit the sewage with a meaty splash and felt himself being enveloped by layers thicker than water and thinner than mud. They sucked his feet, kneaded his stomach, pulsed at his throat and slurped at his face. Swimming against the downward current, he finally broke the oozing surface. While snot-coloured water dribbled from his hair, he craned his head back to stare through the putrid mist. He could just make out the wavering form of Lorna Crail hanging from the ladder's final rung, her body framed by the red light from above.

'GO!'

When she still refused to budge, Cass kicked her fingers from the ladder. Sam had just managed to swim out of her path when she hit the sewage and was immediately sucked under. With the satchel cutting into his chest, he struggled back to the impact point and plunged his hand into murky depths. His fingers snagged Lorna's rags and he yanked her out of the slime.

From behind came another fleshy splash and soon all three escapees were hauling themselves onto the sewer's narrow footpath. They staggered to their feet and wiped the streaming effluent from their faces.

'You hurt me!' Lorna cried.

Cass took the girl by the shoulders and shoved her down the walkway.

'How you doing?' she called back to Sam.

'I'm OK, but we need to keep moving. Dritch—'

The voice of the magician echoed out of the hole and cut him short.

'Yes, you may kill them, but bring back the mirror to me. Now go to your slaughter, Mr Tooms.'

29
The Secret Potion

They were hurrying around a jack-knife bend when the sound of a fourth splash reached their ears. Sam stopped and looked back the way they had come. A mustard mist was caressing the weeping walls while the thin mortar that held the crumbling roof together fell into the sewer like gentle rain. For a moment, all was still.

Then a head broke the creeping surface. Unlike the three who had come before him, Mr Tooms did not rise choking and gasping but slipped slowly, almost peacefully above the slime, as if he felt perfectly at home in that reeking stew. Sam could make out very little of the killer's face, just a pair of hard eyes and a long mane of sewage-slick hair.

The red light from the hole above flickered and died. Moments later, they heard a syrupy slurp—the reluctant sound of the sewer releasing its hold on a warm body.

'Run, little rabbits,' a jubilant voice cried out from the shadows. 'Run!'

Despite the sound of advancing feet, Sam stood frozen to the spot. Something too small to be called an idea—a fragment of understanding, perhaps—scratched at his mind. He did not know the voice and yet those dark cadences made him dreadfully afraid.

He turned to Cass, and echoed, 'Run!'

They scurried on as best they could, Lorna slowing them down with her weakened legs and ceaseless chatter. Kicking through a host of rodents, Sam dared a backwards glance and was shocked to see the pale smudge of a face only twelve metres or so behind. By his rough calculation of the distance through the now familiar tunnels, he knew that Tooms would overtake them long before they reached the winding stair. Only one thing for it then.

He stopped and groped blindly at the sewer wall.

'What the hell are you doing?!' Cass shouted.

Sam scratched frantically at the brittle mortar until his fingertips broke and bled. Still the wall remained intact. From behind came a chuckle, a hoot of victory, and a powerful hand caught his shoulder. Just before he was tugged backwards, Sam felt the wall give and an entire brick came away in his fist. Blinded by a stony spray, he swept the weapon in a wide arc and heard it crack against Tooms' skull. By the time he cleared the dust from his eyes, the killer had dropped to his knees and was tumbling senselessly into the channel.

'Did you see his face?' Sam panted.

'No,' Cass whispered. 'It was too dark.'

'D'you think I killed him?'

'You did what you had to do. Come on, let's get out of here.'

They came at last to the switchback staircase. Sam took the lead and they ascended with as much speed as they could muster, their stinking clothes chilled by icy downdraughts. The adrenalin which had carried them this far was waning and the heavy exhaustion of the fearful slowed them to a plodding march.

'Run, little rabbits! RUN!'

Sam stared over the handrail. There, fathoms below, a figure darted towards the stairway.

'He's alive.'

The web-work of iron rattled under the murderer's stampede. With the mirror weighing him down and Lorna lurching against his shoulder, Sam despaired of ever reaching the upper platform. But then, through the grille of the steps, he saw the slick black head of Tooms pass below and a surge of fear propelled him to the heights of the staircase.

Sam leaned Lorna against the handrail and bolted for the huge iron door set into the wall. He prayed to whatever gods ruled this subterranean realm and, for once, his prayers were answered. With bleeding fingers, he prised open the colossal door which groaned outwards. The rusted hinges were still screeching when he ushered Cass and Lorna into the low corridor beyond.

'And where do you think you're going, little man?'

A sleek, dripping shape rose up from the staircase. Cloaked in shadow, Mr Tooms stepped onto the platform, the clang of his feet like the hollow chimes of fate. Sam couldn't move. To his surprise, he found that part of him didn't want to. Slower footsteps now, cautious and careful, as if Tooms himself walked with trepidation.

'I . . . ' For the first time that harsh voice faltered. 'I didn't . . . '

One more step and the tall man would emerge into the light of the corridor.

Sam moistened his lips. He was afraid, yes, but his heart was still.

A scarred hand pushed out from the dimness.

'Didn't mean to . . . '

'NO!' Sam cried, as he was yanked backwards into the corridor and the door was slammed shut. Cass turned an ungainly key in the lock while from the other side came the pounding of fists and the muted cries of a frustrated killer. Sam lifted his face to the light of the single fluttering bulb.

'I'm sorry,' he said, dazed. 'I don't know what just happened.'

Cass gave him a hard look. 'Are you sure? Sam, you've got to be honest with me now.'

'There's something . . . ' He shook his head. 'I don't know.'

'Well, we better get out of here,' she muttered. 'Tooms'll find his way back to Dritch soon enough and we have to get Lorna home before we can get out of the city ourselves. Do you know where her mother lives?'

'Palisade Court. Number 39.' They turned to the girl slumped against the wall. Her voice was steadier and her eyes had cleared a little. 'Take me home, please.'

The mystery of why the murderer had hesitated on the platform followed Sam into the ruined shell of the great library, where he choked on petrol-tinged air. The walls were freshly blackened and not a single book remained untouched by the riffling fingers of fire. All around, little whiffs of smoke rose up from papery mountains, and dying embers glowed like the final flicker of ancient stars. Was this the madness of the Hydes, Sam wondered, or the work of a frightened world where rules no longer applied?

He stood for a moment and breathed in the desolation, then walked through a broken door and into the gridlocked street. Between empty cars lay discarded suitcases and backpacks, trampled goods and family mementoes, as well as more than a few bodies. Sam and Cass hurried from corpse to corpse in the hope of finding someone still alive. A fruitless endeavour: these people had not simply been killed but butchered with a ferocity that was almost unimaginable. And so the old question rattled again in Sam's mind: *If I'd completed Project Hyde, if I'd transformed, could I have done this?* More than anything, he feared the answer.

Cass found the key to a Renault hatchback in the pocket of a man whose neck had been smartly snapped. While Sam helped Lorna into the back, Cass tried her best to slot the key smoothly into the ignition. At her third attempt, he reached over and took her shaking hand.

'Thought I was coping.' She shuddered and looked down at her filthy fingers. 'But I'm not Cassandra.'

'No, you're not. You're Cassidy, and all this,' his fingertips brushed the body of the jade serpent, 'it's just war paint. It wasn't Cassandra who brought the fight to Edgar Dritch, it was you. *Always* you.'

She nodded. 'We should get Lorna home.'

Apart from a few daredevil motorcyclists zigzagging drunkenly between cars and corpses, they had the streets pretty much to themselves. Buildings burned, people screamed, but the few emergency vehicles they encountered were themselves charred to a crisp. Sam directed Cass away from the main thoroughfare and, after a few twists and turns, they found themselves in the prickly silence of Palisade Court.

He helped Lorna from the back seat and all three passed through the gate of number 39. The little house with its missing roof tiles and unkempt garden was exactly the kind of place Sam had pictured Miss Crail living. He knocked on the door.

'Stay away, whoever you are. I have a shotgun and I'm well versed in using it!'

'Miss Crail, it's Sam. We've got Lorna with us.'

A key turned and the door opened to the limit of its security chain.

'How?' Miss Crail opened the door wide and Lorna rushed into her arms. 'Oh my girl! My little girl...' She turned wondering eyes on Sam. 'H-how did you get my daughter out?'

'Long story, and it'll have to wait. We need to get going.'

'Sam, stop,' Crail said sharply. 'There's something you have to know. Please come inside.'

Cass shrugged. 'I need to make arrangements for our pick-up anyway. Let's see what she has to say.'

While Miss Crail put her daughter to bed, Cass used the phone in the hall. Meanwhile, Sam ducked into the small downstairs bathroom, stripped naked and washed himself as he best he could in the tiny sink. There were clogs of luminous goo in his ears and the reek of the sewer rose from his skin as he scrubbed. He was wondering what on earth he was going to do with his stained clothes when Miss Crail tapped the door.

'I have some of my ex-husband's things here if you need to change. He was tall, like you, so they should fit. Your friend is trying on some of Lorna's clothes. When you're ready, I'll be in the lounge.'

Dressed in a plain white T-shirt and a pair of dark chinos, Sam stepped into the hall just as Cass came downstairs. With her red hair tied back and a long-sleeve check shirt covering her serpent tattoo, the fire girl's beauty struck him anew.

'I've arranged for a helicopter transport,' she said. 'No way we could get out of the city tonight by road. They needed an obvious landmark with a suitable space to touch down—I suggested the roof of the Bluffs. They'll be there in forty minutes.'

'Then we better get this over with.'

They found Miss Crail sitting alone in the dark, surrounded by towers of well-thumbed books.

'Life is strange.' She looked up at them. 'I've been teaching literature for over thirty years and, in the final analysis, *that* is the lesson of books: life is strange. Full of meanings and coincidences, and so often we mistake the one for the other. I lied to you, Sam.'

'When?'

'The day I took you into my office and appeared to confess my involvement in Project Hyde. You probably asked yourself why I was so forthcoming when my daughter was still Dritch's prisoner. The confession was a lure, nothing more.'

'To achieve what?' Cass asked.

'Something very simple.' She passed a trembling hand over her brow. 'To force my favourite pupil to succumb to the mirror. After it became clear that you'd abandoned the project, I received a personal call from Edgar Dritch. He sensed something about you, Sam. Unlike most of the others, your secret self was based on a simple truth, and yet that truth was so profound your transformation would be a shattering one. Of all the Project Hyde participants, this change was the one that excited him most. He insisted that you *must* give in to the glass.'

Sam turned to the window and the dusky firelight that hovered over the city.

'He tried many things to get you to snap so that you'd return to the project. He blackmailed a prison officer to ensure that a letter from your father would find its way to you.'

Sam pictured the envelope with its bright red stamp: **STEMIST MOOR PRISON**.

'He bribed your uncle into mercilessly bullying you.'

Was it because I took the money, Samuel? Is that why you hate me so much?

'But why?'

'Because you refused to give in to your frustrations. When anger failed to deliver you to the mirror, I was instructed to call you to my office.' Miss Crail pointed to the satchel in the corner of the room. 'I take it from the shape that the mirror resides there? Have you seen it?'

'A glimpse,' Cass confirmed.

'Was there anything amiss?'

'A tiny chip near the frame. It wasn't damaged when my father bought it.'

'Dritch told me that the mirror is powerful,' Crail said. 'Almost indestructible, but he is a cunning magician and a minor act of vandalism was within his capabilities.'

'So he chipped the glass,' Sam frowned. 'Why?'

'To take that splinter and grind it into a fine powder. The same powder I then mixed into your tea.'

'The grit.' He'd felt the scrape of it ever since that strange meeting in Crail's office—particles of the magic mirror *inside* him. 'But I haven't transformed.'

'Dritch wasn't sure how you might react. He'd hoped that, as the powder was slowly absorbed into your system, you would change. Obviously that didn't happen.'

Sam swallowed. 'I still feel it. Surely it should've been washed away by now.'

'Magic glass,' Cass muttered, 'who knows how it works? Sam, we should get moving.'

'Please wait, I wish to say something.' Miss Crail rose from her chair. 'Once I can get Lorna somewhere safe, I plan to hand myself in to the authorities. I don't expect your understanding or forgiveness, but I thought you should know I take full responsibility for my part in . . .' She gestured towards the window. 'All of this.'

Caught between his old respect for the teacher and a strong feeling that it was not his place to absolve her, Sam simply said, 'You didn't know how bad it was going to get.'

'Oh Sam,' she sighed, 'but that's the excuse of every coward in history.'

Miss Crail's gate clacked behind them and they were soon heading out of Palisade Court and towards the city. Sam stretched the fingers of his right hand and felt the renewed sting of that old wound. Angered by raw sewage, the cut was bleeding again. *He wanted me especially. Needed me to look into the mirror and change. Needed it so much he bribed Uncle Lionel and then, when that didn't work, forced a piece of glass down my throat. Why? Because he has psychic powers and knew that my secret was so dark, so ugly, so shameful that the mirror would gorge on it?*

By the time he surfaced from his thoughts, they had reached the courtyard of the Bluffs. Cass pulled tight to the kerb and cut the engine. They both got out and stood for a moment below the concrete tower. Solemn, silent, and without a single light to bead its ugly face, the Bluffs rose over the city like a great, featureless tombstone.

Like a memorial to those who had already perished . . .

Sam shivered.

And to those who had yet to die.

30
Sam Unmasked

The lift was out of action, and so they had to climb the thirty-one floors to reach the roof. Sam tried to keep to the shadows. As far as the residents of the Bluffs were concerned, he remained the prime suspect in the murder of Lionel Kremper. Not that any concealment was necessary: twenty-four floors and counting and they had yet to encounter a single soul.

He drew deeply on the smoky air. Was that pollution tickling at the back of his throat or the scratch of the magic mirror?

25

26

The tired numbers painted onto breeze blocks ticked by.

'What'll happen to me,' Sam asked, 'after?'

27

'What do you mean?'

'I have to find out what's inside me . . . ' he hesitated. 'The glass, I mean.'

28

'I'll ask around,' Cass said. 'I've got contacts in the occult world who might know something. Don't worry, we'll get you fixed.'

'And then? I can't go home, not after Lionel and everything else I've experienced these past weeks.'

29

'No,' the fire girl said sadly. 'You can't go back to an ordinary life. Look, I've got money, I can help you start a new life with a new name.'

'You'd do that for me?'

'Of course. Anyway, I couldn't just abandon you to Dritch. If he managed to recapture you—'

30

'I'd never tell him anything. Not about you or the people who've helped us.'

'Not at first,' she nodded, 'and not willingly.'

31

They came to a door marked 'ROOF ACCESS ONLY. STRICTLY NO ENTRY'

'You're one of the bravest people I've ever met, Sam, but Edgar Dritch is a master of manipulation and torture. He'd find you, claim you, drag you back to the Phantasmagorium. Even if it was just for revenge, he'd come up with a thousand ways to make you suffer, and I . . . ' She focused on the door. 'I couldn't bear that.'

Mounting the step, Sam turned the fire girl to face him. Aching for those lips, he leaned in.

'No.' She pushed gently against his chest.

'But why?'

'I told you: love demands honesty.'

They stood in silence for a moment while the sound of nightmares continued to rise up from the city. Part of Sam's mind screamed: *Tell her. Then at least it'll be over. She'll listen to those unimaginable three words and that beautiful face will crack with disgust, but at least you'll know.* But he couldn't. He was too afraid to show her that, although he had not been transformed by the mirror, he was a monster nonetheless.

'Move aside,' he said, renewing his grip on the wheel brace he'd taken from the Renault's boot. Placing the thin end between the door and the jamb, he had tightened his muscles, ready for a struggle with the lock, when the door swung smoothly open. Sam squatted down and examined the frame. In the gloom of the stairway, he had failed to see that the lock had already been smashed from its fitting.

'It could've been done ages ago,' Cass suggested. 'Maybe someone fancied sunbathing on the roof.'

'Maybe.'

Sam pulled the straps of the satchel tight over his shoulders and pushed the door wide.

Fuelled by the fires that raged below, the heat of the night buffeted against them as they moved cautiously onto the flat roof. It was eerily peaceful here, atop the tarnished crown of the Bluffs. Apart from a flashing red beacon and a couple of slatted shed-like structures that housed the tower's heating vents, the area appeared to be empty.

Cass scanned the boiling skyline. A helicopter hovered over the city's main square, an umbilical beam of light apparently tethering it to the ground, but that was a police chopper. She checked her watch and kicked a hail of gravel over the edge of the roof.

Sam moved to the shallow parapet and watched the stones glide into obscurity. Then his gaze shifted to take in the wider view, and the topsy-turviness of the world disoriented him. In the streets below, where virtually all light had been extinguished, a constellation of fires burned against the city's nightscape while in the sky above smoke roiled like a blanket of mist covering the ground. It was like being pulled up suddenly by the ankles or having your reflection flipped in one of those funhouse mirrors . . .

And just like that, he grasped a truth which had so far eluded him: although mirrors had the power to show reality to unwilling eyes, they could just as easily exaggerate and distort. A pimple can become a hideous blemish, a healthy body transformed into a gross monstrosity: it was all in the eye of the beholder. The Stevenson Mirror did the same. It magnified a speck of darkness until that malignant dot had eclipsed everything else, but such darkness was only a fragment of the whole; something which needed to be faced, certainly, but still only part of a much bigger picture.

Cass caught him by the hand and drew him back from the edge.

'What the hell are you doing?'

'Understanding.' He unstrapped the satchel and touched the soft mahogany frame. 'Don't you see, the mirror is—'

'The mirror is me, and I am the mirror.'

They turned together and looked back across the long expanse of the roof. From behind one of the ventilation sheds, a tall man dressed in jeans and a Marvel Comics T-shirt emerged.

'We are one, for I was born of its fragment. But you are my creator too, Sam. Thank you for releasing me at last.'

Mr Tooms came forward. The shadows seemed to slip

reluctantly away from him, as if the jealous darkness was fighting to keep this terrible treasure to itself. The steady pulse of the beacon bathed his form in stark scarlet, splashing light onto his scarred right hand. Sam looked down at his own injured hand. The match was exact.

'Hurts, doesn't it? You were scarred when I was set free, and so I carry the mark too. And I hope you don't mind, but as I was born naked I was forced to steal your clothes. Still,' he laughed, 'I've done much worse things since.'

'You were born,' Sam said slowly, 'while I was unconscious in the art studio. Miss Crail gave me the tea with the powdered glass, I collapsed and then . . .'

'Pain,' Tooms nodded. 'The agonies of my birth. Unleashed by the glass, I pushed and pushed until my fingers emerged from your chest, then my arms, my head, my newborn eyes and screaming mouth. At last, I melted away from your flesh and found myself free of that meek and mewling prison. I was weak, starving, you had given me such meagre scraps to feed on, but I soon remedied that. I took the bag and the change of clothes and struck out into the city. Of course, I should've killed you then.' Tooms stopped dead and the beacon's light flashed just short of his face. 'You were so vulnerable, lying there like a wounded sparrow. I wanted to kill you, yearned to smash in your skull with my bare fists, but I wasn't sure if I would then continue to exist. I needed the advice of an expert.'

'You went to Dritch.'

The shadowy head twitched in Cass's direction. 'Oh, you're a clever fire girl, aren't you? Did you know that's what he calls you?' Tooms' laughter was full of derision. 'When he's gone, when it's just us two alone together, we're going to have lots and lots of fun.'

A flame of anger purer than the Wrath flashed inside Sam. 'You're not going to hurt her.'

'Says who? A trembling coward who hid in the kitchen while our mother was killed? You couldn't stand up to *him* and you can't stand up to me!'

And with that roar, Tooms stepped into the light.

Shaking his head at the horror of it, Sam moved back until the parapet bumped against his boots. It was the face he had glimpsed in the crowds by the Pickman Tunnel. The face he had dismissed as an illusion because his father was locked up in a cell two hundred miles away in Stemist Moor Prison. Pale skin, wiry dark hair, blue eyes, and long, rangy limbs: this thing was his father; this thing was *him*.

'Lionel saw you watching while those Hydes beat him up,' Sam said in an awestruck tone. 'He thought it was me. And Charlie, he told Cass he'd seen me leaving school that morning.'

An easy, unforced smile lit up the mirror man's face. 'Me again.'

'And Mister Tooms,' Sam whispered, picking the anagram apart. 'Stemist Moor.'

'Well, I couldn't call myself "Carrion Wrath". You'd guess who I was right away, and I so wanted to see your face when at last you realized my true identity. As for Stemist Moor?' the dark reflection chuckled. 'That prison contains the truth you could never face: you really are your father's son, and I am that truth made flesh.'

'But you're not like the other Hydes,' Cass said. 'They were transformed while you were separated, their faces changed but yours is the same as Sam's.'

'Dritch explained it all,' Tooms nodded. 'The process was different because Sam swallowed the mirror and so it was reflecting him from the inside out, prompting a physical separation of identities. As for our appearance, Sam has always pictured the Wrath as a true reflection of what he is, therefore his face is mine. Not only that, Dritch told me other things in exchange for my services and the information I provided . . . Oh yes, it was me who informed him about your plan to get into the Phantasmagorium and steal the mirror. Up until the point we separated, I had all of Sam's memories, you see?'

'I betrayed us,' Sam whispered. 'It was me . . . '

Tooms went on as if he hadn't heard. 'And in exchange for my help, Dritch gave me my answer: I am my own person, completely independent of Samuel Stillhouse. Your life is mine.'

'You killed Lionel.'

'I did what you didn't have the guts to.' Tooms stepped back, melting again into that darkness which seemed so much a part of him. 'I am stronger than you, just as Hyde was stronger than Jekyll. And now you will hand over my master's mirror.'

He reached behind the ventilation shed and dragged the bound and gagged Cora Kremper into view. Before Sam could react, Tooms pulled her to the edge of the roof and tilted her over the parapet. Nightmare wide, Cora's tear-streaked eyes flashed between her nephew and the doppelgänger.

'Drop the weapon and slide the bag towards me,' Tooms demanded.

Sam didn't hesitate. The wheel brace clanged onto the roof and he pulled the satchel from his shoulder. He was about to toss it when Cass gripped his wrist.

'Wait.'

He snapped round to face her. 'What are you talking about? He'll kill her if I don't—'

'He'll drop her anyway, once he has the mirror.'

'You know they used to call him "Calamity Sam"?' Tooms bellowed from his perch. 'Such a clumsy child, always tripping and bruising himself. I must have taken a little of that clumsiness with me.'

He loosened his hold and, with a muffled shriek, Cora pivoted forward. At the last moment, he caught her again, his bicep straining as she hovered on the edge of the parapet. Sam turned back to Cass.

'You should go.'

'Are you crazy? I'm not going anywhere!'

'I'll give him both me and the mirror in exchange for Cora. He doesn't want to hurt her as much as he wants to kill me. He won't be able to resist.'

'No,' she wrenched at his arm. 'No.'

'But Cora's innocent.'

'So are you.'

He pointed at his duplicate self. 'Whatever that thing is, it was born of *my* darkness. His hands are mine, and those hands held the knife that killed Lionel.'

'No,' Cass protested.

'I'm responsible,' Sam shook his head. 'Can't you see that? He *is* me, I am him. I have to make amends.'

'No,' Cass said again. 'Don't you understand, Sam? That thing is the very least of you. Could the worst parts of any person, unchecked by the good, betray their friends and murder their enemies? I think they could, and in that you're no different from anyone else. But now you need to take away the strength you've given your darkness. What is it you're hiding, Sam? What is the secret that feeds that creature? You have to face it NOW!'

Sam recognized his own understanding reflected back at him: these Hydes were distorted reflections, seemingly stronger but actually weaker. Tooms' darkness had been inflated by Sam's frustration that he could not admit the simple, hateful truth he had carried with him ever since the night of his mother's murder. Well, he must it admit now, even if Cass hated him for the rest of his days.

Leaning forward, he kissed the fire girl goodbye. Her lips answered his and, in parting, he whispered his confession to her.

'I love him.'

He turned to Mister Tooms.

To Stemist Moor.

To the Wrath.

'I love him!'

Three words and the twisted truth was admitted.

'What did you say?' Tooms' once bold voice shook like that of a frightened infant. 'How . . . *how* can you say that?'

Sam took a step forward, then another, and another until he was striding over the rooftop.

'Because it's the truth. I knew it every dark day of our childhood. L-O-V-E, you see? That hand that hugged and ruffled our hair wasn't felt very often, the other was the one we knew best, but one touch from LOVE and all the cruelty of the bad man was forgiven. I love our father. Though he doesn't deserve one tiny morsel of it, though it doesn't excuse what he did to us and our mother or lessen his guilt one little bit, I do love him strong and I love him fierce.'

'No!' the doppelgänger shrieked. 'You can't say that. You mustn't. He was a monster!'

Tooms tugged his hostage back from the parapet and threw her across the roof. From the corner of his eye, Sam saw Cass dash forward and scoop his aunt into her lap. Part of him wondered if the fire girl's shock had already curdled into disgust and whether Cora was feeling equally revolted. Too late to unsay the words, he pressed on.

'He was a monster,' Sam agreed, slowing his pace as he approached the dark double. 'And that was why I could never admit the truth. How could I sit Cora down and tell her I still loved the man who'd murdered her sister? How could I admit such a sick thing even to myself? Because what would such an admission say about me? That I too was a monster incapable of living a normal life. Because I should hate him. I *should*. He deserves it, doesn't he?'

Tooms dropped to his knees, scarred hand raking frantically through his long hair. Sam took the final step and rested his palm on the creature's heaving shoulders.

'He deserves hatred and I give him love. Deep down, I knew the truth, and the frustration I felt at living this lie gave birth to the Wrath. Gave birth to you. I was angry with myself for being so weak and that anger came flooding out in Project Hyde.' Tears salted Sam's eyes and spilled onto his cheeks. 'You are the rage behind the lie, Tooms, but that's all you are.'

Kneeling, Sam brushed the curtain of hair away from his twin's face.

'I'm sorry.'

'Sorry?' Tooms echoed.

'If I'd been braver you wouldn't exist and Lionel would still be alive. But it's over now.'

'What do you mean, "over"?'

'Haven't you noticed?' Sam reached out and touched the collar of Tooms' oversized shirt. 'You're getting smaller.'

It was true. With every step towards the parapet, Sam had watched the identikit creature wither inside his clothes. It had been a gradual process, so incrementally slow that Tooms had failed to pick up on the changes being wrought on his own body. His fingers were now several centimetres shorter than Sam's and, as he moved to stand upright, his shrunken feet slipped out of their stolen trainers.

'How is this happening?' the mirror man screamed.

'You were born of a secret.' At the back of Sam's throat, the constant scrape of powdered glass began to ease. 'But now the secret's been told. And for you, that means the end.'

'No.' An insane smile lit up Tooms' shrivelling face. 'I do not end. I cannot END!'

With surprising force, the little man caught Sam by the neck and threw him to the gravel. The sharp stones scraped against his spine as he was hauled up and over the parapet. 'Stay where you are,' the creature called back to Cass, 'or he drops.'

The small of Sam's back pivoted on the parapet while his head, shoulders and torso hung over the lip of the Bluffs. Glancing back, he saw Cora sprawled on the ground, apparently having fallen into a dead faint. Meanwhile, Cass had stopped mid-run and now raised her hands in submission.

'She really does *love* you,' Tooms' lip curled upon the word. He inched his creator further over the parapet until Sam grasped the shrinking man's shirt.

'I go, you go.'

'I'm dying anyway,' the Hyde shrugged and lowered his small face until his lips were level with Sam's ear. 'And if I really am your hate made flesh then I should know how much you despise yourself. You do, don't you? Hate yourself for letting him kill our mother.'

'I'll tell you exactly what I feel,' Sam swallowed. 'Lost.'

'You are,' Tooms grinned, and slid him further towards oblivion.

Turning his head to the dizzying drop, Sam saw his tears fall into the waiting arms of darkness. All around, the city burned and shrieked like some hellish thing being born.

'Lost in memories,' he continued. 'Memories of a riverbank and a willow tree. We played tag, do you remember?'

The creature's grip slackened. 'No, I don't remember that. I *don't.*'

'I remember us at seven years old. We're sitting on the carpet while dad shows us how to work a ventriloquist doll. And we're laughing, all of us. We loved him then.'

'No. No, no, no!'

'I remember him buying us our first colouring pencils.'

'Stop it. *Please* . . . '

Sam used his grip on the doppelgänger's shirt to haul himself upright. He was sitting on the parapet now while Tooms continued to wither before him.

'And then we saw him, didn't we? At school on the night of the art exhibition. He was crying.'

'No.'

'Staring at the picture we'd painted of mum and crying. And he said . . . '

'Don't.'

'Proud of you, son. Proud of you.' Sam reached out to the monster. 'You loved him too.'

Roughly the size of a five-year-old child, Mr Tooms looked up with tears of grief and fury. His powerful hands released Sam and he snapped them to his sides, as if suddenly ashamed. While Sam rose slowly to his feet, the creature born of him stepped onto the parapet.

'I . . . I don't understand,' said the little man. 'It's in you, isn't it? Our father's rage. You're going to become him. Become me.'

Sam shook his head. 'That's what I believed: that I was my father's son, that I was fated to end up just like him. But it was the lie that made me angry, not anything inherited from him. We choose our own path, make our own future, shape our own character.'

Tooms looked at him bleakly. 'I'm frightened.'

'I know.' Sam nodded. 'But it's all right, Sammy. It'll be all right now.'

Tooms returned the nod and looked out over the city. And suddenly, in a psychic connection between creator and monster, Sam was seeing through Tooms' eyes: from horizon to horizon, the world seethed and shimmered, the truth of its own complicated self reflected in the light and darkness of seven billion struggling souls. The shrivelled man on the parapet raised its tiny arms to that darkness . . . and tipped into the night.

He grew ever smaller as he fell, the warm air buffeting his frail body, death rushing up to greet him. Now he was a smudge, now a smear, now a speck, and in the final moment, while still metres from the ground, he transformed into a silver dusting that was taken up and scattered by the breeze. In the same instant, Sam felt the last trace of grit vanish from his throat and heard the shatter at his feet. Exchanging a glance with Cass, he took hold of the satchel and tipped it upside down.

Glass as fine as sand ran through his fingers.

'He was made of the mirror, so when he broke apart the fracture spread.'

Cass nodded. 'Maybe that was the only way it could be destroyed. Now Dritch won't be able to use it to ruin any more lives.' She elbowed him coaxingly in the ribs. 'That's not a bad night's work, is it, Sammy?'

'I guess not.' He allowed himself a half smile as they wandered back to Cora. 'Will she be OK?'

Cass brushed a strand of grey hair back from the unconscious woman's face. 'Will any of us?'

Sam knelt down and kissed his aunt's brow. Then, straightening up, he looked Cass square in the eye.

'Do you hate me?'

'Why would you ask that?'

'Because I love him.' And now the tears came, full and fast. 'I love my father.'

She pulled his hands away from his face and made him look at her.

'We can't help who we love, Sammy. We can choose who to like and who to hate, but love isn't a choice . . . and I love you more *because* you love him.'

'But it's wrong and twisted and—'

She kissed him, her lips like a blessing.

'No. Keeping it locked inside was wrong, but shall

I tell you why your love isn't?' She pressed gentle fingers to his chest. 'Because now there's no more Wrath, is there?'

Sam realized that he hadn't felt the Wrath stir since Miss Crail had poisoned him with the mirror tea, and now, where that bright rage had once flared, he could feel nothing at all. Anger would come to him again in time, he had no doubt, but the frustrated fury of the Wrath was gone. He pressed Cass's palm to his chest and smiled.

Fires raged in the city below while high above there was a break in the clouds and the bright, calming face of the moon shone down. Seeing its light reflected in all the darkened windows of the estate, Sam felt a sense of peace. With the fire girl beside him, he watched the moonbeams shimmer over the rotors of an approaching helicopter.

Time to move on, he said to the Bluffs. And his mind echoed the parting back to him. *Goodbye.*

Goodbye.

Goodbye . . .

Epilogue

'To be what we are, and to become what we are capable of becoming, is the only end of life.'

Robert Louis Stevenson

Upon an ocean of clouds, the bruised purple of dawn mellowed until at last all traces of night had been healed from the sky. Turning from this new day, Sam saw his reflection cast sharply in the little window. The recycled air of the private jet caught in his throat as, for a moment, he was reminded of the mirror man who had fallen from the tower. Despite Cass's insistence that his Hyde had been the very least of him and that he wasn't responsible for the monster's actions, Sam knew that he would always carry some of Tooms' guilt with him.

From the helicopter they had been taken to an airport where the private jet stood idling on the runway, and where Cass exchanged a few words with a grim-faced man in an expensive suit.

'You'd better get aboard,' he grunted. 'Some of our psychics are saying that Dritch is on his way here right now.'

They had seen the proof of that prophecy as the plane swept deftly down the runway. As the wheels left the tarmac, a long black limousine had raced onto the grass siding and screeched to a stop. The back door sprang open and a dark-haired boy of about twelve years emerged. Although the distance made it difficult to be sure, Sam was reasonably certain that the strange child had been smiling.

Halfway across the Atlantic, Cora had surfaced from unconsciousness. Taking in the luxurious interior of the plane, she had listened without reaction as Sam tried his best to explain everything that had happened, from his first encounter with Cass to the suicide of Tooms and the breaking of the magic mirror. From that moment to this, she hadn't spoken a word and, although Cass assured him that she would receive the best medical care once they arrived in the States, Sam doubted that the old Cora would ever truly come back to him. She rested now in a seat at the back of the plane, a blanket tucked around her unmoving body.

'If only I'd told her what was happening.' He turned to the girl who sat in the creamy leather seat beside him. Other than the two pilots in the cockpit, they had the jet to themselves. 'If I'd warned her somehow.'

Cass took his scarred hand. 'This isn't your fault.'

'So you say, Cassidy Kane.'

He no longer thought of her as Cassandra. That she had been inspired by her fiery sister was obvious, but the bravery Cassidy had discovered within herself was entirely her own. He believed that she understood that now.

'So I *know*.' She leaned in and kissed him gently on the lips. It felt like a blessing. An absolution. 'The contact we met at the airfield gave me an update while you were getting Cora out of the helicopter. As soon as the mirror shattered, all the Hydes in the containment facilities transformed back to their normal selves.'

'Doreen?' said Sam, sitting up straighter. 'Martin?'

'Both,' she nodded. 'And unfortunately it seems that they remember everything from their time as Hydes.'

'My God. Doreen sent her father crazy, and Martin . . . all those kids he killed.'

'And all the other Hydes who maimed and murdered,' Cass nodded. 'The people who've helped us will do what they can to remove those memories psychically, but that won't be an option for the kids who were captured by the authorities. I'm afraid they will have to live with those memories for the rest of their lives.'

Perhaps they should, Sam thought bleakly. Weren't they responsible for the actions of their darker selves? Even now he wasn't entirely sure.

'Do you think any of them will be sent to prison?'

'Who knows?' Cass shrugged. 'Prosecutors might find it difficult to make charges stick when the perpetrators are now wearing different faces. But maybe this is the beginning of a new world.'

'What do you mean?'

'I mean that Edgar Dritch has orchestrated a supernatural event that the entire planet witnessed. There's solid evidence of the paranormal now: transformations recorded on mobile phones, TV cameras filming Hyde attacks. I wonder . . . ' She hesitated, her gaze roaming to one of the small windows through which the edge of the world showed its blazing brow. Sam felt her shiver and put his arm around her, holding the fire girl close.

'So, what about us?' he whispered.

'A new country,' she smiled, 'a new life.'

Sam felt the plane's soft rumble beneath his feet, sensed the globe turning far below. He believed that a new future was rushing forward to greet them, and that whatever that future held, wonders or terrors, they would face it together.

Sam and the fire girl.

ACKNOWLEDGEMENTS AND ADVICE

In writing about the issue of cyberbullying in *Jekyll's Mirror*, I was incredibly fortunate to be granted a lengthy interview with John Neary, a nurse specialist with the Child and Adolescent Mental Health Services. John's keen and compassionate insights into the blurred distinction between the bully and the bullied, and how the stresses and strains of modern life can impact on a child's psyche, were invaluable (I hasten to add that any errors in the text, factual or psychological, are mine alone).

A second source of information was provided by Sergeant Andrew Hickinbottom of Lincolnshire Police. Andrew, who until he retired last year was a constant presence in Lincolnshire schools, advising teachers and children on the dangers of online persecution, kindly provided a window into this largely hidden world. Not only did he open my eyes to the horrific effect on victims, he showed me that, for this modern law and order problem to be policed in any meaningful way, it *must* be understood more clearly by politicians and lawmakers.

Thirdly, I owe a great debt to my main editors on this book, Clare Whitston and Liz Cross. After a lot of groundwork was put in by the brilliant Jasmine Richards, they then pushed me very hard to concentrate on the central theme of cyberbullying—to examine it as honestly and as boldly as I could. For this crucial contribution I thank them.

To write this book, I felt that I must understand the original intentions of Robert Louis Stevenson, the genius whose immortal tale has been a source of inspiration throughout my writing life. The following books and resources (including Stevenson's own colourful auto-biographical writings) were incredibly helpful: *Dreams of Exile: Robert Louis Stevenson, A Biography* by Ian Bell; *Robert Louis Stevenson: A Biography* by Claire Harman; *Robert Louis Stevenson: The Critical Heritage* edited by Paul Maixner; *The Letters of Robert Louis Stevenson* edited by Bradford A Booth and Ernest Mehew; and the RLS website: http://www.robert-louis-stevenson.org

Finally, I would like to pass on my sincere thanks to a group of people who have asked to remain anonymous. Over the course of six months, and with the permission of schools and parents, I had the good fortune to interview many young people, both victims of online bullying *and* former bullies. With grace and unflinching honesty they spoke to me about their experiences and have allowed me to reflect many of these in *Jekyll's Mirror*. No single history is replicated, but I have done my best to echo the causes and effects, the temptations and the traumas, the hurt and the solace that ran through each and every story.

If anyone reading this is suffering from cyberbullying, please know that there are many organizations that can help. Here are a few:

www.childline.org.uk
http://www.bullying.co.uk/cyberbullying
http://www.beatbullying.org
http://www.cybersmile.org
http://www.kidscape.org.uk

William Hussey, 8 March 2014